BELIEVING
IN BLUE

By the Author

Dreaming of Her

Under Her Spell

Out of This World

Believing in Blue

BELIEVING IN BLUE

by
Maggie Morton

2016

BELIEVING IN BLUE
© 2016 By Maggie Morton. All Rights Reserved.

ISBN 13: 978-1-62639-691-3

This Trade Paperback Original Is Published By
Bold Strokes Books, Inc.
P.O. Box 249
Valley Falls, NY 12185

First Edition: September 2016

Credits
Editor: Shelley Thrasher
Production Design: Stacia Seaman
Cover Design by Melody Pond

Acknowledgments

I'd like to start by thanking everyone at Bold Strokes Books who helped me turn the idea I had for this book into a reality. Big thanks also to Shelley Thrasher—I can't imagine that a more skilled, sweeter editor could possibly be found. Melody Pond has gifted me with an especially lovely and eye-catching cover, for which I'm grateful—after all, some people certainly do judge a book by its cover. And finally, I'd like to thank my dad for his support, my mom for support and her very useful advice on the novel, and my partner, Matthew, for believing in me and supporting me and my writing for ten years come next January.

To Michele and Craig—both of you help, immeasurably,
in keeping me aloft

PART ONE

Chapter One

Wren was lost in the shapely arms of a beautiful girl when the bright-blue raven landed on the sill of her open window. The bird's vibrant, rich blue color and that it was holding what looked to be an envelope made her fantasy fade in an instant, despite the fact that she'd just started kissing her imaginary partner. But a blue, mail-carrying raven excited her much more than a fantasy girl, no matter how good of a kisser she happened to be (not that Wren had much experience in the matter, or, really, any at all). She could always return to the kiss later, whereas this raven might fly off at any moment, so Wren allowed herself to be pulled back into reality…as strange as reality suddenly was. This wasn't even the strangest thing that had happened in the last few weeks, though.

Or at least it wasn't until the lapis-colored raven dropped the letter and said, in an unfamiliar-yet-pleasant female voice, "It's from your father, Wrenny. Read it very soon." Before Wren could begin to accept the fact that a blue, talking bird had just delivered a letter, one that was possibly from her long-gone dad, the bird bobbed its head, turned, and flew off, zigging and zagging until it ducked under some low tree branches and disappeared from Wren's sight.

"Well," she said to herself, alone once again, "*that* was weird."

Weird things had already been happening to her, though, things that were possibly just as weird as what had just transpired. So, with her pulse beginning to quicken, which could have been either from excitement or nerves, Wren picked up the envelope and tore it open, beginning to read.

Dear Wrenny,
*   I must start by telling you—as it is, despite what I am*

about to tell you, the most important fact—that I have missed you terribly these past almost-ten years. I did not want to leave your life, and I hope you believe my words. I had to, though, because if I'd brought you back home with me, you might not even have made it to your ninth birthday, much less your very important eighteenth.

I'm guessing you've gotten your wings by now, and I hope it wasn't too hard keeping them concealed. I also hope you weren't too frightened when they showed up, because although you are from another world, you surely did not know that until they appeared. After all, how could you possibly guess that fact? I couldn't have if I were in your shoes!

I will be sending a girl to help you very, very soon. She will make herself known to you, and then she will teach you how to fly. It shouldn't be too hard, as we Winged Blue always learn quite quickly, and I doubt someone as important to us as you will have a very hard time learning.

Yes, that's right—not just to me, but to all of the Winged Blue, you hold great importance. There is a prophecy, of course, and it speaks of you and your future.

A future that will begin as soon as the thirteenth day following your eighteenth birthday arrives. Which is only a small number of days away, if this letter reached you when it was supposed to.

I could not possibly be looking forward to seeing you again more. I just wish that I hadn't needed to leave your side for all these years. I hope Denise has treated you well, and I can barely believe I'll be seeing you in mere days!

Much love,
Your dad, Torien

Wren didn't know what to think once she reached the end of the letter. First her wings had appeared, that one late night in the woods just days ago, and now her missing father was suddenly back in her life…if only slightly. And then there was this prophecy, one in which she apparently held great importance. A prophecy that seemed to state that she mattered, immensely, to however many Winged Blue there happened to be.

Now so many thoughts were all rushing around in her head that it took a while before one decided to dominate all the others and push its way up to the very top of her consciousness.

What the…what the hell is going on?

CHAPTER TWO

The weather was far too nice to be trapped inside, so Wren couldn't have been happier to exit her high school that afternoon and start walking toward the café where she worked after school. The feel of the gentle breeze tossing about her long hair and skirt was almost as delicious as what she would be drinking in about ten minutes.

She'd been looking forward to her before-work treat all day, an iced, blended mocha with extra whipped cream she was planning to enjoy at one of the outdoor tables in front of the café. She could enjoy the silky-warm June air and people-watch.

And perhaps she could reread the letter from her father, which she had folded up and pushed to the very bottom of her skirt's front pocket shortly before leaving for school that morning. There was no way she was going to leave it at home, where her mother Denise might have a chance to stumble across it…as unlikely as that was. Her mom almost never went into her room, instead vegging out in front of the TV every single night until her multiple nightcaps often knocked her out. And on those nights, Wren would need to help guide her up to her bedroom and into bed, Wren's stepdad Tim usually nowhere to be seen. If she was unlucky enough for it to be a night where he was actually at home, Wren just had to hope that he would avoid the two of them and hide out in his gross-smelling den, filling it with the scent of cheap cigars and, Wren imagined, pent-up rage.

Rage that unfortunately wasn't always "pent-up." Not when he got into an especially bad mood and took it out on Wren or her mom. He was never violent physically, but words, Wren had come to realize, could do a rather impressive amount of harm if they were chosen just right.

But today it was lovely out, and Wren had just arrived at the café, so she turned her thoughts to sunshine and delicious coffee and away from whatever might be waiting for her at home later that night.

Her boss Shawn stood behind the counter when she entered the well-lit, yellow-and-orange–themed restaurant. Shawn was wearing her usual uniform, a button-down, black work shirt and loose jeans, her look finished off with her favorite baseball cap, which sat on top of her close-cropped, sandy-blond curls. Wren had been confused at first, when she'd started work there two years ago, with how Shawn liked to dress. But she was also confused about why she liked looking at her pretty female classmates more than her supposedly hot male classmates, and so, once Shawn had mentioned a girlfriend, it had all begun to make more sense. After copious online research and sneaking some of Shawn's lesbian magazines home, Wren felt fully informed, or as informed as a young lesbian like her could become without any equally thorough research in certain *other* areas.

"Hey there, Wren. You want your usual? You have a nice, long twenty minutes before it's time to start behind the counter. And I'm feeling generous today, so if your friend Nicole comes at her usual time, her drink of choice is on me." Shawn grinned at Wren, her wide smile lighting up her tanned, handsome face.

But as believable as Shawn's smile was, and as happy as Wren was to see her boss and friend, there was no way she could tell her about the two supernatural events that had occurred in the past couple of weeks. She wanted Shawn to continue to think of her as sane. Even a woman as cool and kind to her as Shawn wouldn't want to be friends with a crazy person. Or at least a person who *sounded* crazy, because as impossible as her new wings and the blue raven still seemed, they also were definitely one hundred percent real. And Wren figured that their realness was far preferable to her falling off the narrow ledge of sanity, a ledge upon which she'd felt quite precariously balanced ever since her dad had left.

So she didn't even consider telling Shawn, as much as she liked the older woman. Instead, she took the icy glass from her boss, sucked a small mouthful of whipped cream off the top, and thanked her.

"No prob, hon. Enjoy your java, and I'll see you back in here soon, right?"

"Of course. Thanks, Shawn." Wren grabbed a spoon and went outside, sitting at one of the metal tables in a chair made hot by the sun. She sighed as she relaxed into the chair. Then she saw the girl.

She looked to be about Wren's age, or she could have been older.

It was hard to say, precisely, because she was turned slightly away from Wren. But even the half-view she had of the other woman's face told Wren enough about her features to know that if the young woman ever looked at her head-on, she would be gorgeous. The girl had dark-brown hair with strands of garnet red, all of it pulled back into a loose bun with a few locks hanging down around her perfectly curved cheekbones. Her lips were set into a subtle smile, thinner than Wren usually liked but so nicely shaped their lack of fullness didn't matter. Her eyes could have been either hazel or green—Wren couldn't tell from this far away.

Wren thought about her own looks, then: her hair, black with slight red highlights, but nowhere near the exciting color of the girl's, and it had also never made up its mind between being straight and curly; her coffee-and-cream skin, which, while *she* didn't have a problem with it, had still made her stand out at her practically all-white school, most of the Caucasian kids tending to either insult her or avoid her; and her shape, not nearly as curvy or thin as she might have liked. But despite her notably lesser attractiveness, she almost called out to the girl, hoping to get a good look at her entire face before she left or before Wren had to go back inside to work.

It turned out that Wren didn't need to get the girl's attention, because said attention was headed in Wren's direction right that moment. Wren watched as the girl stood, adjusted the gray T-shirt she was wearing over darker gray slacks, and then she felt her stomach tighten as the girl began to stride straight...toward...her.

"May I sit here?" the girl asked in a sweet-yet-certain tone. She sounded like Wren wouldn't possibly say no, and, well, she was right.

"S-sure. Yes. Please." Oh God, Wren thought, was she blushing as much as she thought she was? Her face suddenly felt much hotter than her sun-heated chair, but the girl either didn't manage to notice or didn't care.

"You just looked...interesting," she said as she moved the chair to the left of Wren's, dragging it until it was directly across from where Wren sat. Once seated, the girl formed her perfect lips into an equally perfect smile, and Wren realized then that her eyes hadn't left the girl's face for a second, a fact that she quickly remedied by looking at her company's feet instead. The sky-blue flip-flops the girl wore couldn't compete with her looks, but their color did manage to distract Wren momentarily, as she found herself thinking of the raven from the day before.

"Do you like birds?" the girl asked.

Wren's eyes shot back up to the girl's face. But this time, instead of checking her out, she searched her for signs of hidden intent, signs of secrets or mysterious plans. "Yeah," she finally answered, failing to see any of those things in the girl's shockingly green eyes. "Yeah, I do. Especially…ravens."

"Ravens, huh? Do you like Edgar Allan Poe's poem?"

"Never have I liked it more," Wren said, then took a big swallow of her mocha in hopes that a large, whipped-cream mustache would at least slightly distract the girl from her stupid joke.

Instead of giving her a weird look and then leaving, as Wren had expected, the girl chuckled, her laughter managing to make Wren feel like much less of an idiot. "Cute joke. So, would it be okay if I told you a story my mom told me about Poe when I was little?"

"I'd like that," Wren said in reply. Had she sounded as excited to hear the story as she felt?

The girl placed her elbow on the table and rested her chin on her fist, looking slightly off into the distance as she began to speak. "You see, when I was about thirteen or so, I began to feel like I didn't fit in, even when everyone my age was nice to me. I was different, you see, in a way that I didn't want anyone to find out about, because it embarrassed me so much, how different I was. So my mom, despite me being a little too old for stories, made one up for me one night when I was crying to her about how hard it was to feel like I didn't fit in. And so, this is the story mom told me." She cleared her throat, glanced at Wren, and then looked off into the distance once more.

"When Edgar Allan Poe was little, he found a raven in a field. He didn't have any friends, my mom said, so he decided the raven would become his friend instead of the mean kids at school, the ones who always called him 'strange' and even meaner things.

"The raven was always affectionate toward Edgar, nuzzling him and making soft clicking noises as it did so. So Edgar decided to see if he could help the bird out, to show it he loved it in return. He taught it how to hold a pen and how to write, and by the time ten years had passed, it had begun to make up entire stories, writing them in sloppy, loose capital letters. But they were still legible, of course. One night, Edgar came up with the idea to pass off the raven's writing as his own, so he began to sneak its pages out of his home while the raven was sleeping.

"After a number of years, the raven noticed Edgar leaving their home with its writing, and it followed him to the building where Poe had been dropping off the raven's stories and poems. Once Poe got home, the raven confronted him. It told him that, although Poe had always felt different, the raven had felt different too, having all of these stories trapped in its head and with no way to let them out. It told Poe it was different in another way, too—the raven told Poe that though he was a male raven, he preferred the company of male ravens to female ones. Poe burst into tears upon finding out that he and the raven shared the horrible feeling of not fitting in within their species. He begged the raven to forgive him, but that night, under the light of a full moon, the raven left him, its feathers turning from black to a rich, dark blue as it flew off into the bright moonlight, never to be seen again. It was possible that the raven had come from another world, Edgar thought. Mr. Poe decided that night to come clean about the truth of 'his' writing, but he never got the chance, as he died the very next week.

"My mom told me this story because she knew how *I* was different, and she didn't want my fear of not fitting in to stop me from living the full life she said I deserved."

While the girl told her story, Wren had been completely transfixed. She'd always loved a good story, but she wasn't at all expecting a tale that seemed only the slightest bit removed from her own newly changed reality, a reality that was quickly replacing all that was ordinary with things that were truly exceptional and magical. And did the mother's story mean that this girl was gay, like her? What about the raven in it, blue like the one she'd met the morning before? Was the girl possibly hinting at some involvement in the new, bizarre changes in Wren's life?

"My name's Sia, by the way," the girl said, standing and reaching behind her head. She pulled out the two chopsticks that had been holding her hair up, and it began to fall down around her in a rush of garnet and dark-amber waves. "I hope to see you again really soon," she told Wren.

Then Sia turned and walked off, and before Wren could even come close to recovering her cool, much less call after her like she wanted to, Sia had disappeared around the corner and was gone.

Wren was still holding her mocha midair a while after the girl was entirely out of view, and it was a struggle to return to the world even once Sia had been gone for a few minutes. Then she became aware of the time and that she'd have to finish her drink quickly if she was going to make it back inside the café in time to start work. She only had two minutes till her shift began, so she gulped down the rest of the mocha. Wren wondered if the beginnings of brain freeze might possibly manage to push all the disruptive thoughts of Sia out of her head. There was no way she'd be able to concentrate on work if those thoughts stayed this firmly in her imagination. Wren's last thought of her before she rose from her chair was a question. Could Sia be the person her father had told her about? But now all she was supposed to be thinking about was coffee, customers, and making change.

Once she had reentered the café, Wren lifted up the counter to the left of the dessert case and went into the back room, where she put on a stiff, black apron and her best smile. It might not have been as real as the one she'd give to Sia if she ever saw her again, but it would have to do.

It likely was the effect of tourist season on Wren's town that caused the almost constant flow of customers that afternoon, and Wren was pretty tired by the time 5:29 rolled around. But right as she was heading to the café's front door to flip the OPEN sign over, her friend Nicole burst through it, and the sight of her familiar, freckled face brought back some of Wren's energy.

"Hey, Wren. I hope I'm not too late?"

"No, your timing's fine, Nicole. Please, come in!" Her friend wrapped Wren in a sweet-smelling hug, her signature perfume comforting and welcome as Wren took in its slightly strong scent. "Do you want dinner?" Wren asked her. "I'll have to fix mine and my parents' at home, but I could treat you to a sandwich or something. And extra cornichons, of course."

Nicole walked over to her usual table, sitting down in one of the faux-velvet-cushioned chairs, and she winked over Wren's shoulder, where, Wren saw, Shawn was just coming out of the back.

"Nicole! Hey there, gal pal. Can we get you something?" Shawn took off her apron and laid it over the counter next to the register. "How about a chai latte? I can add some raspberry syrup. It sounds kinda gross when you hear about it, but trust me, it's absolutely wonderful."

"That sounds great, Shawn. And how about a bagel with lox and cream cheese, hold the onions?"

"Got a hot date?" Wren's boss whisked the last bagel out of the case and put it into the toaster behind the counter.

"Yeah, do you? With James?" Wren pulled a chair closer to Nicole and sat down, getting ready for the usual combination of jealousy and joy she experienced whenever her best friend's boyfriend came up. Yes, she didn't want her own *boy*friend, though a female partner would have been more than welcome. But between her school's lack of racial diversity, its lack of queer awareness, and its lack of acceptance of people who even seemed gay, it had been clear to her that dating wasn't a good idea, or even an option. It would have to wait until after school ended, she'd decided, and maybe once she was out of high school the locals would be more forgiving of her orientation. Forgiving enough for a first date and then, hopefully, a first kiss.

"James is…he's taking me out tonight, and he told me he had something important to tell me. We're going to eat at Le Nuit."

"Hot damn, Nicole, that place is fancy," Shawn called out from behind the counter. "What do you think he's going to tell you?"

"You don't think…you don't think he's going to ask you to marry him, do you?" Wren asked. She knew there was no way her college-bound friend would want anything to stand in the way of her four heavily-planned-out years. "Would you say yes, if he did? And if you did say yes, would you move to the school he's going to?"

"Whoa, Wren, slow down. First, no, I do *not* think he's going to propose. Second, I would definitely say no, but I would let him down easy. And finally, ain't nothing that would keep me away from Stanford. I've wanted to be a doctor ever since you or I can remember, and an offer of a ring and James's hand in marriage, no matter how much I love him, isn't going to stop me."

"Good. High five?" Wren raised her palm in the air.

"Sure, you geek, but don't let anyone know I still high-five you. It would ruin my reputation."

Wren and Nicole's palms met with a sharp slap, both of them grinning and laughing. "So, Wren," her friend asked, "what's new since I saw you three hours ago?"

"Lots, believe it or not."

"I thought so." Shawn was coming up to their table with a steaming mug of pale-brown liquid and a plate holding the food Nicole had ordered. She put them down in front of Nicole and flipped a chair around, crossing her arms over its top as she sat across from the two of them.

"What do you mean, 'I thought so'?" Wren asked.

"I saw you with that girl, outside. You looked like you were either in heaven or about to throw up when she walked over to you."

"That pretty much sums it up." Wren laughed and looked down, unable to meet either of her tablemates' eyes.

"So, do you have a hot date for tonight, too?" When Wren looked up at the end of Nicole's sentence, Nicole wiggled her eyebrows at her and nudged her in the ribs with her elbow a few times.

"Not at all. She left before we could even have much of a conversation. I don't think I'll see her ever again," Wren told them, although as she said those words, she realized she didn't truly believe them.

Nicole pressed her for information, and during the next ten minutes, Wren had to lie to her friend about her entire conversation with Sia. She couldn't tell her about the story, because even if she left out her own opinion of the girl's tale, she didn't want to make her sound nuts. After all, even though she didn't know the first thing about Sia, she had a good feeling about her, and she didn't want her best friend or Shawn getting the chance to talk her out of her new crush.

Right around six, once Wren finished doing her share of that day's cleanup, she got ready to say good-bye to Nicole and Shawn. "I'm going to try a new recipe for meatballs tonight. It calls for fennel seed, and I just picked up a bottle of it at Nancy's Fancies."

"Your stepdad doesn't deserve food that nice, you know," Nicole told her, her smile and squinted eyes replaced by a much more serious look as she stared Wren down. "And you shouldn't be spending any of your income from here on expensive ingredients."

"I...I know that. I like doing it, though, and at least I enjoy the added complexity of the food's flavors. But I have to go now," Wren told her. Neither Nicole nor Shawn knew even half of what she had to deal with at home, just that it wasn't always all that great. Despite her closeness to Nicole, she'd never told her exactly how bad her stepdad got, or how much her mom drank, instead keeping her friend as far away from her home and the truth as she possibly could. "My stepdad's going to be home at eight, and he likes to have his dinner ready when he gets there."

"I don't know why your mom can't make it. Didn't she used to cook dinner for you and your dad every night?"

"Yeah," Wren said as she reached the door, holding in the sigh that was desperately trying to escape her lips. "She's the reason I'm such a good cook."

As Wren started her walk home, she thought about her dad's letter, and Sia, and the fact that as close as she and Nicole were, there were far too many things she could never, ever tell her friend. But she'd kept things from Nicole for years, so she was used to lying to her, despite the fact that all her secrets were often fighting hard to come out.

At least with her wings, and her dad's letter, and Sia's possible involvement in everything…at least with them, she knew she was doing the right thing. Nicole couldn't know about these three things. No one on the entire planet could find out. Because she'd either get locked up in the loony bin or locked away in a government lab to be studied, and she wanted to find out if the letter she'd received the day before held the truth. She wanted to know if she was finally going to see her dad again.

And she wanted to know if, just like her, he had wings.

CHAPTER THREE

Her mom was in the living room watching TV when Wren got home, her breath smelling strongly of vodka when she kissed Wren hello on the cheek. It was no longer a surprise to come home to her mom and have her be drunk. And her stepdad Tim's insults, both to her mom and to her, were also something Wren had gotten used to. Not that they had ever stopped hurting, but at least she wasn't as surprised as she used to be when one came flying in her direction.

So Wren expected tonight to be business as usual: a delicious meal that Wren would make all by herself, a drunk mom, and a stepfather who wouldn't even care how much effort she'd put into the food.

Denise did care, though, proving this by asking Wren the question she made a point of asking every single night. The one that let Wren know she was still deeply loved, her mom's voice full of that love, even if she always chose to be intoxicated when she asked it. "What's for dinner, sweetheart? I'm looking forward to it already, whatever it happens to be."

"I'm making spaghetti with meatballs, and garlic bread. I'm trying a new recipe for the meatballs, too," she told Denise, a weak smile finding its way onto her face while she looked down at her mom.

"That sounds great. I'm pretty hungry, too, Wren. When will I get to eat your delicious meal?"

"I'm going to head upstairs for a bit. Then I'll be back down a little before six thirty, and if you want, you can come into the kitchen and watch." Wren always extended this offer to her mom, but the answer was always a kindly worded "no."

"Oh, hon, I'm so sorry, but I'm really, really tired." Her mom sighed and turned her eyes away from Wren and back to the TV. "Rain check?"

Wren knew "tired" was code for "drunk." She also knew her mom would never join her in the kitchen the way she wanted her to. She would never kick Tim to the curb, either, and so Wren was in charge of making sure her mom had it as easy as she could make it for her. It was why she wasn't going away to college. Someone had to make sure Tim never got worse. She thought of her dad's letter, then. Could she actually abandon her mom, even if an entire world was depending on her?

It was a world where she'd never been and a father who had abandoned *her*, even if both were desperate for her help. But maybe it was time to place all of this torture firmly in her past.

Instead of breathing any of these thoughts to Denise, she squeezed her on the shoulder and started to leave the room. "I love you, Mom. See you in short while."

"I love you too, Wren. Have fun in your room."

Wren went up the stairs and into her bedroom, where she shut the door and turned on her stereo; her favorite oldies station was in the middle of a song by a band her dad had gotten her into while he was still around. His leaving made sense now, or at least it seemed like it did. If he was telling the truth in his letter to her, she would gladly forgive him. She'd been mad at him for far too long, but her anger had never managed to overcome how much she missed having him around.

After lying on her bed for a while, she pulled her journal out from under her mattress and began to write.

Dear Me,

First the wings, and then a letter from dad. From Torien, who I haven't heard anything from, anything at all, since he left me and Mom...abandoned us. I wonder if he would have done that if he'd known what my stepdad would be like and how hard it would be for Denise to scrape by and keep me fed and in clothes until she met my jerk stepdad. I'd love to leave Tim behind, far behind, but my mom? Could I really force her to stay here, without me to help? All alone with HIM?

I guess I am mad at her for staying with Tim, I think. But I still love her, very much. Just like Torien says he loves me. But I don't know. I just don't know!

At first, I thought the wings were really cool, but now they seem like a problem. Sure, maybe someday I'll be able to fly, which is pretty awesome.

But my mom can't fly...she doesn't have wings, and I can't leave her behind.

If I even end up going...and if this girl even shows up, whenever that's supposed to happen. God, was my dad's letter ever vague about everything that may happen to me! I mean, WHY am I so important? Why do I suddenly matter so much?

And speaking of girls, I do wonder if Sia...if that's even her real name...is THE girl who's supposed to show me the way into this other world, or at least teach me how to fly. I've tried every night in my secret spot, but although I have been able to release my wings from my back on command every time now, I haven't had any luck at all with lifting off the ground. I'm probably just doing it wrong...and this girl, whoever she is (please, please let her be Sia!), may not even be able to teach me, maybe because I'm not in the right world to learn. No wonder I never felt like I fit in. I'm not even human!

Wren closed her journal and hid it back beneath her mattress. Usually, no one came into her room, except for her mom on rare occasions, telling her that a show or movie she liked was on TV. Her mom did still love her, but not enough, not enough to leave Tim or to stop drinking. So maybe it was time to let go of all of her ties here and go to a place where she mattered, very much, to everyone there.

But in this world, the way she mattered right then was in her ability to get a meal onto the dinner table in the next hour. She got up off her bed and steeled herself to go downstairs, to fix dinner for a mom she loved and a stepdad she pretty much hated. At least two out of the three of them would enjoy this dinner, as long as her meatballs turned out well.

Wren walked down the stairs and past the living room, into the house's large kitchen. She had been excited about the kitchen at first, looking forward to cooking with her mom on the fancy stove, shiny silver and brand-new. She'd also been excited at first about not being poor any longer, but although she stayed excited about the kitchen, her mom only cooked in it with her for about six months, before the bottle made her lose her interest. And the money, that had never made up for Tim being such an asshole. Not even close, not even when he had treated her to the occasional front-row-seat concert tickets or a fancy coat. It was almost as if he'd still wanted to earn her love, but that hadn't made any sense, because it had been clear for a long time that he didn't love her. No one spoke like that to someone if they cared about them.

Wren got out a pan and sliced an onion, then crushed a clove of garlic. She poured what she hoped was the ideal measure of olive oil into the large pan, then added a bay leaf and a small spoonful of oregano along with the onion and garlic. While they browned, she turned on the kitchen stereo and tuned to her "cooking station," one that was always playing lively, danceable jazz. It was music she'd always thought was perfect for both cooking and kissing, although she'd never done the second to music. She'd never kissed anyone without it, either. She continued to make the sauce, humming a few notes here and there when slightly familiar songs came on, and even belting out the lyrics to one of her favorite songs from the forties. She might have been off-key, but that had never stopped her before, at least while she was alone.

Once the sauce was ready to simmer for the required hour, she started on the meatballs. She was really hoping the recipe would turn out well—she always got a little nervous when she tried a recipe for the first time. A little of that nervousness came from not wanting to eat something gross. But most of her apprehension was from her stepdad's responses all the times she'd either ruined a meal when she was much younger or when he'd said the meal was inedible crap, despite the fact that she'd followed the recipes perfectly. Her mom always seemed almost overly appreciative, proud of her cooking and then some. However kind her compliments happened to be, though, they had never quite made up for Tim's polar opposite and often furious responses.

The meatballs were almost ready after about forty minutes, and during the brief break while they were baking, she read the beginning chunk of a novel Shawn had given her, about a young lesbian woman with magical powers. It was both surprising and a bit thrilling to suddenly have something in common with a character who could do magic, and a lesbian one at that. She fell in love with the book only a few chapters in. Her comfortable kinship with Lynne, the spunky protagonist, kept a smile on her face the whole time she was reading.

Soon enough, the meatballs and sauce were done, and so was the spaghetti she'd started cooking in the middle of a painful break from her reading. She knew she'd have to hide the book before Tim got home from his office: he'd made rude comments about the occasional lesbian character on TV, insults that soon branched out to include Wren and her assumed "dyke-y-ness." He might have been correct in his assumption, and she'd learned that people of her orientation occasionally used the term "dyke" for themselves, but Tim didn't have the right to use it in the cruel taunts he directed at her. She'd tried to tell him this, while leaving out the fact that, however much he meant it as an insult, she *was* a dyke. And thanks to Shawn and Nicole, she knew there was nothing wrong with being gay. Even Tim hadn't managed to convince her otherwise.

Dinner was ready, now, and just in time, because she heard the front door open and slam shut. The loud sound made Wren jump slightly. It wasn't the sound as much as it was the person who was causing it, and the fact that whenever Tim slammed the front door that loudly, he'd likely had a bad day at work. Next, she heard him talking to her mom. Wren was unable to make out his words through the kitchen door, but perfectly able to hear his pissed-off tone of voice. This was not good. Hopefully he'd eat his dinner quickly, and then Wren could go back upstairs and hide until it was time to catch a few hours of sleep. The best part of her entire day would come then—the part where she went to her spot in the woods, and let out her wings, and was free from everything but the magic her body now possessed.

It wasn't midnight yet, though, not even close. So she plated up the pasta and sauce, making sure her stepdad's plate had the most meatballs, and threw together a salad as quickly as she could manage. Then she took everything into the dining room, placing each plate of food and then the salad bowl on its polished, dark surface. She felt like a maid, sometimes, instead of a stepdaughter, one who was expected to cook, clean, and be quiet. Tim had trained her to be as quiet as she could around him, because the more she spoke, the more she drew his harsh attention.

Only a few minutes after the table was set, Tim came in and sat down, placing his usual mug of whiskey and Coke next to his spot. From what little Wren knew of alcohol, his particular drink of choice seemed kind of inexpensive for someone as rich as he was. But if it was a low-class drink, it fit him perfectly, she joked to herself. As she was thinking this, she smirked a little, which soon proved to be a mistake.

"What are you smiling about, smart-ass?"

Wren's small smile turned into a slight frown. "Nothing, Tim, nothing. Should I go and get Mom?"

"Aw, who gives a rat's ass. I'm hungry, so I'm going to start eating whether she gets her lazy ass out of that armchair or not." Tim speared a meatball and stuffed it into his mouth, barely bothering to chew before he swallowed. "These are mediocre, but much better than what you made last night," he told her around a following mouthful of spaghetti. That was the closest to any praise she was going to get, so her tense shoulders relaxed a little as she went to get her mom.

"Dinner's ready," Wren said when she reached the living room.

"Thanks, sweetheart. I can smell it from here, actually. Did you put anything into the spaghetti sauce?"

Wren told her mom about the unique ingredient in the meatballs as Denise slowly got up, wobbling a little once she was standing. During dinner, her mom complimented her cooking at least five times, but Wren still couldn't wait to get upstairs. And more than that, she couldn't wait to go out into the balmy night air; she couldn't wait to let out her wings and finally become more herself than she'd been all day long.

CHAPTER FOUR

Everyone had eaten quickly, especially Tim. Thankfully, he had only fumed silently for the better part of the meal, his usual scowl showing that while he wasn't ready to blow up just yet, Wren would probably be hearing some yelling while she tried to take a catnap.

And just as expected, his usual outburst had begun shortly after she went upstairs, and she heard his loud, angry voice on and off until ten thirty. It was then that she was finally able to sleep, shutting off the light and setting her alarm for midnight.

She woke to the Beatles, singing about strawberry fields, which wouldn't have sounded like a half-bad place to go if she didn't have an even better location in mind for that night. Her spot might have not been all that special to anyone else, but she'd gone there often during her years of living on the edge of the woods in this giant and lonely house. She didn't feel lonely in the woods, even after her wings had appeared. She was used to secrets, after all, and unlike the ones she'd already kept from Nicole and Shawn about her home life, this one felt almost good to keep. No, it felt *wonderful*.

After shutting off her alarm and resetting it for seven a.m., she changed into what she'd started calling her "wing shirts." She'd torn right through the shirt she was wearing when they first came out, and so she'd taken a few of her least-favorite tops and cut out most of their backs, to make room for her new, highly distinctive body parts.

The night air coming through her open window let her know that the night would be cooler than the early evening heat on her walk home had promised, so she added a light sweater to her outfit. She put on some sneakers and grabbed her house key, stuffing it into her pocket. Then she left her bedroom and headed for the back door.

The one nice thing about living in such a large house was that her mom and stepdad's bedroom was conveniently located far down the hall from hers. The stairs were well made and new enough that there also weren't any squeaky steps, but she kept her footsteps light and soft all the same. She didn't know if Tim would care about her sneaking out, but he sure would be mad about her waking him in the middle of the night!

So she shut the back door quietly, too. She never bothered to lock it, even though she always brought her key—their neighborhood was incredibly ritzy, and besides, she didn't want to risk forgetting her key one night and getting locked out. She had no interest in spending the night in the woods, however much she liked to go out into them for a few hours every night.

Wren went to the back gate and opened it, its slight screech as it swung shut a welcome sound by now. It was far enough away from Tim and her mom's room that she knew neither of them would ever hear it. Once she was free of the yard, she also felt free of everything else. It was time to free her wings, too, and she felt lighter than she'd felt all day as she started down the narrow dirt path, the one that led to her wondrous midnight freedom.

Tonight the moon was almost full, so she hadn't bothered to bring the flashlight she had hidden under her bed right next to her clean "wing shirts." She walked down her special, secret path quickly, her excitement growing with each step toward her equally special, equally secret spot. And about ten minutes later, after reaching the very end of the dirt path, she was there.

As summer nights went, it wasn't an especially warm one, so Wren shivered a little when she removed her sweater. There was no way she was okay with wrecking it—it was one of her favorite pieces of clothing, and as she'd learned the first time she'd let her wings out, they weren't stopping for anything, not even a jean jacket. So far, they had seemed to be the most powerful part of her body, but they still weren't powerful enough to lift her off the ground. At least, not yet.

She placed the sweater on the rock she sometimes had sat on to read in the past, shut her eyes, and told her body it was safe now…her wings could be released.

It always began with a slight itching, like a slowly growing discomfort that didn't lessen as time went by. But then the itch would turn into a tightness, and the tightness would lead to a lovely release, one like falling into sleep when you were completely exhausted, or like how she imagined it would feel when she kissed someone for the first time.

In the moment her wings began to come out of her back, and as they spread to their entire, vast size, Wren smiled. The smile didn't come from the calming relief she experienced when her wings felt the summer air for the first time all day, or at least, it didn't come entirely from her allowing her wings to exit her back. She was also smiling from the thoughts of that kiss, so lost in her imaginings of it that when a voice, seemingly from out of nowhere, said, "Hi, Wren," she practically jumped out of her skin.

"Holy shit! Who's there? Are you going to hurt me?" She quickly opened her eyes and found herself face-to-face with the girl from the café. Sia. But she was clearly no ordinary girl, because she had wings just like Wren's. Their intense-blue feathers glowed in the moonlight just the same way Wren's much-paler wings had glowed each time she'd come out to her special spot. It might have still been special, but it clearly wasn't a secret anymore. Nor were her wings.

"I was hoping I'd see you here tonight," Sia told her. "No, actually, I was expecting it. You sure chose a perfect spot, you know. Plenty of room to take off once I get you flying." She was wearing an outfit that looked like a combination of a form-fitting dress and a robe. It was dark gray and fell almost to her ankles, with a square neckline and loose, wide sleeves, along with what looked like tight-fitting pants underneath, the hems of them stopping right above some elegant sandals the same color of her robe-dress and pants.

Wren tried to coax her breathing back to normal while her uninvited (but not unwelcome) company sat on the rock and crossed her arms. "Your dad did tell you he was sending someone, right? I didn't want to try to sneak a peek at his letter before I delivered it. Some things are sacred, of course."

"Of...of course. I'm glad you didn't read it." Wren *was* glad she hadn't, very glad. No way did she want a complete stranger reading everything her dad had written, even if the stranger seemed to know Torien, and even if the stranger was so incredibly attractive. It wasn't only Sia's wings and her sudden appearance that had given Wren a little trouble with breathing regularly, but Wren wasn't quite ready to admit that to anyone, least of all herself.

"Anything for a new friend. We *are* supposed to work together, after all, and so it's important that you trust me. It's always important for the Winged Blue to trust the one who teaches them how to fly. After all, where we're going in just a few short days and nights is pretty damn high up in the air. Wouldn't want you to get so nervous then that you forget how to fly!" Sia chuckled, but Wren didn't really find her words all that funny. Nor were they especially reassuring.

"High up?" she asked. Then a more important question came to Wren, making her forget about her first. "So, um, you mean you're going to teach me how to fly? I've been trying for almost two weeks but haven't had any luck." Wren walked over to the rock and sat down, tucking her wings into each other a little so they didn't bump into Sia's.

"We Winged Blue never teach ourselves, so it's no wonder you weren't able to learn on your own. And you seem pretty good at letting them out of your back by now, at least, so that only leaves us getting you up in the air. Should be no problem at all, as our not-yet-flying young ones almost always learn in just two days!"

"I don't have two days, though," Wren told her. "Not all at once, at least. I have school, and graduation, and my mom, despite her... distractions...would notice if I was gone for that long."

"You'll be gone a lot longer than two days, I'm afraid. But your mom will be fine, I'm sure, and besides, you have a world to save. Two, actually!" Sia grinned, almost looking a little proud, Wren thought. But she couldn't possibly be proud of *her*, as she hadn't even flown yet, much less saved the Winged Blue's world, or whatever other world Sia happened to be talking about. Wren was in no way ready to save even just one entire world. Right in this moment, she felt as if she couldn't even save herself from her small, meaningless life.

"So, are you ready to get started?"

Wren nodded, making eye contact with Sia for a few seconds, whose bright-green eyes made her look much happier to be there than Wren was right at that moment.

"Great!" Sia clapped a few times, then jumped onto her feet. "To start, I want you to watch me, to see how I look when I go about it. Does that sound good to you?"

"Yes!" Wren couldn't keep the excitement out of her voice, as the idea of watching her new acquaintance fly sent a flicker of fluttery thrill through her chest.

"Great, great. Okay, please get up and stand behind me, so you can see firsthand what my wings look like when I first take off."

Wren stood and got behind Sia, wondering if her own wings looked as gorgeous as Sia's from the back, hers a blue almost as dark as the night sky. Wren's were merely the pale, watery blue of the sky as the sun was first rising, or at least the parts of them she could see when she looked over her own shoulders.

But now she stared at Sia's shoulders instead, her clothes seemingly cut perfectly around where her wings left her back, although Wren couldn't understand how they came out without tearing the fabric around their base. Maybe…maybe they were magical clothes. Maybe the impossibilities this world came with didn't just include…what was it Sia had called them? Blue…Winged Blue.

"Okay, Wren, you watching closely? And you might want to back up a few feet. I don't want to whack you in the face when I start to lift off the ground."

Wren hadn't realized she'd been standing so close to Sia, so she shuffled backward as fast as she could. "Is here good?" she asked. She now stood near the very edge of the clearing, Sia a good eight or so feet in front of her.

"Much better, Wren. Here I go!"

Wren's jaw dropped the second Sia's feet left the ground. All it had taken were a few strong-looking flaps of her wings, and she'd been able to achieve flight. That had looked downright easy! It had looked so easy that Wren was almost certain she'd be able to learn that very night.

Oh, was she ever wrong. First, Sia had taken a few leisurely, smooth laps around Wren, although instead of running slow circles around her, Sia was *flying* slow circles around her. She'd landed slightly in front of Wren and told her, "Now, you try. Remember, it only takes a slight push-off from the ground. At least for beginners like you."

Wren really was a beginner, because even with the hardest push-offs she could make with her tensed knees and sneakered feet, she only managed to make a fool of herself in front of her pretty teacher. And as a grand finale, she fell flat on her face after almost an hour of trying.

"Oof!" She began to get up on her own, but then Sia helped lift her off the ground, adding insult to (slight) injury by flying a little as she helped Wren stand back up.

"I think…I think that's enough for one night," Sia told her, and Wren had to admit, she really was ready to stop. Sia squeezed her hand lightly before she let go of it. "You'll have better luck tomorrow, I'm sure of it. Now, why don't you join me on the rock again? I have something I need to tell you, and you might want to be sitting down for it."

"What? Is it bad news?" Wren began to worry, then, that it might have to do with her dad.

Sia patted the rock to her left. "Just sit, please, and I'll tell you everything you need to know."

"Sure, okay, I will." She went over to the rock—*her* rock, as she'd thought of it until then—and got ready for the worst.

"First, I'm guessing this will come as a shock to you, but your mom…I mean, you must think she's your mom, right? Well, Denise isn't actually related to you."

"What? She isn't?" Wren was very glad that she'd listened to Sia about sitting down, because this wasn't at all what she'd been expecting to hear. She hadn't known what to expect, to be honest, but now she knew that just about anything could be told to her next, so she steeled herself for the existence of giant flying badgers that the Winged Blue could turn into at will.

Instead, Sia said, "Your dad told me he got lonely after a few years alone here on Earth, raising you by himself, and then he met Denise and felt much less alone. She might not have been his true love, the way your actual mom was, but she filled some of the space in his life that your mother had left empty when she disappeared."

"Disappeared? So he doesn't know where my birth mom is?"

"No one knows. She was with him when he left through the portal to come here, but it seems she didn't make it. The sky above only knows where she might be…or if she's even…well, I don't want to worry you about her. Just know that she loved you very much and wanted to protect you just as much as Torien did. And does."

"I'd always thought my dad had a rather unique name, you know. Now that, along with how he seemed slightly different from other… other *human* dads, I guess I should say…well, it makes a lot more sense."

"I'll bet it does!"

"Do…do you know why I'm so important to the Winged Blue? My dad said I was, and you seem to think so, too."

"From what little I know of our prophecy, you're very important to everyone's safety, but I don't know why. At least our part of the prophecy doesn't state why."

"You have only one part of it?" Now Wren was even more lost. What new and confusing fact about this other world would crop up next?

Sia nodded. "Yeah, only one. We don't know where the other section is, just that it's missing. Although it's very likely that the Winged Red have it."

"The...Winged Red? Are they kind of like the villains of the Winged Blue's world?"

"Villains? That's one word for them, but I can think of a lot of more fun words you could use. I've been trying to cut down on my swearing, though. Don't want to scare off any girls with delicate sensitivities!"

Wren laughed. "You don't have to worry about that with me. By the time I was fourteen and a half I'd probably heard far worse than anything you can come up with."

"Then to fucking hell with it, I won't hold back!" It wasn't just her looks Wren found attractive by that moment—Sia could also clearly make her laugh. It almost seemed like she believed in Wren, too, and Wren's importance. Wren realized then that it almost felt, for the first time in longer than she could remember, as if she mattered. A heck of a lot, if she was to believe she was going to save an entire world...or two of them, as Sia had actually told her.

"Anyway, I should also tell you that you need to learn how to fly by the time we're supposed to *take off*," and Sia wiggled her eyebrows with these words, "because the portal you'll travel through kind of ends up on a platform. A high one. A very, very high one. And you'll need to fly down from there, because I won't be able to catch you if you fall from that far up above our home. I may be strong enough, but my wings can pretty much carry only me and something around half your size. They can't even come close to keeping me in the air along with you! I mean, not that you look all that heavy, or at all bad at your weight... whatever it is," Sia added quickly, looking slightly embarrassed at her words. Wren knew she wasn't the thinnest girl in the world, as her stepdad had made clear to her on many occasions, so it was wonderful to have her somewhat-crush reassure her about her looks.

"So, let's see, what else..." Sia fell silent, tapping her leg a few times before she spoke up again. "I need to meet with you here at least three more times. Are you free tomorrow afternoon and night, sometime around now?"

"I come out pretty much every night to this spot, and tomorrow afternoon will be fine." Wren was going to get out from her last day of school about noon, and that night was her graduation, where she would walk with Nicole and be handed a diploma. The diploma meant a lot to her, but she knew it couldn't lead her toward a bright future the way it might for her other classmates. At least Nicole was heading off to college the way Wren wanted to, so that was something to be happy about.

"I'll see you tomorrow afternoon, then? At, say, two thirty, let's meet here. Bring your wings, and don't be late, 'kay?" Sia got off the rock and started heading out of the clearing. "You did great tonight, even if you didn't learn right away like some of us thought you might. But I'm sure you'll have it down by the end of tomorrow night. And one more thing...the Winged Red may not have a portal into your world the way we Blue do, but still, be careful who you trust over the next few days. Just because they can't come to your planet, your world, they have at least some power here, or so Torien believes. Be careful, will ya?"

"Sure, Sia, of course. I...I'm looking forward to seeing you again," Wren told her, hoping her honesty wouldn't draw scorn from Sia.

"I am, too. Bye!" Sia waved once and then disappeared in the opposite direction of Wren's path.

She tried to fly one last time but had no luck. Not that it was at all likely that she'd be able to without Sia's help. So, struggling a bit more than usual, Wren pulled her tired wings back into her shoulders and left the clearing. Then, with a familiar feeling of disappointment, she went back to her yard, back inside her house, and back upstairs and into her room.

Before she changed into her pajamas, she thought about her crush on Sia. It didn't seem like a good idea, even if Sia sounded like she might be gay, too. No, she needed to concentrate on more important things, like learning how to fly and saving not one, but *two* entire worlds.

As she lay in bed, trying to sleep, Wren ran the entire night over and over in her head. She finally let go of these thoughts and worries around two and drifted into a shallow slumber to the beginning sounds of rain.

❖

Sia headed back down the path she'd taken from her cabin ever since the first time she'd gone to watch Wren. She'd wanted to reach out to her sooner, but Sia knew patience was best, and the Seer had told her to wait, that Wren would surely learn in time, and to let her get used to having her wings before she tried to use them. It might have not gone very well that night, Sia thought to herself as she pushed through the thick brush, but they still had the next afternoon and three more nights. It would have to be enough.

She reached her cabin after about ten minutes of walking. Torien had discovered it on one of his long, solo hikes through the woods, and he'd decided it would be a good base of operations for the somewhat-distant future. It was decidedly cozy, with its thick, lace-trimmed curtains and a rather comfortable bed. She'd brought flowers to the cabin every afternoon while she was waiting for the time when she'd first make contact with Wren, and today's bouquet included Stargazer lilies and bright-orange roses. As she entered, she inhaled the fragrant perfume they filled the cabin with, then shut the front door and sat down in front of the magic mirror propped against the room's table. Torien had left it there on his last day in this world, having been someone who liked to plan rather far ahead.

Now that she was seated, Sia put a pen to paper and began to write her latest letter to Torien. She would have to lie to him, because she'd contacted Wren beyond the woods, going against the rules he'd given her. She just hadn't been able to resist approaching her student while she sat outside the café. Even though Sia was aware that showing her face in public might be a bad idea, she couldn't think of any reasons for it to be so. Besides, she'd found Wren almost irresistibly cute, sitting there and staring off into space while she drank her mocha, a charming whipped-cream mustache only adding to her appeal.

That memory made her sigh. *You aren't allowed to like her, silly Sia. She's far too important for that.*

To distract herself from all these thoughts, Sia returned her attention to the letter she was composing. It was time to write the person who had sent her here and tell him all the latest developments. All of them except how much she liked Wren's smile.

Dear Torien,

    I've made contact with your daughter, now. She seems very smart, a chip off the old (not that old, of course) block. She looks a bit like the way you've described her mother, and a bit like you, not that her resemblance to you and her mother is strange. Or important.

    Never mind that. Anyway, we tried to get her flying, and it seems that my brother will win his bet with me after all, because although I wanted her to be able to learn in one night, it just didn't happen. After my years of helping our young Blues, I guess I found it unlikely that someone learning how to fly for the first time at such an advanced age would learn super-fast, to be honest. She seems willing to try as hard as her wings will allow her to, and we still have many more hours for me to teach her. So, nothing to worry about.

I haven't seen any sign of the Winged Red here, although that doesn't mean I don't have my eyes and ears constantly open for the possibility. It still doesn't seem likely to me that they would be able to see into this world without a portal, but who knows? Stranger things have happened.

I'll be meeting with your daughter tomorrow afternoon and night. It's obvious that it won't take very much longer for her to take wing and leave the ground. She is your *daughter, after all, isn't she?*

Sia signed off and placed the letter against the blue-surfaced mirror. It started to disappear through the mirror after a moment, and then it was gone. Now, thankfully, she could get some shut-eye. Sia went into the bathroom and washed her face, then brushed her teeth.

Once in bed, she ran over what she might try that afternoon with Wren, to help get her off the ground. And even though both this world and her own were depending on her, this fact didn't keep her awake for much longer than it took her to place her head on the pillow and close her eyes. She'd let herself sleep in late, she decided right before she drifted off. And then, maybe brunch at that café where Wren worked. The food there had looked *so* good…

❖

A few hours after Sia had fallen asleep, her mirror's surface began to ripple, with subtle, flowing circles emanating from its center. The ripples started out blue, but slowly, little by little, they changed hue, until the mirror was blue no more. Two sets of eyes, eyes the same shade as the mirror, now stared out of it. Shortly after they had become visible, two ravens' heads appeared in the midst of the mirror's now-murky glass. Each raven tilted its head in one direction and then another, as if they were taking in the room and the sleeping girl.

The raven on the right was the first to speak, and its voice was that of a younger woman. "Do you think she's learned how to fly yet?"

"Only time will tell, of course. The prophecy just stated that she'll learn in time. But I'm sure she'll be here in our world soon enough, and then we can set the rest of my plan in motion."

"*Your* plan?" If a raven could be said to glare, that's what the younger-sounding raven seemed to be doing as its head turned toward the larger raven.

"It is mostly mine, you should remember. You know I've been shaping its parts since quite a while before you were born. The prophecy said that would be necessary, and who am I to disagree with such important words?"

"Yeah, I guess so." The raven sounded slightly annoyed, almost as if she'd heard that line a few times too many. "By the way, you should know that I've finally succeeded—I can send the power to the female human I found and guide Wren to her."

"I still don't want you to enact your idea. It wasn't in the book. I want us to just wait till she's here and follow what our prophecy says. Otherwise, we might startle her, stop her from even wanting to travel to the Winged Blue's land in the first place."

"I may be young, but you should know by now that I'm smart enough to see that it can't hurt to get a head start on things."

"Can't hurt? You would be wise to remember that we don't want to push her too hard, or things won't fall into place like we want them to. Like they're supposed to…like they must."

"I'm…sure you're right."

With those words, the mirror began to ripple again, and its surface became blue and calm once more.

Sia had slept through her uninvited visitors' entire conversation, although a slight frown and a furrowed brow showed she wasn't completely unaware that all was not right.

CHAPTER FIVE

Wren had never been much of a morning person, and after her lengthy late-night excursion, that didn't seem like it would change on this particular day. She mumbled a curse and, after a bit of a struggle, found the snooze button, giving her a decidedly useless extra ten minutes of sleep. The second time her alarm went off she shoved herself upright and stretched. Then she stumbled off to splash some cold water in her face and see whether she had any especially noticeable dark circles under her eyes. Once the splashing and checking had been taken care of, she trundled downstairs in search of strong coffee and cereal. She was grateful that her mirror-aided assessment showed her looking far more awake than she usually did after a midnight trip to her spot in the woods.

Maybe it was the excitement the last night had contained. This was her guess as she ground some dark-roast coffee beans in her stepfather's top-of-the-line grinder. Lost in thought, she ground the beans a little too fine, but they would have to do—no way was she wasting any of her special coffee stash, which she'd bought at Nancy's Fancies along with the fennel. It seemed more like an investment than a purchase, she'd told herself. Even if it had been an unwise impulse buy, her first cup—splash of cream, no sugar—made the price of the coffee seem more than merely fair in her opinion.

Her taste buds and body now much happier, she poured a bowl of granola and sat down next to the messy pile of newspapers her stepdad always left near her favorite spot at the table. Instead of going for the paper, she returned to the book she'd been reading the night before. The girl in it had just found out exactly how important her powers were going to be in her fictional world. In Wren's much-less fictional world, her own powers were supposedly also very important. Perhaps somewhat more so, considering the girl was living in a book and Wren was not.

Before she'd learned of them, it would have seemed like her wings and her supposed importance could have been right out of a novel. And there were parts of her life she still wished only existed in between some book's covers, that much was for sure. But change was on its way into her life, clearly, change and then some.

"Change" would have to wait, though, because despite her strong urge to skip school, she put on some jeans and a black tank, and brushed her hair and teeth. All of these things, all of these normal everyday habits, had suddenly become exceptionally ordinary actions in comparison to her no-longer-ordinary life. She almost wanted to let her wings out right now, but she'd have the chance soon enough, and she'd much rather take them out in the presence of a certain new acquaintance.

But instead of Sia, her father Torien was the main occupant of her thoughts during her walk to school. There were traces of Sia in them, of course, but she was thinking of her father as she walked through the school's double doors and started down the hallway. Halfway down it, a woman's voice from behind her called her name, and Wren stopped walking, and stopped thinking about her dad and Sia as well.

"Wren?" the voice said again.

She turned around and saw the school counselor beckoning to her. The woman had been trying to get her in to her office for a long time, but Wren had dodged her every request. Wren didn't want to talk about her home life to anyone, not even her friends, so why would she spill it all to a complete stranger?

"Wren, do you have a minute? I thought I'd give it one last try, just for the heck of it." The counselor, Jamie, gestured toward her office, but Wren shook her head.

"Sorry, Jamie, I have somewhere to be."

"I just wanted to hear about your plans for after you graduate. I try to meet with all the future graduates before the year's up, and you haven't made it into my office yet."

There's obviously a reason for that, Wren thought, but after a glance over her shoulder at the freedom beyond the doors she'd just walked through, she sighed and started in Jamie's direction. "Why not?" she told the counselor, following the short woman through the door to what was presumably her office. Presumably because she might also be planning on cooking and eating Wren, and instead of a couch and an armchair, the room might contain a human-sized roasting pan.

But the room didn't contain anything that scary, even if it seemed like it should have. Instead, two ugly brown armchairs and a cheap-looking love seat sat opposite each other, and enough large, potted plants to fill a small greenhouse were barely contained within the small room's four walls. "Are you a gardener?" Wren asked her.

The petite, graying counselor settled into one of the armchairs, looking far more at home than Wren felt at the moment. How had this seemingly unassuming woman managed to get her in here? Jamie smiled, gesturing at the plants. "These are my babies. Just like your fellow students, I help them find their way into the healthy form they're meant to be in."

"So, am I a ficus or a bonsai? Maybe a fern?"

"Oh, I don't know yet. I'm pretty sure you're not a plant, actually, but a high-school senior who's about to graduate and is probably looking forward to moving into the future."

"You're right, I am excited," Wren told her, the words slipping out before she had a chance to stop them. They actually seemed to be the truth, too, another regrettable fact. But considering Jamie's gray hairs, she'd probably had at least a few years' practice ferreting out high schoolers' secrets.

Wren braced herself for whatever the counselor's next question happened to be, but Jamie just smiled at her and said, "That's exactly what I like to hear. Do you have any special plans for your future? Anything you'd like to discuss?"

"N-no, nothing special," Wren stuttered out. She broke eye contact with Jamie and started scanning the pots of greenery on the wall to her right, trying to decide exactly what lie to tell the counselor. "I'm, um, I'm going to work at the café I've been working at all year for the summer, and then I think I'm going to…I'm going to…I just remembered, I have somewhere to be." With those words, Wren moved away from her spot across from Jamie, and with the calmest steps she could manage, she went over to the door and turned the knob.

"See you later," she told the counselor, although that was a lie, too. She wouldn't be seeing her later, Wren thought as she quickly made her way back down the hallway. She heard the counselor calling after her as she got closer to the double doors, but Jamie's voice grew quieter and quieter as Wren began to speed up, breaking into a run as she slammed open the left front door.

There was no way she could have told Jamie the truth, she thought as she ran. She couldn't tell anyone, but that didn't mean it was a bad secret, not at all. It was a secret that lent a bright, precious light to each pounding step she took across the sidewalk. It was a secret no one on Earth would understand, but that didn't make it any less special. Because Wren also felt special, for the very first time since her father had disappeared from her life. Now her future shone as radiantly as the secret that would lead her there, the secret that would lead her to her true home.

CHAPTER SIX

In a different part of the region, deep in the woods beyond the town, Sia was sitting in front of her mirror. She was equally deep in thought, using her newest journal to try to remove one topic in particular from her head. It didn't seem to want to be removed, because all she'd been able to write about for the last hour was that she liked Wren, and not just in a friendly way, not just in the way she was allowed to. She hadn't expected Wren to be so attractive, and she hadn't expected her to be gay, either. And now the combination of these two facts, fluttering around in her brain like a pair of lovesick birds, had made for an annoyingly distracted beginning to her day.

Only one thing worked when her mind was this impossible to control, and so she closed her journal, went to her window, and shapeshifted, letting her ravenform take over.

Anyone who saw her fly out of the woods wouldn't have seen a dark-blue raven, as her feathers looked the typical black to any human's eyes. Only fellow Winged Blue could see the subtle difference in her plumage. She didn't have to think about whether a Winged Red would see her unearthly color, thankfully; the last thing she needed was to be detected in a world without any fellow Winged Blue. And their protection.

But as she flew above street after street, she knew that wasn't entirely true. Wren was in this world with her. She was even in the same exact same town that stretched out below Sia's flying form.

She was apparently in the exact same section of it, too, because with a few more flaps of Sia's wings, Wren appeared below. She was sitting just a few feet away from the telephone pole that Sia almost flew right into.

This flight had been intended to clear her mind, Sia grouched to herself as she landed on the phone wires directly above Wren's head. *Clear* her mind, not fill it with the entirely current and three-dimensional sight of her inconvenient crush.

To make matters worse, Wren somehow chose that exact moment to look up from her biscotti and coffee. Then the only person on the entire planet who could see through Sia's disguise gestured to her and called out, "Hey, Miss Raven, you like biscotti?"

Sia didn't know if she did, or if finding out was a good idea, but she went ahead and flew down to Wren's table on the off-chance that biscotti was as good as her brother's crumble-cake. Just a few bites of the unfamiliar, oblong cookie, and she would be off. It was the only polite response to Wren's offer, after all.

"It's dark-chocolate and almond, my favorite kind. I hope you like it." Wren broke off a few small pieces of the biscotti and put them in her cupped hand, which she held out to Sia's beak. Sia glanced around—good, no humans were paying any attention to her and Wren's interactions. They were all too lost in their cell phones or laptops to even glance at the girl talking to a bird. She dipped her head down and took a small beakful of the cookie crumbs. *Hmm, pretty good.* She took another bite, bigger this time. *No, really, really good!*

Her world and Wren's contained similar animals and plants, but not all the same recipes, as she had learned shortly after arriving here. And this was another delicious discovery to add to her already lengthy list of delectable Earth dishes. It ranked slightly below chocolate-chip cookies, but she decided that biscotti wasn't too far down on her "Must Eat Again" list. Not that she was likely to return to Earth: this might have been her first visit, but it was probably also her last. If they were going to protect Earth from the Winged Red, they needed to use the portal as infrequently as possible. Even opening it to bring Wren to Shyon held great risk, but not nearly as much as leaving her behind on Earth.

Sia took another few nibbles of the biscotti and then bobbed her head once at Wren, who seemed to understand that Sia was saying good-bye.

"Nice to see you, Sia," Wren said softly. And then Sia was off, back in the sky and coasting along on the occasional updraft. It had been a pleasant diversion, running into Wren, but she needed some time to think. More important than getting rid of her mild (but possibly growing) crush on Wren was figuring out what she'd done wrong in her teaching attempts the night before, and how to turn things around in time. Wren had to be flying in just a few days, days that were slipping past minute by minute.

At her temporary home once again, Sia changed back to her more human form. She made herself a ham sandwich, another new favorite human dish, and sat down to wait until it was time for Wren to arrive and for their next flying lesson.

Her trip into town had been merely a momentary distraction from the importance of the next few days and nights. She could only hope that this afternoon's lesson would be successful, but she found so far that the certainty of speedy success she'd begun her trip to Earth with was somewhat diminished since her first lesson with Wren had failed. Just slightly, though, because she told herself shortly before two thirty that today she *was* going to achieve her goal.

Sia chose to hold on to that optimistic thought as she left her cabin and headed toward the spot where she and Wren were to meet. The spot where Wren would obviously learn in mere minutes today. *Obviously*...

Chapter Seven

When Wren got home, her mom was in her usual spot for pretty much any time of day. This afternoon she was watching one of the trashy shows she settled on whenever, according to her, nothing good was on: an unsolved-mysteries reality TV show. Wren had enough unsolved mysteries of her own to not pay it more than a few seconds of attention, but she did take a moment to lean down and kiss her mother hello on the cheek.

The familiar scent of vodka was on Denise's breath when she greeted her. "Welcome home, honey. 'S nice to see you. I wanted to ask you, is there any chance you could pick me up some tonic at the grocery store today? I'm fresh out, and I just don't have it in me to get it myself."

"Sure, Mom, but I don't know if I'm heading into town today. I'll do it if I get the chance, I promise." Wren didn't like helping her mom with her drinking habit, but Denise was always so grateful when Wren picked the tonic up for her that it was worth it. Besides, even though she didn't like her mom's drinking, she'd come to understand it. It was a reasonable thing to do when you had someone like Tim around so much of the time, even if there was an obvious solution that was both healthier and more permanent. But Denise obviously wasn't capable of making that choice, so Tim was here to stay, at least for the time being.

But Wren wasn't, beginning with going out for a short while this afternoon. And possibly, in the very near future, forever. She still hadn't made up her mind, not completely. It was especially hard to decide what to do whenever she was reminded of her mom and where she would be abandoning her if she were to leave Earth for the world of the Winged Blue.

But she had something important to do this afternoon, far more important than her mom's errand, and so Wren ran up the stairs and let Denise return to her TV show and her drink. Once she was in her room, Wren changed into one of her wings-appropriate shirts and put a blouse on over it. Then she grabbed the fantasy novel she was already over half done reading, and with one last stop in the kitchen for an apple, she left the house the same way she had the night before, more than ready to escape.

She was more than ready to see Sia again, too, but it was only 2:10 when she reached the clearing. She'd known she'd be early, hence her book and her snack, but in her excitement to see Sia again and to try to learn to fly, she'd made it there in what could be called record time. A little sad that she had so long to wait, she took off her blouse, sat down on the clearing's narrow rock, and opened her book, placing the apple on her knee for later.

She was so lost in her book that she only noticed the floating apple once it reached the level of her face. As she'd never seen an apple levitate before, especially in such a startling way, her mouth fell open and her book tumbled out of her hand, dropping with a light *thud* at her dangling feet.

"Go ahead," said a voice from a few feet behind her. "Take a bite. I hear flying apples taste better than normal ones."

"S-Sia? Is that you? And do you actually expect me to eat this apple? Its…its molecular structure might be completely different now, since apples aren't really supposed to fly. It might taste like rotten fish now."

A familiar-looking blue raven landed on the rock next to her. "I'm sure it's fine. After all, I've eaten lots of flying food before. Keeps your hands free if you're reading or playing sports. Go ahead, it won't kill you, not even if it does taste like rotten fish."

The apple, bobbing up and down a little, floated closer and closer to Wren's mouth, so she decided to be brave. She leaned forward and took a small bite. Yep, it still tasted like apple, she thought. *Thankfully.*

While she was chewing the bite, the apple landed back in her lap. Sia startled her yet again when she stuck out a suddenly visible arm and wiped some juice off Wren's chin with her sleeve. Wren really hadn't wanted the next time she touched her to involve cleaning food from her face. That was a mother's job, not one for a romantic interest. A very charming and pretty romantic interest. Wren attempted to take the gesture in stride, though. People whom you wanted to kiss you at some point probably didn't want to be compared to your mom, either.

"Much better," Sia said. "May I take a seat?"

"You can even have some of my apple, if you want."

"I don't think I've had one of your world's apples yet. A lot of my world's language and yours is the same, as we often traveled back and forth through our portal to Earth, and we've managed to grow a lot of the same food and raise a lot of the same animals. Many, many years ago, people on Earth and people on our world interacted, at least the ones we could trust. But times have changed over the centuries, and now no one but you knows of us here. Sad, really, as I like your world almost as much as I like mine. Minus all the war and violence and bad television."

"I hear you there," Wren told her, taking another small bite of her apple, which was now under the pull of gravity once again. "So, want some?" She held the apple out to Sia, who took it from her and took a bite twice the size of either of Wren's.

"Sorry," she mumbled around it, wiping some juice off her own chin. "Didn't mean to eat so much of it. It just looked really good."

Wren thought she'd looked particularly cute wiping off her wet chin, but she kept that thought to herself. "Yeah, Pink Lady is my favorite type of apple."

Sia was wearing the same robes she'd had on the last time Wren had seen her in the clearing, and now that she had her composure back, she noticed that Sia's wings were out, too. They looked luminous and glossy in the dappled sunlight coming through the trees. Wren realized she'd never seen her own wings in the sun. She had always gone out to the clearing only under the cover of night, when she knew she wouldn't be noticed entering it. She hoped that no one had seen her going into the woods this time, but it seemed unlikely, and even more unlikely that someone might have followed her.

Instead of allowing herself to worry about it, she relaxed the spots on her back where her wings hid throughout the day and felt them slide out and unfold.

"So, before you get started, I'm guessing you're wondering about the floating apple, maybe?" Sia handed the apple back to her, smiling in a way that implied she was about to tell Wren something juicy.

"Yeah, I totally am. What…is it magic or something? Did you do a spell when I wasn't looking at you?" Wren placed the apple in her lap, giving Sia her full attention.

"Something like that. We Winged, we all have a power, along with our wings, our ravenform, and our hysterically funny sense of humor."

"Your…that was a joke, right?"

"Guess it's not that funny after all. Anyway, we all get our specific powers shortly after we learn how to fly, so you should get yours soon enough. Probably a little after you arrive in Azyr, our capital and where your dad and I both live. They're genetic, too, so we all get the power of one or another of our parents, and occasionally, very rarely, we get the power of foresight, too, the ability to see the future. Or possible futures, at least. But I doubt you'll get that—it's a pretty rare extra. You'll probably have your dad's power, which is power over the wind, because your mom, Passea, never gained a power, for some weird reason. No one knew why, and even our city's strongest Seer, Piru, had no clue why that was the case. He never saw her getting one, either. Not that it ever stopped her from helping with anything she could, which is partially how your dad became the leader of the Winged."

Sia paused to take a deep breath. "So, any questions?"

"Millions. But I guess I have just one main one. How are we getting back there, to your world? Mine, too, I guess. How does this whole portal thing work?"

"Well, we have one above our land. It used to be able to take us to lots of places, but now we can use it only to come here. I took it here just a short while ago, and I have this to help me return." Sia reached into her robe and pulled out the bottom of a mid-length, silver chain, the top of which had apparently been hidden under her robe's high collar. Hanging from it was a perfectly round orb, which looked a lot like a marble, with circles of interlocking blue and gold contained within. "Go ahead," she told Wren. "Take a closer look, if you want to."

She held it out to Wren, and Wren reached for it. Their hands touched for a few short, electric seconds. Once the orb was in Wren's hand, she began to examine it. The round pendant felt surprisingly warm to the touch, and as Wren brought it closer to her face, she saw that the blue and gold rings inside it were slowly rotating back and forth.

"Cool, huh?" Sia sounded like she found it just as impressive as Wren did, and Wren nodded in answer, but she didn't want to take her eyes away from the glowing movements of the blue and gold. "Anyway," Sia said, "all I have to do is tell it to open my—our—way back, and it'll make a passageway from here to your home. Your real home, that is. And then we can take care of the small pesky matter of stopping the Winged Red, and after that maybe we can have some cake or something. I think you'll deserve some once you've succeeded."

If she succeeded. Which Wren doubted was possible in the slightest. But that thought never needed to reach Sia's ears. She didn't want her to know that their world was counting on someone who was probably going to fail, and fail hard. So instead of sharing her thoughts of self-doubt with her teacher, she kept them to herself.

When she handed the portal-opener back to Sia, she was as gentle with it as she could be. As it left her hand, there came the same flush of warmth and nerves when she felt Sia's skin against hers this second time. Touching her soft hand almost felt magical, but Wren kept that non-sharable thought to herself, too.

"So, how 'bout we get you and those wings into the air?" Sia asked.

"Okay, sure. And I might have better luck today, since I'm not so tired. Coming out here during the day instead of at the middle of the night sure is different."

"I'll bet. Yeah, if the little Winged were woken up at midnight to learn, I bet they wouldn't do too well at first, either. Let's give it a go, then!"

She gave it a go, all right, for three-plus hours. Clearly, she had been wrong about the afternoon being different than the night. Finally, Wren sighed, letting her disappointment at her failure to fly get the better of her, and she went back over to her rock, grateful to rest her wings and her legs for the first time in far too long. She just hoped that Sia wasn't as disappointed in her as she was in herself. But Sia's smile, even if it did look a little forced, was joined by the words, "I'm really proud of how hard you tried, Wren, and I'm sure you'll manage it tonight."

Thankfully, Wren's stepdad was going to be out of town the whole weekend, so it would just be her and Denise, whom Wren still thought of as her mom. After all, how could you call someone your mom if you'd never even met them before, and if someone else, another woman, had raised you and called you hers? It might not have been easy, with Tim in their lives, screwing everything up so badly, but at least Denise hadn't been gone for almost all of Wren's eighteen years.

Denise was sitting in her recliner in a loose T-shirt and slacks when Wren got back, so at least she had bothered to get dressed today. Maybe that was because Tim was out of town, because Wren noticed she hadn't refilled her glass yet, either. The lack of tonic water never stopped her from just drinking alcohol straight if she had to.

"Hi, Mom. You about ready for dinner? I was just going to throw together some salad and defrost some of my pesto, maybe with some angel hair. That sound okay? I'm kind of tired, or I'd fix something better. I promise tomorrow night's dinner will be an improvement on tonight's mediocre meal."

"Oh, sweetie, you never have to do anything extra for me. I'd be happy eating tuna right out of the can as long as you're eating it with me. Not that…not that I don't love and appreciate everything, everything that you fix…cook, I mean. When would you like to eat? My show's just ending now, so I can come into the kitch…the room while you cook, if you'd like."

"Sure, Mom, that would be great. I'd really like the company."

Denise grabbed her tumbler and followed Wren into the kitchen. She winced when she heard her mom stumble a bit as they entered the room. Apparently she'd had more to drink than Wren had assumed. Oh well, at least there would be no Tim here tonight to push her mom even further. Maybe if she got out some of the blood-orange soda she'd bought at Nancy's Fancies and served it with the meal, her mom might be satisfied with that.

But after Wren had fixed the meal and they'd sat down to eat, Denise poured about two inches of gin into her tumbler before Wren had the chance to serve her the soda. Her mom was still very attentive, considering how drunk she was getting, praising what Wren thought of as a rather lazy meal, telling her that no, the pesto didn't taste in the least like it was months old, and of course the meal was wonderful. Why would Wren think otherwise?

After dinner, Wren cleared the table and started washing up, her mom telling her she had a surprise for her on television tonight and to try to make it into the TV room before eight. It was only when Wren was placing the last plate in the drying rack that she realized it: she'd missed her high-school graduation. Her best friend—her only friend— had been forced to walk alone.

Wren cried as quietly as she could, muffling her sobs with the damp kitchen towel as she asked herself how she could have been so stupid: to forget her friend, to forget her high-school graduation, to have let her friend down so badly. A friend who was one of the few people who clearly cared for her. When her last tear had fallen, she saw that it was 7:55, and she hoped her eyes didn't look too bloodshot. She didn't want to worry her mom, after all.

In the TV room, her mom's tumbler was half full, but while the liquid it in was the bright color of the blood-orange soda, it didn't look any paler than Wren's had. Maybe her mom had decided to slow down her drinking on her own, at least for whatever surprise she had planned.

"Look, honey," Denise said as Wren entered the room, and Wren noticed that her words were slurred less than they usually were this late at night. Denise gestured toward the TV screen. "It's your favorite movie from when you were little."

Wren recognized it instantly. *"The Princess Bride!* Thank you, Mom."

"Maybe I should join you on the sofa tonight, sweetheart. How's that sound?"

Wren was worried she might start crying again, but the only tears that fell were caused by the movie, and this time she spent with her mom almost made up for her disappointment about missing her graduation.

When the movie was over, Wren saw the time and knew that if she was going to take her usual nap before heading into the woods, it had to happen right then. She thanked her mom again, who said, "Sweet dreams, hon."

But neither sweet dreams nor even bitter ones seemed to be in the cards. Wren lay in her bed for thirty minutes, trying to shut down her brain, but it was rather insistent, telling her again and again to worry about the future. Like, how would her mom…her stepmom, that was… how would she manage, with only Tim for company? With no Wren to take some of the weight of his anger? How would she react when, suddenly, her only daughter (stepdaughter?) was gone, potentially to never return?

Yes, how could she possibly leave her mom, or at least the woman who actually deserved the title, in such a horrible position?

Wren had found journaling to be incredibly helpful whenever her brain was stuck on such a challenging problem, and since sleep refused to come to her, she took out her journal and a pen and began to write.

Dear Me,

    I can't believe I'm even considering going to another world. How could I, with the situation with Tim and my mom? What kind of shitty daughter would do that? She might have chosen to stay with Tim all these years, which I don't understand or approve of, but there's no way I can go so far away when she'll be stuck here on Earth, living with him and without me to take on some of his cruelty. No good daughter would do something like that, and I may not be very good in many areas, but I do love Denise, entirely, even despite her failure to rescue us from that jerk. So, what to do? How can I leave her behind?

Or, actually...how can I take her WITH me? I know Sia said there was no way she could carry me down to her—and my—city, but maybe...maybe the two of us could manage it together? Mom is super petite, after all, in a way I'll never be, so maybe...maybe it's possible. It's better than going away without her, far better, and then I won't have to hate myself for the rest of my life, although that might not be long considering the bit I know about the Winged Red. But there's no way I can NOT take her with me, she so doesn't deserve that, so I think I will just have to find a way to get her out to that clearing on the morning of the eighteenth. Maybe, hopefully, I can come up with a good solution by then. I'll have to, because I can't abandon her to his abuse, and I can't stand the idea of never seeing her again, either.

Wren stopped moving her hand for a moment as she looked out her bedroom's window, past the sill where Sia had landed only days ago and delivered the letter that had changed everything. She didn't write down her next thought, because if she was right, there was no way, no way at all, that she could go to this other world without this woman, birth mother or not, who had raised her, almost entirely alone, and whom, even including her imperfections, Wren loved so incredibly much.

Because I don't know if I'll ever be able to return to Earth.

CHAPTER EIGHT

When the alarm went off at midnight, Wren was already awake, feeling just as excited as she had been the last time she knew she'd get to see Sia. But she was also excited about the chance of flying tonight, especially because she had a feeling that tonight would be the night.

Or would it? She found her hopes of taking flight that night plummeting fast when she woke up further.

As she pulled a sweatshirt over her wing-shirt and put on some pale blue flats, her brain quickly returned to a more clearheaded and typical place. No, there was no way she'd learn tonight, but at least she'd get to see Sia, even if it was inevitable that they'd both end the night disappointed. And Sia wouldn't even be getting anything out of it, not like Wren.

She was reminded of the only thing she would gain that night as she entered the clearing. Sia's striking wings were even more noticeable under the fuller moon, and her slight smile when she turned to Wren outdid even their beauty.

"Good to see you, new friend. You ready to get into that warm night air, see what the treetops look like?"

Wren wasn't ready, though, and her small hope of taking flight sank deeper and deeper into the ground each time she failed to take off. Sia even suggested she try jumping off the rock they'd sat upon yesterday, but Wren barely managed to avoid a twisted ankle when she hit the ground hard, and Sia wound up helping to save her from making the pathetically rough landing even more disastrous. And embarrassing.

"Guess tonight isn't the night, then. Well, it's not surprising." Sia nodded once, as if she were even more certain of her statement than she'd sounded.

"It's…not?"

Wren couldn't hide her pain at Sia's statement, but Sia either didn't notice it or didn't want Wren to know she had. "Yeah," Sia told her, placing a warm hand on Wren's shoulder. "There's no way even a quick learner like me could've learned this fast so far from home. But you're Torien's daughter, so I know that by a little after midnight tomorrow, you'll be laughing about how tonight didn't work from hundreds of feet above where we're standing, don't you think?"

"I…I guess?" Wren attempted a smile, but only one half of her mouth managed to rise, and the possibility that Sia was misjudging the breadth of Wren's meager abilities felt more and more true as each moment passed.

"I know just the thing to cheer you up, Wren. Why don't you hand me your sweatshirt?"

Wren had taken it off when she'd first arrived, and it had been on the clearing's rock until her fall off said rock had knocked it to the ground. She picked it up, dusted off some clumps of dirt, and handed it to Sia. "Sorry it's so gross."

"Totally fine. Now, check this out." Sia let go of the sweatshirt, but it stayed in the air. Wren found she still knew how to smile as the shirt began to dance, the sleeves bobbing up and down in a very merry way. Her mood began to lift as Sia grabbed its sleeves.

Wren wouldn't have believed her eyes even a mere month ago, but she just sat on her rock and relaxed, watching as her shirt led a beautiful, winged young woman in a slow, graceful dance across the moonlit ground.

Back at home and in bed once more, Wren pictured Sia dancing, only she wasn't dancing with Wren's shirt. In her fantasy, Sia spun Wren back and forth, moving as gracefully as she had in real life, and Wren drifted off just as Sia was leaning down to kiss her at the end of their dance.

❖

Sia's walk back to her cabin took less time than usual, some of her tension from her last meeting with Wren bleeding out of her and into the indentations she left in the ground. Yep, she'd sure…what was it the Earthlings said? Ah, yes—she'd sure screwed the brooch on this one. Falling for the one person she couldn't, what a sorry cliché. And even if Wren liked her back, she would surely forget about Sia once they arrived in their home city of Azyr. Because between the fact that Wren would be somewhat like royalty and the fact that she would have their world's fate pretty much riding entirely on her shoulders, she wouldn't have any time for Sia.

And so Sia had to shut down those feelings for the pretty young woman, because they wouldn't lead to anything good in the end. Besides, with Wren still not having taken flight, they couldn't afford any distractions from this most crucial of goals. It was far more important that Wren get into the air by the eighteenth than it was for Sia to get the kiss from Wren she so wanted. The kiss she'd been picturing since she'd first noticed Wren's subtle beauty.

Wren's beauty was growing less subtle by the day, though, and so Sia slammed the door of her cabin behind her. Then she plopped down into the cabin's sole chair and sighed in a way that she noted was rather melodramatic. She barely knew Wren, after all, and it would just be a kiss from someone she liked, not from someone she loved or anything. Wren was only a crush, after all, not true love or anything silly like that. And when it came down to it, Wren wasn't important to Sia in a romantic way, or at least that wasn't where her main importance lay. No, she was important because Wren was needed in their world. And so Sia decided a bath was in order, to clear her head and, possibly, hopefully, to help her relax.

Once the claw-footed bathtub was full of hot water and lavender-scented bubbles, Sia placed her clothes on the chair she'd brought into the room and sighed as she sank into the water, its heat already doing the work she'd hoped it would. She spent the next while blowing the occasional bubble from the bath into the air and turning each one into various things with her power.

But her unicorn was lopsided and her ice-cream cone started to deflate and then popped only seconds after she'd formed it. Piru, her grandfather, had warned her that her powers wouldn't be at their best in this world, so that was obviously what was causing her problems with the bubbles. It had nothing to do with her inability to empty her head of the young woman with the bright, sky-colored wings.

She was half-asleep from the heat of the bath when she heard something from the cabin's only other room. Had that been a voice? Quickly, she jumped out of the tub, drying off as fast as she could, and then she wrapped the towel around herself and cautiously left the bathroom.

Her mirror's face held a cloud of red, and Sia took a stumbling step backward. They couldn't have found a way to use her mirror, could they?

Then the red disappeared, and in its place Sia saw herself holding her bow and arrow, her face twisted into a look of fear. "Wren, no!" the mirror version of her cried out, and the bowstring in Sia's hand slipped, and the arrow left her bow and shot toward the mirror's surface.

Sia flinched reflexively, even though she was certain that image hadn't been real. Had it been a vision? She wouldn't have thought herself to be one of the rare Winged Blue to receive such a gift, but if she was, it felt more like a curse at the moment. Her grandfather did have The Sight, but she'd never expected to have it herself.

She knew, though, that there was no way to know what the image meant, or even if this event would play out in reality someday. Someday soon, it seemed, because the image of her didn't look one iota different than she did right then, her current self now reflected in the blue-tinted glass.

Should she tell Torien? No, she wasn't ready to trust that this image had actually been real. She would sleep on it and decide tomorrow if it was right to bother such a busy man with something that, quite likely, had no need to be shared with anyone.

Instead, she kept her nightly note to the Winged Blue's male leader short, only telling him that Wren still hadn't learned. She left out her thoughts of the small yet growing possibility that Wren wouldn't learn in time, and that Sia would fail to teach a Winged Blue to fly for the first time in her life.

About half an hour later, she got a message in return. It was also short and to the point.

Sia—

You are aware of how much we're depending on you, I'm sure. I know you will be successful, dear friend. I also know that you must *be successful, because your grandfather has had a vision. He has foreseen that we don't have long until the Winged Red take action, not long at all, and so I offer you my sincerest wish that you can hold on to your faith in yourself and in your ability to teach the Winged Blue to fly.*

CHAPTER NINE

The bow didn't feel comfortable in Wren's hands. And the many red eyes staring at her as she took aim didn't help. Her hands were starting to shake from the strain of holding the bow. Then she couldn't hold on to the bow any longer, and so she dropped it and it fell to the ground.

"Welcome home, daughter," a woman's voice said.

And then Wren woke up. The sheets were twisted around her, like she'd been tossing and turning in her sleep. As she fully woke, the dream faded fast, until, even as she tried to grasp its final subtle remnants, it was completely gone.

Wren got dressed slowly that morning, the memory of the missed graduation hitting her like a hard slap, again and again. As she went downstairs, Wren decided that the only way to lessen the pain of her forgetfulness would be to call Nicole as soon as possible, and maybe her friend would still be glad to hear her voice, if she was really lucky.

It turned out that she was. "Hi, Wren! God, I was so worried about you last night when you didn't show up," Nicole said, and Wren could hear the concern in her voice, her words made believable by its obvious presence. "What's up? Why didn't you come last night? Is everything okay?"

"Just some…just some trouble at home," Wren lied, the words coming out easily. Like they always did, she thought with a twinge of regret. But by now her untruths left only the slightest ache in her stomach as she said them.

"Is it your stepdad again? Oh, Wren, you really need to get out of that house. For good." Nicole sighed, loud and long.

Wren felt like sighing, too, but she stifled her reaction as usual, instead telling her friend, "I'm so sorry that I didn't make it. I hope you can forgive me?" She nibbled on her lip as she waited for Nicole's answer.

"Of course, silly. Of course. So, anyway, I have family visiting this weekend, way too much family, actually, and because of that I'm going to be super-busy till Monday. Any chance we could meet up then?"

"Definitely!"

Wren didn't fail to notice the sound of pure desperation her answer had held, but this would be her last chance to see Nicole before she left Earth, and perhaps it would be Wren's last chance to see her ever again. And poor Nicole didn't even know that, nor did she have any clue what was going on in Wren's overly complicated life. She didn't know about Wren's wings, and she didn't know about Wren's father's wings, either. Or that Denise was actually her stepmom, for that matter.

Well, Wren could fix at least half of that, with at least a small portion of the truth. "Hey, so, I've been meaning to tell you that I'm going to be getting out of my house for a while after all. I'm leaving town to visit my dad. He wrote me a letter, explained why he's been gone for so long, and I've forgiven him." *Mostly*.

"Wow, Wren, that's awesome! What happened to him? Why was he gone? And where is he living right now?"

Wren obviously couldn't tell her he was located in a completely different world, so she lied again and said, "California, actually, in San Francisco. I'm really looking forward to going, too," *another lie*, "because of the huge gay community there. He told me all about it, said that we could visit the gay neighborhoods any time I wanted."

"But what...why..."

Wren heard a voice calling out Nicole's name, and Nicole said, "Damn it, I have to go. Can you tell me the rest on Monday? Over lunch maybe, around noon?"

"Yeah. How about a picnic in the woods near my house? The weather's nice enough for it. I'll provide the food, too."

"Sounds great, Wren. Okay, gotta go, bye!"

And before Wren could say good-bye back, Nicole hung up.

Well, that was a huge weight off her shoulders. She hadn't ruined things with her best friend after all. That fact and the warm weather lifted Wren's spirits enough for her to decide to go into town for breakfast. She scribbled out a note to her mom and put it on the fridge.

Denise never got up this early, even though it was nearing ten when Wren shut the front door behind her and locked it.

It really was a lovely day, just warm enough to be pleasant, and the sky was empty of even a single cloud. Wren made her way down her street, her bright mood inspiring her to whistle a little as she walked. It seemed she reached her favorite diner in less time than usual, possibly because her thoughts were lighter than they tended to be. The cheery jingle of the bell over the diner's door announced her entry, and a short-haired, smiling waitress approached her. "Any table you want, dear, and the specials are on the board." She gestured at a blackboard with elegant cursive announcing a tilapia omelet and blueberry pancakes.

"Just a ham-and-cheese croissant and coffee," Wren told her.

"Don't need to write *that* down. Okay, honey, your order will be here quick as a blink, since, as you can see, you've missed the breakfast rush by about forty minutes."

When the waitress had left, Wren reached into her purse, where she'd tucked the novel she'd been reading for the past few days. She was almost finished, only about fifty pages to read, and in the time it took for her to savor her rich croissant and some rather good coffee, she reached the book's final page. It had a very satisfying ending, the girl in it managing to vanquish the dark fairies and win the hand of the city's eldest princess. She'd have to thank Shawn for suggesting the book… if she ever saw her again.

Wren's mood fell a little at the thought. Done with both her food and the book, she paid and got up, making sure to leave a good tip and thank the waitress as she left. The sun might have still been out when she headed back down the street, but Wren's mood was starting to cloud over.

Near the end of the street, she spotted a house she hadn't noticed there before. An older, redheaded woman in a long crimson dress was sitting outside the small, one-story house smoking a dark-brown cigarette, and she narrowed her eyes at Wren as she began to walk past. "Hey, girlie, you look like you'd benefit from having your tea leaves read. I'm having a good day, so I'll read them for you, for no charge, if you'll just follow me inside." The woman rose from the chair, dropping her cigarette and grinding it out with a gray boot. As Wren made eye contact with the mysterious-looking female, she felt almost as if she were being pulled toward the woman and her offer of a free reading.

"I guess I could come inside," Wren said, beginning to head toward the house's front door.

"Wonderful! Follow me, girlie, and watch your step." The woman went up to the doorway and then turned back for a moment. "The hallway's uneven, you see. Don't want to trip and hurt yourself."

Wren followed her, the woman's slow gait and swishing skirts moving in a hypnotic way as she led Wren down the house's long entryway. The hallway ended at a small door, and the doorknob looked to Wren as if it were coated with rust. But that might have just been a trick of the low light and lack of windows. The woman turned the knob and opened the door, and its creak sounded vaguely familiar, almost like the cawing of a crow.

Or a raven.

Wren shook her head at the thought and, instead, began to examine the room. It had three round windows, but they were all quite dirty, and so the space wasn't much brighter than the hallway had been. She saw a lumpy couch in one corner and a crooked, darkly hued painting of a castle that hung a few feet above it. In the middle of the room sat two metal chairs and a cloth-covered table, which held a black crystal ball, along with a steaming teapot and two mugs. Wren could smell the tea from there—it was the only appealing thing in the entire room, its scent floral and rich, like nestling your nose within a fresh, full-bloomed rose.

"Have a seat, please, and I hope the mess doesn't bother you. I'm always trying to keep up with it, yet it never lets me catch up." Wren couldn't see any mess, as the room didn't hold anything besides the couch and the table and chairs, but she didn't mention this to the psychic. There was also what might have been a mirror in the far corner, but if it was, its surface was tilted toward the wall, and Wren didn't want to annoy the woman by asking her about it. Besides, what did it matter whether it was a mirror or not?

She sat down on the closest chair to the door, and the woman moved the other until it was only a few inches away from Wren's, her movements graceful as she slid it into place and then sat down. She lifted the teapot and poured a small serving into each of their cups, the tea a rich, ruddy brown as it flowed from the spout. Wren lifted the cup to her lips, blowing on it softly, then took a small swallow. She'd been hoping that its taste would match its scent, but the tea was rather bitter, more like a black tea that had been forgotten about for twenty minutes too long.

"Sorry about its taste," the woman said, but she didn't drink anything from the cup she had poured herself. "I like my tea strong, and bitter tea is better for readings. More tea leaves, you see."

"Ah." Wren felt a subtle tension tightening her shoulders as she took her second sip, and it only grew with each mouthful of the overly strong brew. The woman had poured so little tea into her cup that after about a minute, she was done, and she placed the almost-empty cup back on the table. The pull that had led her to enter this woman's house almost seemed like it was reversing itself, now pulling her back toward the outdoors, back toward the brightness of the sunny day. But Wren wanted to have her fortune read, even if it was just going to be a lie. She wasn't fanciful enough to believe in things like tea leaves telling your future, even if she now believed in winged people and magic. And since she now believed in those things, did that mean that fortunetelling was possible as well?

"So, let's see…let's see what's in your future," the woman said, interrupting Wren's thoughts. She grabbed Wren's cup off the table and held it close to her face, squinting at its contents. "I see…I see a young woman in your future, more beautiful than you've ever seen. And…I see red…red…red!" The woman flung back her head, and her irises spun upward, and now Wren could see that her whites were filled with spiderweb-thin veins that matched her repeated word. "Blue feathers, all falling, falling, falling down, and you will have to choose, between woman and man, between true and false, between the wrong and the right. Choose Red! You *must* choose Red!"

But Wren heard a voice in her head then, a voice that drowned out the last of the woman's words, telling her, *Run, Wren, run!* Instead of staying in her chair another second, she heeded the voice, because she could feel through and through that she wasn't meant to be there, and that it wasn't safe for her to stay another second.

Wren's chair fell to the floor behind her with a clatter as she jumped up, dashing to the room's door and slamming it open. She heard fast footsteps following her down the hall and through the cottage's front door, but she didn't look back, or slow down, until she was about half a block from the house. Then she paused to catch her breath, and she heard a voice behind her call out, "Wait, Wren, I haven't told you the most important part! Wait!"

But she didn't wait. She ran for as long as her breath allowed, not stopping until she'd left the woman and her home far behind. She realized only when she had stopped running, right outside a used-book store, that somehow, the creepy fortuneteller had known her first name.

CHAPTER TEN

Because bookstores always made Wren feel safe, she opened the large front door and went inside. In the back of her head she also thought she didn't want that woman, whoever she was, knowing where she lived.

Unless the woman already did.

But the comforting scent of shelf after shelf of used books calmed Wren quickly, and she lost herself in the store, leaving all thoughts of anything other than the beckoning of the many rows and uneven towers of books back at the building's front door. Her house might have been what she thought of as "home," but books had long been her true home, and this bookstore held more comfort than the house she lived in could ever provide.

Wren walked down the rows of novels, seeing a few favorites here and there, and wandered down another few rows—memoir, history, and self-help—until she came across a section on birds. One particular book caught her eye: *Ravens in Winter* by Bernd Heinrich. Without even glancing inside the book, she decided to buy it. It was only once she was handing her cash to the balding man at the register that she decided to give the book to Sia. Hopefully it would come across as a joke, but deep down, Wren knew this gift she had chosen for her teacher meant something more to her than that.

She wandered around the area surrounding the bookstore for another hour or so, before deciding that she'd have to go home eventually, considering that she didn't want to end up sleeping on the street. She would have loved to spend the night in that wonderful bookstore, but she figured the owner might have disagreed with her about it being a good idea. After a moment of hesitation in front of it, she followed the street until she reached her own neighborhood, and with one final glance over her shoulder to make sure no redheaded soothsayers were lurking behind her, she went down her street and up her front steps.

Her mom was sleeping on the couch in front of the TV, a glass with what looked like diluted blood-orange soda on the floor near her dangling arm. Wren moved it to the table next to the couch, making sure to put a coaster down first, and took the stairs much slower than she had that morning. Her nerves were acting up again, but after a few minutes of pacing and glancing out her bedroom window's curtains, she decided that she was being silly, and the woman couldn't possibly have followed her all the way there.

At least, she sure hoped not.

The book she'd purchased didn't contain anything about blue *or* red ravens, or a city named Azyr, but as Wren read the first few chapters, she learned many things about this world's much more ordinary ravens. Not too ordinary, though, as they seemed to be far more intelligent than she ever would have guessed.

Wren put down the book after about an hour of reading, because thoughts of the future had started to draw her attention away from all the interesting facts about ravens. But one thought in particular never seemed to go away fully: would she ever get to return to her home world? Then came another penetrating thought, right on the coattails of all her other worries.

How was she going to get her mom...her *step*mom...how was she going to get Denise out to the clearing, so she could take her through the portal with her? There was no way she would come along if Wren just asked; Denise barely left the house anymore, and she obviously wouldn't be up for a stroll in the woods in the middle of the night. Her mom tended to pass out around ten or eleven most evenings. With that thought, Wren began to form a plan.

What if...what if she turned up the heat in the living room that night, maybe set it for eighty, or eighty-five? It would probably be a warm night again, so the combination of the indoor heat with the already warm outdoors might make her mom woozy enough to get her out to the clearing. The few times her mom had been awake until midnight, she'd been pretty out of it, sloppy and slurring and more awkward than ever. So maybe, just maybe, Wren could get her to the woods and to her secret spot under these conditions. It was better than nothing, and in fact, she decided, it just might work. For the first time in a while, Wren paid herself a compliment, proud of herself for coming up with such a good plan in such a short period of time.

But then, just like a hungry, circling shark, the first worry came back to Wren. She went downstairs after deciding to brew some chamomile tea, because as this worry swam closer and closer, its sharp teeth looked as though they wouldn't let go willingly.

While the tea steeped, Wren ran over the same thoughts again and again. She didn't want to leave everyone but her mom behind, even if "everyone" only consisted of Nicole and one other person, her aunt Mary from her stepmom's side. By the time she'd finished her tea, drinking it before the water had much of a chance to cool, she had managed to reach two conclusions.

First, she would have to ask Sia about this: would she ever be able to come back? And she could take care of the second with a phone call to her aunt. She dialed the familiar number and smiled when Mary answered after only two rings.

"Hello? That you, sweetie?"

"If by 'sweetie' you mean Wren, yeah. Hi, Mary!"

"Hi, Wren. It's great to hear from you. How was graduation? So sorry I couldn't make it, but my back is only just recovering from that slipped disc two weeks back."

"I know, and I'm really glad you're recovering so soon." Wren tapped her foot as she waited to see if her aunt would notice her failure to answer Mary's question.

She was in luck. "Me, too, Wren, you *betcha*. So, what's up?"

"I was hoping I could come by for a visit, maybe tomorrow, if you're free? I have some really important stuff to tell you, about my dad." The words were out before Wren could stop them, but she realized it was okay and that Mary deserved to know she'd be leaving town.

"Wow, Wren. Does that mean you've finally heard from your long-lost pop?" Her aunt sounded surprised, perhaps even startled. Wren couldn't blame her. She'd been shocked to hear from her dad, too, although Wren's surprise came with a lot more knowledge than she was willing to share with Mary, even as close as she and her aunt were.

"Yeah. I heard from Torien a few days ago."

"Well, I'll be damned. You simply must come over, in that case. I'll make lunch. Just bring yourself and whatever you can tell me about this sudden reappearance of your father. I can't wait to see you, and

I can hardly wait to hear what you have to say about your dad, too. When's good for you?"

"Noon tomorrow? Would that work?"

"I think so. Okay, Wren. I'll see you then. Ciao!"

Wren hung up the phone, her head full of an intense brew of swirling, disparate emotions. She felt excited about seeing her aunt and about seeing Sia again that night; worried about getting her mom to the clearing; and concerned whether she'd ever set foot on Earth again, or ever see Nicole, or Mary, even once, after she had left with Sia. Finally, she found herself thinking one of her most common questions. Would she even be able to learn how to fly? She had only two nights left to learn, after all, and then it was either fly or fall (presumably, to her death) once she reached the Winged's world.

Her poor head could hardly contain all these various thoughts, and she was starting to get a bit of a headache. So she went with what she thought was the wisest plan possible and walked upstairs to take a nap.

CHAPTER ELEVEN

The moon was even fuller that night, and it was the warmest night yet that month, so Wren had foregone her usual cover-up over her wing-shirt, risking someone seeing her chopped-up top. They would probably think it was just some weird teenage fashion attempt, not a clothing alteration made out of sheer necessity.

"Wren!" Sia called out when she entered the clearing. Her teacher was sitting cross-legged or, more accurately, flying cross-legged, because she was a good three feet off the ground. "I think tonight is the night, Wren, I just know it. You ready to take on that big bad sky, do some dips and dives, some loop-de-loops? You ready to show gravity who's boss?"

"I...I guess." Wren found she smiled far more frequently when she was around Sia, and she was smiling even now after seeing Sia for only a very short time.

It was also only a very short time until the portal to Azyr would be opened, and so Wren tried harder tonight than she had on any previous night. This time it was three hours before she gave up, and Sia looked almost as exhausted as Wren felt.

They'd even tried some visualization. "*See* yourself in the sky, Wren. You're weightless, only your strong wings keeping you in the air, and you're way up, *so* high, miles upon *miles* above the ground."

"That's...that's kind of scaring me, Sia," Wren had told her.

Back in the present, Sia was clearly doing her best to reassure a crestfallen Wren. "Well, you obviously tried really hard. I think tomorrow night will definitely be the night." Sia didn't have to add the words, "because it has to be." That fact was just as obvious left unspoken as if it hadn't been. "Why don't you sit down? Maybe something's bothering you." Sia went over to the rock and sat down, patting the space beside her. "It kind of seems…well, I may be wrong, but it kind of seems like you're only partially here, especially when you're trying to fly. Maybe there's something about what's in the back…or front…of your mind that's keeping you on the ground."

"I'm too tired to try anymore tonight, anyway." Wren sat down next to Sia, their bodies only inches apart. She wanted, so badly, to place her hand on Sia's thigh, to kiss Sia. She also wanted to leave the clearing. Anything was better than telling this young woman with the kind smile on her face the truth.

"Hey, I won't judge what you tell me, I swear. I just want to get you into the sky, where you belong."

"I…I've never told anyone this before, you should know." Wren paused, and then she decided it was time. It was time to tell someone, and despite the short time she'd known Sia, she trusted her, more than she'd trusted anyone she'd ever known. "My stepdad, he's a really bad person. When my mom…when Denise was abandoned by my real dad, Torien, she fell apart. She loved him, deeply, strongly, and so he left an unfillable hole in her, and that lasted for years. Finally, I talked her into moving on, when I was only twelve, mind you. And so she did, around the time I turned thirteen, with Tim. He seemed nice enough at first, really generous, warm, sweet, and he showered my mom with presents, me as well."

Wren took in the gentle look on Sia's face as she spoke, and she knew then that she'd made the right decision. So she continued. "About a year later, late one night while I was studying, they had a huge fight. Their bedroom was too far down the hallway for me to make out what was being yelled back and forth, but I could tell my mom Denise was really holding her own. The next day, Tim was gone, and my mom told me he wasn't coming back.

"But that wound up being a huge lie, because after a month, my mom went out to dinner with him. Apparently, something he told her, or maybe a few somethings, struck the right note with her, because after that dinner, he convinced my mom to quit her job, and we moved in with him into his huge, fancy house.

"At first…at first, everything was fine. He was back to his usual generous habits and was openly affectionate toward Denise. But then, after a few months, the fighting started. Only, this time, my mom didn't yell back. One night, I came downstairs for dinner, but instead of it being fixed, Mom was almost passed out on the couch, the drunkest I'd ever seen anyone, and she begged me to make it myself, because Tim would be home soon, and he would be furious if it wasn't on the table.

"It was then that I had to take over everything my mom had done in the past. Cooking, cleaning, grocery shopping a lot of the time. You better believe it was challenging getting the groceries home with no car and no bicycle, as Torien left right when he was in the middle of teaching me, and Denise never had the time to finish what he'd left unfinished.

"After that night, my mom was drunk every night. Some were worse than others, usually when there had been a lot of muffled yelling and screaming coming down the hallway to my room. I was still holding out hope that Torien would swoop down and rescue us, but that letter, it took way, way too long to get here. I feel…I feel broken, from the way Tim treated my mom."

Now came the hardest part, the part Wren wasn't entirely sure she was ready to share. But when Sia slipped her arm through the small space between Wren's wings and her back, and laid her warm hand on Wren's shoulder, the rest of the truth came pouring out. "And from the way he treated me."

"Oh, Wren." It was then that Wren noticed that Sia was crying, one tear sliding down each of her moonlit cheeks. "It's all okay now. It's all going to be okay. You'll be safe from that bastard forever now, I promise." She pulled Wren to her chest, squeezing her tight, and then Wren allowed herself to break down and cry. But this time her tears weren't from Tim's cruelty or her mom's clearly immense pain. These tears were tears of relief, of the freedom from the weight she'd been carrying by herself all these years.

It was then that Wren knew she also wanted to fly for her own reasons, too. To fly away from this world and her house. To fly away, far away, from Tim, forevermore.

Finally, the tears stopped. Sia pulled back from the hug. The look of concern on her face was so intense Wren almost felt like she was going to cry again, from the sheer gratitude she felt to have someone listen to her story and still want to be around her.

"How about I show you something, something from your world, so you can stop thinking about that horrible bastard? How'd you like to see some magic?"

There was no other way to answer, at least for Wren. "Yes, I'd love that."

"Follow me, then." Sia got off the rock, and Wren followed her down, finding that her feet still worked but were a bit confused about how this whole "walking" thing worked. Between the three hours of failed flying attempts and sharing those painful truths for the first time, she almost regretted her decision to follow Sia into the woods, but her friend's swishing hips and occasional smiling glances over her shoulder quickly changed Wren's mind.

Her mind was changed even further when Sia led her into the small, rustic cabin she told Wren she was currently calling home. "It's not much, but I don't need much," she said as Wren took in the simply furnished room. Only a short table, a wooden chair, and a small, quilt-covered bed were in the room.

Then Wren noticed a piece of furniture that, strangely, her once-over had missed: a large, ovoid mirror was balanced between the wall and the small table. And this was no ordinary mirror, Wren could tell, because within the blue haze flowing around beyond its glass, an image was slowly coming to life.

Soon, a woman appeared in the mirror. She didn't look familiar, as Wren would have remembered a woman that striking. She looked to be about forty, with chin-length, jet-black hair and a perfectly shaped, rosy mouth, topped by a delicate nose and two almond-colored eyes, their irises ringed with gold. "Hello there. You must be Wren," the woman said, with a voice that sounded like it could command an army or tame a tiger. Wren wished that she could sound that confident. It seemed unlikely she ever would, at least right then.

"He-hello." Wren turned to Sia then, hoping her face said what she was thinking: *Who on Earth is that? And is she even* on *Earth?*

It seemed like Wren's look was clear enough. "That's Rysha. She's one of the two heads of the Winged Blue, along with Torien."

"And I'm his partner, as well." The woman's intense features turned gentle as she said these words.

As corny as it sounded, Wren could see the love, plain as anything, on her face. Love that made Wren think of Denise and everything Torien had put her through.

That jerk had just moved on? Without a word to either Wren or her mom? She tried to relax her features, because she couldn't allow the anger in the pit of her stomach to reach her face. She couldn't show this woman the instant and fast-growing dislike that had sprung to life by meeting her.

"It's wonderful to finally meet you, Wren," Rysha said. "I look forward to meeting you again when I can actually shake your hand."

Her smile, perfect or not, was not going to win Wren over, and neither were her kind words. But Wren put on her most cheerful face, grinning at Rysha and hoping the annoyingly attractive partner-stealer in the mirror wouldn't know her smile was fake. "It's nice to meet you too, Rysha. Where's my dad, though? When can I see him?"

"I'm afraid I didn't know you'd be in the cabin, or I would have brought him to Piru's," the woman in the mirror told her. "He's at his house, actually, but I can tell you quite honestly that he couldn't be more excited about seeing you again."

"That's good to hear. I…I hope I haven't disappointed him by not learning how to fly yet."

"Hey, Rysha," Sia said, glancing at Wren before she continued. "Maybe you could come through the portal and use your power. I mean, it's worth a shot, right?"

"What power?" Wren asked Sia, but Rysha answered her question.

"As I'm sure Sia has told you by now, all us Winged Blue, and the Winged Red too, I'm afraid, have a power along with our birdform and our ability to fly. Mine happens to be the ability to control the Winged's wings, but it only works sometimes, as I'm not exactly the most powerful of the Blue. Not like your father. But for all of us, with our powers, well, they aren't always able to come out. Especially when we need them most." Rysha chuckled.

"Well, *that* doesn't sound good," Wren said. Sia made a gurgled, choking sound at her words, and she looked like she might have been fighting to keep a grin off her face. She turned back to Rysha and the mirror. "Why can't you use yours to help me, then? Is it just because you're weak?"

"Well, no. I just think it's best that you learn to control your wings yourself, and your father agrees."

The fact that this father-stealing jerk had talked about Wren behind her back made Wren like her even less, but she still managed to keep the artificial smile plastered on her face. She realized then that she didn't ever want to see Rysha again. But that would be impossible, seeing as how she was co-leader of the Winged Blue. So maybe, if Wren was lucky, Rysha wouldn't be around much…or if she was, maybe she wouldn't try to interfere with Wren's life anymore.

"I should add that your father would love to see you, but it would just be too painful for him to just see you through the mirror. We can pass things back and forth between your world and ours, but nothing living, and we can only use the portal to get you to our home world

Shyon, as it just isn't safe for us to use it anymore. We're worried the Winged Red will be able to locate it if we do, and the last thing we need is for them to be able to travel away from our world."

"But what if they already can?" Wren blurted out. She'd been thinking of the fortuneteller when she said this, and she saw Sia and Rysha share a worried glance.

"What do you mean, Wren? Has something happened to you? Something to do with the Winged Red?" Sia's words had rushed out of her mouth in their quick-moving train of queries.

"May…maybe. I was in town yesterday morning, and this woman, this supposed 'fortuneteller,' she talked me into entering her home and having my tea leaves read. But when I went inside, things got really creepy, and she said all of this stuff about seeing red, and falling feathers, and me. I'm sorry, but I don't really remember all of it. She really scared me. I took off pretty soon after she started saying all these things, and…and I wish I remembered more, but I don't."

"That's fine, Wren. I will ask Piru about this, as it could imply that this woman was one of our enemies, although I have no idea how she possibly could be in your world if she was. I am almost entirely certain she was human, and maybe it was just a strange coincidence or something of the sort. Piru will know, I think." Rysha looked down for a moment, as if deep in thought, then brought her eyes back to Wren's face. "Wren, it's so late at night here that I should be getting home and let Piru, and you two, get some sleep. I just wanted to discuss something with Sia first, in private, so Wren, if you could please step outside for a moment?"

Wren had no idea what Rysha would want to keep from her, nor did she understand how she could possibly be so rude. But did she really have a choice? "Sure, Rysha," she muttered, and she left the cabin. Shutting its door behind her, she sat down on the cabin's low porch to wait for Rysha's secret conversation to be over and done with. She could hear the muted voices of the two women traveling through the window to her right. So she got up, walking over to it as quietly as she could, and placed her ear against its surface.

Their voices were still challenging to hear, but Wren managed to make out a few words here and there. First, she heard Rysha saying something like, "…why she can't fly?…need to…or we will fail."

"I know!" These words she heard perfectly clearly, Sia sounding angry for the first time since Wren had met her. Sia's voice was still raised enough for Wren to hear her easily when she said, "She'll either learn or she won't. But I believe in her, and I'm trying my best. I have an idea, one which may work, so if you can *just be patient*, please!"

"I'm sorry, Sia." Then Rysha's voice lowered again, and Wren couldn't decipher anything else until she noticed the cabin's door swinging open.

She jumped back from the window, hoping Sia wouldn't see her, but the first thing that Sia said was, "How much did you hear?"

"Just you defending me." Wren was grateful for the low light in the forest, because she could feel herself blushing a bit from being caught.

Sia tilted her head slightly, then sighed. "Don't worry about the eavesdropping. I don't blame you. I just can't believe Rysha has the nerve to doubt you, even despite what all the prophecy said. Well, I don't doubt you, not one bit. Tomorrow will be the night. In fact, I'm going to try something with you that I think just might work. Do you have a portable radio?"

"A radio?" *How on Earth could a radio help me learn to fly?* But Wren was willing to try almost anything at this point. In answer she told Sia, "Yeah, I think there's a wind-up emergency one in the back of my bedroom closet. It was my dad's, and I just couldn't get rid of it, even if I didn't foresee any need for it in our current ritzy neighborhood."

"Well, I wouldn't call this an emergency, but it will be required the next time we meet up. I'll see you at midnight, same time, same place, of course. And sorry, but I can't meet you tomorrow afternoon. I'm going to be visiting Shyon, and I won't be back for a while. I need to talk to my grandfather, Piru, about some stuff."

"I'll *bet* you do," Wren said softly.

Instead of calling her on her obvious rudeness, Sia just laughed. "Yeah, after that talk you heard part of, you better believe I want to talk to Rysha, too, tell her off again for you."

"Once was plenty. And thank you. For everything." *Especially for believing in me.*

"You're very welcome. Oh, one last thing," Sia said as she went to her cabin's open door. She turned to Wren, a happy look on her face. "A very important one." Wren got ready for whatever she had to say. "Have you ever had a chocolate-chip cookie? They're the best! If you know how to make them, maybe you could teach me back in Azyr."

"I promise to."

"Great. See you soon!"

Once Wren was back at home and in bed, her exhausted body told her she'd spent far too much of the night outside of its soft, welcoming sheets. But despite this, she still had some trouble falling asleep. She couldn't stop thinking of the unforgettable fact that it was tomorrow night or never: she had only one night left to learn. And if she didn't, if she failed, she would never be able to save her father, and Sia, and even Rysha, and all the other Winged Blue.

It also was likely, and she was almost certain of this, that she would never see Sia again if she failed. After all she'd shared with her, all those deep, painful secrets she'd laid bare, the thought was far too painful to think about anymore.

For once, Wren was in luck. Her mind soon caught up with her fatigued body, and she fell asleep just as the sun was beginning to rise.

CHAPTER TWELVE

As much as Sia wanted to believe in the abilities of her new friend and student, she just couldn't trust Wren as completely as she would have liked. So after a night of poor sleep and a quick shower, she did what she knew she wasn't supposed to do except under dire circumstances: she opened the portal to her world.

Even though she'd only been up on the portal's platform one time, it still felt far more familiar than any part of Wren's world. That "Earth" place is nice and all, but it isn't home, she thought once she'd returned. Landing softly on the large metal disc that lay beneath the glowing opening to Earth, she gazed down at her city with a fair amount of pride. Azyr was beautiful, beautiful in a way that nothing on Earth really was.

Except for Wren.

Sia pushed that silly thought out of her head and dove, headfirst, off the platform's edge, enjoying the rush from her free-fall down toward Azyr. The city grew larger and larger the farther she fell, and after she'd had enough fun, she pulled up with a few strong beats of her wings.

She first touched down only a few feet from her own front door. As much as she had missed her family, she was hoping they wouldn't be home. She didn't really want to see them again when she'd just be going back to Earth in a few short hours, because this was the longest she'd ever been separated from them. Maybe someday she would move to another part of the city, but for now, her home's familiar blue door and the scent of baking bread in the front hallway told her she was in the right place for the first time in many days.

Earth was the right place too, though, and she reminded herself of this as she made her way to her bedroom. The baking bread's rich, comforting scent beckoned to her, but she still had to pick up what she'd come here for and then make her way out of the house and down to Piru's. And she had to do so before anyone noticed she'd come home. She didn't want her family judging her, either for failing to teach Wren to fly or for using the portal when it was likely quite dangerous to do so. She knew she'd made the right decision, though, or at least she *thought* she had.

"Who's there?" came an intimidating-sounding voice from the kitchen. But Sia wasn't frightened, because nothing about her brother Kriss was intimidating in the slightest, least of all to his younger sister. She heard a chair being pushed back from the table in the kitchen, and then Kriss tilted his head out of its doorway, with a charming dash of breadcrumbs located on the left side of his mouth. "Sister? What are you doing back, Sia? Did you already teach her to fly? But…I thought you weren't supposed to come back here till the Earth's eighteenth, and I know that isn't for another two days. Is everything okay, sis?"

"Take a breath, and don't choke on your bread, dear brother." He had spoken the entire barrage of words around what must have been a rather large mouthful of bread. "And what kind of bread is that? It smells terrific, whatever it is."

"It's a recipe from Earth, from some woman named Jool-ya Child. I believe it's called 'French bread.' Would you like some?" As he headed down the hall toward Sia, he held a huge slice of hard-crusted bread with an equally huge bite out of it.

Sia had taken for granted what her brother looked like her whole life, so seeing him approaching her, his bulky form covered by an equally large, flour-bedecked robe, she felt struck by his size for the first time. "It's really good to see you, Kriss."

He ruffled her hair and then pulled her in for a hug, practically enveloping her whole body in his muscular, long arms. He smelled just like the bread he'd been baking, but her brother had always smelled somewhat like baked goods…in the best way possible. It felt wonderful to be hugged by a brother she hadn't seen in so long, and so she just enjoyed his comforting scent and the hug for as long as it lasted.

Then Kriss pulled back and took another bite of the bread. "Srry," he mumbled, "'s juz sho gud!" He chewed a few more times and then swallowed. "You miss me? You miss my cooking? You miss Azyr?"

"Yes, very much, and too much to measure."

"Nice to see where I stand, then. Slightly beneath my cooking or *way* beneath it?"

Instead of answering him, Sia reached up and dusted some flour off the ends of his chin-length brown curls. "Looks like you need a shower, brother."

"So, what are you doing home, then, sis?"

"It's that…it's just…I haven't been able to teach her, Kriss. So I needed to talk to Grandfather Piru, to make sure it'll happen in time. To make sure I can do it. I do have an idea to try tomorrow night, which I think maybe might work."

"What is it?"

This time it was Sia who mumbled. "Dancing with her."

"Did you just say, 'dancing with her'? Ooh, little sister's got a crush on the Savior! You do, don't you?" Kriss gave her a light knuckling on her head, which she remembered the Earthlings called a "noogie." They weren't well liked on Wren's planet, either, from what she'd read in her imported Earth novels when she was younger.

But she put up with this particular knuckling better than usual; she was so glad to see her brother that it barely bothered her that he was giving his nineteen-year-old sister the same unpleasant greeting he'd given her since she was six. At least this time, the knuckling came *after* the hug.

"Listen, I've got to head straight to Piru's, and then I'm back to Earth. Don't tell anyone else I'm here, okay? Please? It'll look really bad to anyone other than you and Piru that I used the portal."

"You're darned right it will, but he and I, we know how smart you are and that you wouldn't take a risk like that if it wasn't necessary. 'Sides," Kriss said after taking another bite of bread, this one thankfully less of a mouthful, "I know he'll need to make physical contact with you in order to work his magic. So I don't blame you, especially since you haven't been able to teach Wren how to fly yet. I know you'll get it down…or up, that is…in time, though, even if you do only have one more night. But you haven't taken any other risks, have you? Like trying to teach her during the day?"

"No! No, of course not." Apparently even her free-spirited brother drew the line somewhere in terms of her breaking the rules.

As important as her brother Kriss was to her, she had something to do instead of spending time with him till darkness fell. She would be leaving as soon as she'd taken care of things with her grandfather. She went into her bedroom and stuffed something from a drawer into the knapsack she'd brought with her, which already held a few treasures she'd brought for Piru from Earth.

It took all her strength to say good-bye to Kriss, and she knew that parting with Piru wouldn't be easy, either. She had to keep reminding herself that she'd be back in about two days and would see everyone again soon. And there was also the fact that someone she had grown to care about was waiting on the other side of the portal she'd just come through.

She reached the top of the hill that her grandfather's house sat upon soon after taking off from her house and landed at the bottom of the small house's steps. It almost blended right in with the sun-filled sky, painted that particular hue because it was Piru's favorite shade of blue.

Before she could knock, the front door opened, and her bespectacled, barely five-foot-tall grandfather stood there before her, wearing a bright-green, flowing caftan and a welcoming grin. "Ah, Sia, just in time. My pancakes are done, and I just squeezed the last orange for our juice. I know you've been gone for only a short while, but you still take your coffee black, correct?"

"Seems like much longer than a 'short while,' Piru. It's really good to see you." Sia leaned down and gave him her customary cheek-kiss hello, her grandfather squeezing her shoulders when she bent down to his level.

"I guess it does seem that way, my dear granddaughter. I should have guessed, knowing you as well as I do."

Piru knew Sia somewhat better than the rest of her family, due to his special sight, a fact that sometimes made Sia uncomfortable. Especially right now, because she didn't want him finding out about her growing feelings for Wren. Nor did she want him to know about her growing doubt about whether she could actually teach her student how to fly.

His hands were still on her shoulders when he said, "I'm sure you'll have stopped worrying about that by the time you head home, Sia. Now please come inside, as I'm guessing you're pretty hungry."

"Your psychic powers tell you that?" Sia asked him as she followed him into his sunlit living room.

"Nope, just your growling stomach."

Sia laughed. "Must've been the bread my brother had just baked when I got to my house."

"He does make some pretty darn good bread," Piru said. "Now, why don't you follow me into the breakfast nook, and we can dig into the food and relax. I know you need it, after all your hard work on Earth with Wren."

Sia went into the kitchen with her grandfather, where the small, bright-yellow table in the sunlit nook was covered with food: a fruit salad, a large pile of pancakes, a pitcher of orange juice, and a carafe of that wonderful invention "coffee," for which Sia would be forever grateful to the Earthlings. There was also the Winged Blue's head gardener of a hundred years ago to be thankful for; it was he who had planted and tended the many rows of coffee plants in their large gardens, just so that future Winged Blue could enjoy it in their home world.

Sia poured her first cup, took a sip, and sighed. No one in all of Azyr made better coffee than her grandfather, and she hadn't had any on Earth to rival it, either. She did know he made some sort of secret addition to it, something spicy that added a little kick, but this was a secret he had never told her. It didn't seem fair, him keeping anything from her, when all of her life was laid bare the second he touched her skin.

"I hope you don't mind my learning about your time on Earth," Piru said as he pulled back the chair across from Sia. "You know how hard it is for me to shut off my ability, at least with people I'm so familiar with, such as yourself."

"No, no, it's fine, I guess. I'll just have to tell you to keep out of my head if I ever manage to finally get a girlfriend."

"I was late to the dating game as well, Sia, but boy, it sure was worth it. Your grandmother Nikka was such a catch. I know you'll meet someone of her quality soon. I've seen it," he added with a wink, then quickly added, "but not who it will be. No clue there, I'm afraid."

"Well, *that's* great. Thanks for that huge, mysterious teaser, Grandpa."

"I suppose sometimes I should just keep what I've learned to myself, huh?" Her grandfather's grin was lopsided and perhaps a bit sheepish. As it should have been. He held out the plate of warm pancakes, which Sia took to be a peace offering of sorts.

She speared the largest one with her fork and put it on her plate, covering it with fruit salad. "Maybe you should. But just so you know, it's still good to see you. Very good."

"It's nice of you to say so out loud, Sia dear."

They both dug into the food, which was delicious as usual, and Sia was able to relax almost fully for the first time in a while. All that was required of her in that moment was allowing herself to enjoy the comfortable silence with Piru and the soothing view of his pond from the breakfast nook's large window. The pond was always kept clean enough to swim in, and Sia made use of that fact as often as she could in the summer. This particular year, she wouldn't have much time for such laziness, so she planned to take advantage of the brief lull before the storm hit Azyr, the one Piru had warned Torien and Passea about all those years ago.

"I…this is a lot of weight on my shoulders, you know," Sia said once she'd cleaned her plate and drunk her coffee and juice.

"I do, of course, I do." Piru placed his hand atop Sia's. "But, my dear girl, I know you're up for it. And further, I have strong feelings that you will be successful in teaching young Wren to fly."

She'd tried to keep her mind blank once his hand was touching hers, but like usual, it was hopeless. It was like trying not to think of a pink raven—completely impossible.

Piru pushed back his chair and smoothed the folds of his caftan. "Why don't we retire to the living room? I noticed that you brought your knapsack, and I'm curious to see what's inside it."

"A few surprises for you, and a treat for me," she told him, and she took out her gifts once they were back in the living room.

"*National Geographic* and potato chips? You do know how to spoil your grandfather, don't you?" Piru took a moment to flip through the magazine, then placed the gifts on the couch's side table. "So, Sia, I know we just ate, but why don't I get some sparkling water from the fridge, and then you can use my bathroom to change into your swimsuit…if you brought it," he quickly added, but it was already obvious that he knew she had. He probably even knew which one it was, Sia thought.

All annoyance at her grandfather's aggravating abilities faded away as soon as her bare foot first dipped into the shallows of his pond. It always felt better than she remembered as she edged her way into its cool, welcoming waters, which her grandfather sometimes joked had healing properties. They did manage to heal Sia's worries on that afternoon, at least for the hour or so she spent swimming and then relaxing on a towel at the pond's edge. It was the first true respite she'd felt since she'd been told of what lay in the Winged Blue's future and what lay in hers.

Once she was done swimming for the day, she knew it was time to return to reality and to get ready to try, one last time, to teach Wren. Maybe that Earthling saying about "third time's the charm" was wrong, and it was really the fourth time when everything finally clicked into place.

Based on what Piru had told her, this would likely be the case, and so it was with renewed faith that she flew up to the Winged Blue's portal and prepared herself for what lay ahead that night: her final chance to get Wren into the sky and her last night on Earth, whether she could teach her…or not.

CHAPTER THIRTEEN

Wren gazed out the window of the bus as it sped toward Mary's lower-income neighborhood. Her aunt's house was too far away for Wren to walk, or at least it was too far after her long night of flight attempts…and failures. At least she wouldn't have to tell Mary about that. She still didn't know how she'd manage to keep the parts from Mary that would make Wren sound crazy, while still filling her in on her imminent departure and her dad having reentered her life. Mary was eccentric, for sure, but there was eccentric and then there was insane; her aunt was definitely not the latter. Nor did Wren want her to think that her favorite niece was, either.

Wren had been sure that Mary told all her nieces they were her favorite, but when, at the age of fifteen, she had finally worked up the nerve to ask, Mary had taken her hand and told Wren in a very serious voice, "I don't know who convinced you of your lack of value, young lady, but you are very, very special, and you should never, ever forget that."

Being around Mary was one of the few instances when Wren still felt special. Although now that she'd come clean to Sia, and had felt the reassurance in her hug, she had realized that maybe it wasn't just her aunt who was capable of thinking Wren mattered.

Mary's appreciation of Wren, and her joy at seeing her "favorite" niece, were clear as the bright-yellow sun when she answered the knock at her apartment's front door. Her blond curls were pulled back into a frizzy, full-bodied ponytail, and her orange velour track suit was partially covered by an apron that said a certain swear word starting with the letter "F" followed by the words "The Cook."

"Wren, darling! Come in, come in! It is *won*derful to see you… it's been far too long." She enveloped Wren in a tight hug against her ample chest, the accompanying cloud of her favored strawberry perfume comforting, as usual, despite its overpowering, saccharine smell. "Now, we have cucumber and aioli sandwiches, vichyssoise with potatoes and caramelized onions from my deck, and Bundt cake for dessert. I hope you've brought your appetite, Wren, because there is a *lot* of food. Now, come to the kitchen with me, and we'll dine in style while you tell me your shocking news. I mean, really, Torien? Back in your life after all these years?"

Wren wasn't ready to talk about her dad just yet, so she evaded Mary's questions with the words, "I'm sure it's really good food, Mary, like always." She followed her aunt into her neon-orange kitchen, which today smelled strongly of the pink roses that sat in numerous large vases scattered around the small room. She sat at the faux-marble counter across from the small sink, two-burner range, and the puce-colored fridge with a slightly dented freezer door. The kitchen was in no way as fancy as Wren's stepdad's, but the company and conversation here more than made up for it. "Your cooking is always great," Wren said.

"Well, your mother and I learned from the same woman, after all. That Tina Mae, she sure was a whiz in the kitchen. And a wild woman outside of it, just like your auntie!"

"Yeah, I still remember that story you told me about her streaking in college."

"Yes, imagine that, in her era! She was a huge feminist, too, as you know, something I'm afraid skipped your mother, although hopefully not you, sweetheart! Have you gotten around to reading that book I loaned you, *The Feminine Mystique*?"

"Not...not yet. You did only get it to me a week ago, and I've been kind of busy, so I'm really sorry. I'll read it soon, I promise." If I can even manage to take it with me, Wren thought to herself. Which reminded her of why she'd come. She took a cucumber sandwich and bit into it, mulling over how to tell her aunt while she chewed.

The bite of sandwich was delicious, of course, not that her aunt's food was ever anything less than amazing. Wren tasted basil and saw some fresh green slivers of it sticking out of the sandwich. The aioli was obviously homemade, as Mary had taught Wren how to make it herself only a few months back. And the thin layer of goat cheese added the perfect final touch of richness to offset everything else. She wouldn't have thought it was a good idea to add the aioli along with the goat cheese, but her aunt had made the right choice.

"This is wonderful, Mary."

"Thank you! Coming from a primo cook like yourself, it means a lot."

"Oh, Mary, I'm not *that* good," Wren told her, as she started to feel flushed at the sudden compliment. "I still make major missteps when I'm cooking."

Mary took a seat to Wren's right, shaking her head as she reached for a sandwich half. "All young cooks make them, no matter how good they are. I did tell you about my rock-salt-coated lamb, didn't I?"

Wren chuckled. "Mmm, yeah, and I'm surprised you didn't die of dehydration when your father insisted that you finish it up."

"Well, Wren, we weren't exactly rich, growing up. I don't think that's what attracted my sister to your stepdad, you know, but I can appreciate, from living a life of barely scraping by from birth to this day, that money does offer some comfort that even the most loving arms cannot."

"I guess." Wren scooped up a spoonful of the cold, creamy soup, making sure to savor its subtly complex taste before she swallowed. "I mean, I remember when she and I were poor, after Dad disappeared, and it wasn't easy on her. That's why, at least partially why, it was such a relief when she met Tim."

"I know you've had a lot of trouble with Tim over the years, but I still don't quite understand why. He doesn't seem like that bad a person, despite what you've told me about him."

"Um, yeah, you're probably right." Wren had told her aunt very little about the indignities she'd had to suffer from her stepdad, and now didn't seem like the best time to tell her the rest, no matter how much she wanted to. It also wasn't the best time to tell her about her wings, or Sia, or Shyon, or all that her future might hold. Wren didn't want to add more to her aunt's worries once she'd told Mary about her planned departure, especially if those worries included wondering if Wren had lost every last one of her marbles.

But she could tell her loving aunt at least some of it, and Mary deserved to know that much. "You already know that my dad has gotten back in touch with me, right? Well," she said before her aunt had a chance to answer her, "he sent me a letter a few days ago, and he invited me to come stay with him. Mom will be driving me there, and so you might not see either of us for a while. A long while."

Possibly never again. Wren couldn't tell Mary that, though, not with the immeasurable number of lives that depended on her traveling to Shyon, because then her aunt might try to stop her from leaving.

"Wow, Wren. I mean...are you sure, after all your dad put both of you through? And this is all okay with your mom, after how your dad broke your...I mean, I'm proud of Denise, for being able to face that jerk after all this time. I hope she gives him a good what-for and maybe a swift slap, too!"

Wren surprised herself by saying, "I almost want to give him one, too, but I also really, really want to hug him."

"Oh, honey, I'm so sorry. I shouldn't have said that. It wasn't appropriate. You know how I'm always running off at the mouth, saying things I shouldn't. Your father actually was a dear man, and I'm sure he has some sort of valid excuse for why he left. Or at least I hope he does."

"Oh, yeah, he sure does." Wren shut up the moment after she spoke, afraid all the rest of the unbelievable story would follow if she didn't lock her lips tight and throw away the key.

"What is this very valid excuse he's given you then, dear?" Mary asked, idly stirring her soup while she stared at Wren.

"It's...he...I can't tell you. I'm sorry, but I can't."

Mary tilted her head and narrowed her eyes. "You can't, or you won't?" Then her face relaxed, and she reached forward, tapping Wren on the arm with her spoon. "I guess it doesn't matter which. You've always been a particularly smart girl, so I'm sure you have a good reason for keeping *his* good reason from me, don't you?"

"Yeah, of course I do." Wren basked in her aunt's compliment for a few moments, enjoying the feel of someone thinking of her as "smart." She did want to tell Mary, tell her everything, but at least there was one thing she could tell her without risking almost anything. That is, as long as her aunt responded the way she wanted her to. "I have something else to tell you, too."

"What is it, Wren? My, it's nothing but shocking secrets today!"

"I'm hoping that this one won't shock you, actually...I'm hoping it will be fine with you, too, because I'm pretty sure it will, but..."

"But what, Wren? Go on, spit it out. It can't be very bad, knowing you as I do."

"I'm...I'm gay."

"And the sky is blue, and I'm eccentric."

Wren's mouth fell open. Mary *knew*? "It's that obvious? Really?"

"Oh, only to other gay people, dear."

Her aunt was gay, too? It couldn't...it couldn't possibly be true. But then, Wren realized, there was the fact that her aunt hadn't dated anyone since her divorce ten years ago. At least not anyone Wren had been made aware of. And then other things began to click into place, things that Wren had read about in her boss Shawn's magazines. "You mean that you—"

"Yes, Wren, welcome to the club. We're glad to have you, and I hope you're glad to have us...to have me." Her aunt sighed and squeezed Wren's hand. "Now you know why you haven't met any of my romantic interests since my ex-husband was firmly ejected from my life. I've only dated two women since him, both of them from out of town. This is not a good town to be gay in, so I'm glad you're going somewhere else. I hope you can stay there, because this was not a great place to put down roots, let me tell you!"

"You thought I would judge you, even when you believed I was a lesbian, too?"

"I guess I got so used to hiding it from everyone that you just got thrown in with the others." Mary sighed and shook her head, then looked into Wren's eyes as she said, "I'm sorry, for what it's worth. Incredibly sorry."

Wren pulled her aunt into a tight embrace: it seemed like the only acceptable response to her aunt's heartfelt apology. She was doing her best not to cry, because that just wouldn't do, even if Mary might have handled it fine.

The tears would have been okay, except she had just learned that she and Mary shared such an important trait. Wren also would have been crying for the loss of Mary in her life, for the days, weeks, months, or, perhaps, the eternity she would be gone. So Wren held them back. She could always cry later, once she was alone. Like she always did.

"It's fine, Mary, really," Wren said to her aunt once she'd let go of her. "I'm just glad that you were willing to tell me and that we have this in common. And...I've kind of met someone I like recently, a girl about my age, but I don't know if she likes me back, or even if she's gay. I don't really know how to tell about that kind of thing, not at this point, at least."

"Well, I know that if this girl is gay, she would be an idiot to not have feelings for you, Wren." Her aunt grinned at her and looked downright proud of her niece.

Wren wanted to tell Mary that she was the one who was probably the idiot, but she kept her opinion of the truth quiet, and instead, she said, "She's actually visiting from where my dad lives. She's the one who got me back in touch with him."

"How strange! Do they know one another well? Is she perhaps a new stepdaughter or something?"

"No," Wren told her, as another half-lie headed straight out her lips. "She works for him, and they're good friends, but he's with someone new now."

Mary looked almost like she was about to choke on her latest mouthful of soup, but she managed to get it down, followed by a large gulp of water. "Oh my, Wren. How do you feel about that, your dad being with someone new?"

"Not all that great. I don't know how Mom will…is handling it, either. I just want it to be okay with her to have him back in her life." Wren found then that she wanted Torien more than merely "back" in Denise's life. She wanted them to get back together, even despite the fact that her dad had seemed to move on. As had Denise.

That didn't mean they didn't still have feelings for each other, though, she thought, and it didn't mean they couldn't work it out. Wren prayed in that moment that they still had a chance.

After their lunch was long gone, late in the afternoon, Wren told Mary good-bye, holding back her tears until she was back at the bus stop. Thankfully, she didn't get any weird looks for crying openly in public. Instead, an old woman sitting next to her offered her a tissue, after asking her if everything was okay.

The woman might have been nice, but she wasn't exactly observant. "I'm guessing it's boy troubles, my dear. Well, I'm sure he didn't mean to hurt you. You know what cads boys can be, especially these days!"

Wren made her best attempt not to laugh at the sweet old lady's words, who, despite her kindness, couldn't have been more wrong about what was making Wren cry. Instead, she thanked the woman and took the tissue, her tears slowing as the bus moved closer to Wren's house.

Where only her mom waited for her, thankfully. And a short distance from her house, Sia, who Wren would be seeing in just a few hours, also waited for her. As she stepped off the bus, she found herself picturing what it would be like if she ever got the chance to dance with her fellow Winged Blue, in place of her floating shirt. It would be lovely, she decided. But that couldn't possibly be what the radio was for…could it?

Chapter Fourteen

Wren ate upstairs in her room that night. Her mom had been snoring loudly on the couch when she'd gotten home, and she hadn't wanted to wake her. Besides, Wren was getting more and more nervous as the morning of the eighteenth drew closer, and she didn't know if she could hide the tension from her mom. Not even if she happened to be as intoxicated as she always was by this time of night.

There was more riding on Wren learning to fly than just the saving of two worlds: she also had to save her mom from Tim. And save herself, too, from Tim, and from this town where she would never fit in well enough. She knew she had only tonight left to learn. So many things depended on her succeeding that the idea of failing was firmly planted in the realm of the unacceptable.

Wren managed to sleep just long enough for her midnight awakening to be vaguely doable. She was more tired getting up this time than she had been in a while, likely due to all her heavily interrupted sleep those past few nights. As she changed into her last clean wing-shirt, her thoughts turned to her friend Nicole. How would Nicole react, were she to see Wren's wings?

Nicole had always been decidedly open-minded, accepting Wren's gayness like it wasn't even slightly a big deal. But this...her wings, her coming from another world...it would be hard for anyone to accept, open-minded or not. It wasn't the right time for her to make up her mind about how much to say, she decided. Figuring out whether to tell Nicole would have to wait, because she had a new friend to meet. And wings to release from their cage, wings that she desperately wanted to lift her into the sky. Once she was dressed, she stuffed the Bernd Heinrich book into the large front pocket of her oversized sweatshirt and walked to her bedroom door.

Just as she began to turn the knob, she remembered that Sia had asked her to bring her radio. After what seemed like far too long, she managed to unearth it, hidden under a seemingly unending mountain of shoes and old clothes, next to an ancient bag of cookies that couldn't be referred to as "chewy and fresh-tasting" anymore, Wren thought with a slight smile. Or "edible."

Radio in hand, she made her way downstairs, lost in thought. Among her distractions were concerns about Nicole, along with worries about her mom, and those things were soon joined by everything she could possibly find to worry and wonder about. She didn't expect her tense thoughts to cease for a moment—they were constant company as she walked down the familiar, wooded path. But her mind cleared the second she laid eyes on her lovely new friend.

Sia was standing in the middle of Wren's special spot, staring up at the full moon. At first, Wren assumed Sia hadn't noticed her, but then, in a distant, wistful voice, she spoke up. "Our moon is gold-colored. I always thought it was one of the prettiest things I'd ever seen, but your moon puts it to shame." Sia's voice sounded dreamy, almost like she was lost in thought, too. Then she turned to look in Wren's direction, and Wren could see it wasn't dreaminess in her voice, just tiredness.

"I'm sorry you have to be up so late," Wren told her. "I wish it had been possible for me to get away at an earlier time, but even though it's only my mom at home tonight, and even though she's probably passed out by now, I don't want to risk her noticing me leaving the house."

Sia looked as if she were about to ask a question, which would likely be one that wouldn't be too much fun to answer. Wren turned her gaze from Sia to the moon and decided that if she managed to say just the right thing, she wouldn't have to talk about her mom's drinking problem any longer. "You're right, our moon really is beautiful. But yours is gold? 'Cause that sounds pretty great, too. I'm looking forward to seeing it."

"I hope you'll like it, then." Sia walked up to Wren and reached out toward the radio. "Is it tuned to a good station? Something that's… something that's good for dancing?"

Sia looked nervous for the first time since Wren had met her, her face normally so filled with confidence that it was a shock to see her features expressing doubt. Was it because she thought Wren would fail to fly again? And if she couldn't— "Wait, did you say dancing?" Wren had just noticed that word in Sia's last sentence, and she tensed while she waited for Sia's answer. She *had* to have heard her wrong.

"Yeah, yeah, I did. So maybe you could turn on the radio and find a good station?" Sia looked away now, her eyes settling on the ground in front of Wren's feet instead of the moon. There was nothing Wren wanted more in that moment than to have Sia's eyes turn back toward hers. But Sia didn't look at her again, so Wren busied herself with winding the radio, its handle's loud whirring making up for the silence between them.

It wasn't hard to choose which station to tune to, because a few minutes ago, her bedside alarm had alerted her to the fact that her usual oldies station was playing love songs for the next two hours. It was probably presumptuous for her to pick something so romantic, but she certainly didn't want to try to dance to anything more challenging. After all, it was her first time dancing with anyone, at least other than her dad before he'd left. And this time actually counted. This was her first time dancing with a woman, with someone she loved to look at, someone whom she wanted to kiss.

"It's perfect," Sia said after "I Only Have Eyes for You" had been playing for a few seconds. It was the very beginning of the song, and Wren hoped the dancing would last till it ended. She placed the radio as carefully as she could on the rock to her left and then approached Sia. As she did, Wren quietly took in how graceful Sia looked in her slightly loose robes, how beautiful her wings were in the moonlight, and especially how Sia was now holding out her hand.

She took Wren's left hand in her right, her fingers somehow both gentle and firm in their grip. "Now, you just need to let out your wings and close your eyes. I hear dancing is best when your eyes are closed." It was then that Wren finally accepted that, yes, Sia did want to dance with her. Maybe not as much as Wren did, but even if she didn't, it still was enough to bring a soft smile to Wren's lips as she closed her eyes and released her wings.

Once her eyes had been shut for a few seconds, she felt Sia place her hand near where Wren's right wing was attached to her back. Wren risked laying her head against Sia's shoulder, and Sia didn't tell her to remove it, instead starting to slowly sway back and forth in a circle. Wren was so lost for the entire rest of the song, she barely even noticed when it drew to a close.

The show's host spoke after a second song had come and gone, and then Wren slowly opened her eyes. She was hoping to see Sia grinning, perhaps, or at least a small smile, something to let her know that Sia was glad to have her there. But that wasn't what she noticed first when she opened her eyes.

The trees they'd been standing near weren't where they belonged, it seemed. While Wren tried to make sense of that confusing fact, Sia pulled away from her, letting go of her hand and moving a few steps back from where they'd stood.

No, not a few *steps* back, but a few *feet* back, because now the strangeness of the trees made sense. Wren was floating a few feet above them, the ground seeming like it was miles below her, a horribly far length down, and Wren was…she was…

"I'm flying? I'm…I'm flying!" She could feel her wings flapping behind her, each of their beats strong and steady, like they'd always known exactly what to do, if only she'd relaxed enough to let them. And that's what the dancing had done. It had allowed her to let go of all the worries that held her down on the ground, tethered to the earth, tethered to everything that was wrong with her. But those tethers were gone now, and she felt weightless for the first time since her father had disappeared.

Perhaps because she almost was.

"Wanna take those bad girls out for a spin?" Sia asked, the pride in her voice unmistakable to Wren's happy ears.

All of her was happy, she found, and she only grew more joyful when Sia grabbed her hand and took off, pulling her along at a fast but surprisingly comfortable speed. Wren found she had gotten used to the trees being so far below them, and it was only mildly uncomfortable to also see her home as so tiny and so far beneath her feet.

Being in the air in such a wondrous way allowed her to let go of everything that had happened in that house, everything that had kept her tethered to the earth and tied to her pain. Maybe it would return when she landed again, but for now, she was full of hope, for the first time in far too many years.

"How do you like flying?" Sia asked her, a wide, pleased smile now directed straight at Wren.

"I love it! I feel so…so free!" She didn't add that the best part was holding Sia's hand as she flew, but that particular pleasure was only slightly stronger than the fact that she'd finally learned. Now she would be able to go to Shyon: to see her dad, finally, and to help her mom, Denise, be free, too. It might not feel as good to her mom as this—as flying, flying and holding Sia's hand in hers—but she knew that for her poor mother, anything would be an improvement over being stuck here with Tim, and her drinking, and all the problems that came with living in this particular world.

Flying might have felt like a new start to her, Wren thought as she and Sia touched down back in the familiar clearing, but the real new start would be happening very soon. The new start she'd always wanted, and one that included the dad she wanted to see again, and yes, the world that was her true home.

"Thank you," she told Sia when she let go of her hand. It didn't seem like enough, just those two simple words, but it was all Wren could give her then. Later, sometime in the future, maybe she could give her more. Maybe she could give Sia what all these lessons had really been for. Maybe she could actually save the day, the way Sia seemed to think she could.

It felt strange, to have someone believe in her the way Sia clearly did. Not just ordinary, everyday faith, the type her mom or Nicole or her Aunt Mary might have had in her. No, this was something else entirely. This was someone who believed Wren was capable of being a hero.

Wren hated the fact that she had to go home now and leave Sia's side, but she cheered herself up with the fact that she'd be spending a lot more time with her friend soon, now that she could fly. Fantasies of what might transpire between them in Wren and Sia's home world floated through her head on the walk home, which made it pass by much quicker than it ever had before.

Back at home, Wren slowly changed into her PJs, and then she turned on her bedside radio, still tuned to the oldies station. She'd listened to it for years, but now it had a new, special meaning to her. Now it was the station she'd been listening to when she learned how to fly. More importantly, though, it was the station she'd been listening to when she'd danced with a girl for the first time. As she was climbing into bed, she realized she'd forgotten to give Sia the book. Hopefully her finally learning to fly would be a good enough replacement. Besides, could they even take the book with them? After all, their arms would be quite full with keeping Denise in the air once they'd arrived.

The station's DJ spoke the last words Wren heard before she fell asleep. "This is our final song of the night, all you lovebirds. I hope you'll be listening to it nestled in the arms of someone you adore."

CHAPTER FIFTEEN

Wren woke up much later than usual the next morning. It was half-past eleven when she finally managed to pull back the covers and go downstairs. Denise was already in front of the TV, dressed in short-sleeved flannel pajamas and holding a mug of what was likely coffee.

It was incredibly rare for Denise to be up before Wren, but her mom didn't seem to notice the lateness of her stepdaughter's rising this morning, or even the fact that Wren had entered the room. All that would surely change once they were in Azyr, though, and Wren found she couldn't wait for the plethora of imminent changes that would come once they left Earth behind.

But first it was time to say her good-byes to Nicole. She had barely enough time to get dressed and make the picnic for their meal out in the woods. It would be her very last meal with Nicole, for however long this whole adventure to her home world would take. It would either be only a few days or perhaps, and Wren hoped this wasn't the case, forever. She wished she could take Nicole along with her mom, and Mary, too, because they were among the few people who had made her time in this town—and on Earth—somewhat more livable.

That wasn't enough of an excuse to rip them out of their own lives, though, so instead of thinking more about how much she would miss a few very dear friends from her no-longer-home planet, Wren got to work on making lunch. She sliced some salami, three types of cheese, and half a baguette, and washed some grapes and strawberries, which she then cut up and put into a container with the grapes. She would have liked to have thrown together something fancier for her last meal with Nicole, but her friend would arrive in only a few minutes; Nicole was almost always right on time.

Just as Wren was putting two mugs into the top of her backpack, she heard a knock on the front door. She rushed to it, more eager to see her friend than she had been in ages. It seemed Nicole could see how excited she was, as in the middle of a tight hug, she told Wren, "Whoa, Tiger, I'm glad to see you too, but maybe you could let me breathe while you hug me?"

"Sorry, Nicole, sorry," Wren said and let go and quickly backed away.

"So, when's lunch? I'm pretty hungry, actually, because I jogged here."

Wren noticed then that her friend was dressed for running, wearing a dark sports bra and thin, skin-tight shorts. Nicole had never been her type, a little too feminine for her taste, but her workout habits were clearly working for her, with every visible inch of her body completely toned. Wren had gone running with Nicole a few times over the years, but it had never come easily enough to her, especially when those runs had included having to keep up with her speedy friend. After getting the worst charley horse she'd ever had, during a heat wave the previous summer, she'd turned in her jogging shoes for good. Wren began to wonder then if flying might be an equally good workout.

"Lunch will be really soon, I promise," she told Nicole, turning slightly toward the kitchen. "I just have to go get my backpack. I didn't have time to fix anything fancy, though."

"Totally fine, Wren. You never have to go all-out for me. Just your company is enough. Besides, it's hearing all about your trip to see your dad that I'm excited about, even as hungry as my run made me."

"I'll be right back, then," Wren said, and she went into the kitchen and grabbed her bag full of food.

The walk into the woods felt like it took a little longer than it had the last few times, and Wren realized it was probably because of her current company. No matter how much she cared about her best friend, Nicole didn't cause the level of excitement to spread throughout Wren's body that Sia did. She didn't make Wren's pulse race when she touched her, and she wasn't someone Wren wanted to dance with, either.

The clearing was almost too warm where the sun managed to reach the ground, so Wren laid out the blanket she'd grabbed from the hall closet in the shade instead. She figured Nicole would be pretty warm from her run, and the heavy bag and the summer heat had made eating in the sun unappealing to Wren as well.

She unpacked her backpack and poured each of them some soda, and they dug into the food. Wren found her appetite wasn't at its usual level, but Nicole more than made up for her, remarking between bites about how delicious everything was. When they were both done eating, Nicole drained the last of her soda and turned to Wren, her face more serious than Wren had seen it in ages. "So, now Torien is back in your life, and you're going to go see him. Time to spill, Wren. Tell me *everything.*"

So Wren shared as much as she could, telling Nicole that her stepmom (although she made sure to still call her "mom") was driving her there, a fact that made Nicole gasp. She knew a bit about Wren's dad's departure and the havoc it had wreaked on Denise's and her lives. Wren had to admit that the idea of Denise driving her to see her dad after her immense heartbreak was rather unbelievable. So she told Nicole that her "mom" was choosing to leave the past in the past. She said Torien wanted to fix things, not just between himself and Wren, but also with her mom. Wren wished her lie were actually the truth, and she also almost told Nicole her plans for trying to get them back together, if Denise could ever forgive him enough to let that happen. She wouldn't blame her if she wasn't able to, though, and that part she did tell Nicole.

"I wouldn't blame you if *you* couldn't, either," her friend said, and she looked as though she meant it. "I'm not sure you're making the right move here, but I can understand your choice, at least, to go see your long-lost dad. I don't know if I could ever forgive my own dad if he'd done something like that. You're made of pretty tough stuff, Wren…pretty damn tough stuff." Nicole wrapped her arm around Wren's shoulder and squeezed her against her side. Wren knew in that moment that she had to tell Nicole everything, or she'd never be able to forgive herself. Nicole had to know that she might not be coming back, no matter how high the cost might be for her revelation.

"There's more, you know. There's something I've been keeping from you for a while, and it's time I told you the entire truth." Wren got up from the blanket, reaching for the bottom of her tank top, ready to pull it over her head.

Right when she began to lift her shirt, she heard some rustling in the trees behind her back, and a familiar female voice said, "I'm the entire truth."

Sia stood in front of the path they'd taken to her cabin two nights back, wearing a loose, summery dress and a less-than-believable smile. Normally Wren would have been glad to see her, but she'd been so ready to reveal her wings to Nicole that this interruption wasn't as welcome as it could have been. In fact, as Sia walked over to Wren and took her hand, she realized it wasn't welcome at all, despite how good her new friend's hand felt against hers. "I'm the one who convinced her dad, Torien, to get back in touch with Wren. And Wren and I, we're kind of seeing each other now."

"Really? Wren, that's great! Why don't you join us, uh…"

"Sasha. I'm Sasha. Sure, I'd love to. After all, I'm happy to meet any friend of Wren's." Sia, or "Sasha," flowed into a cross-legged position on the blanket, with a level of grace Wren felt she'd never attain herself. The sudden appearance of her attractive teacher had completely prevented Wren from following through with her big reveal, and she wondered if Sia's showing up was intended as more than just a pleasant surprise. It certainly seemed that way, especially as Wren was pretty sure they weren't "seeing each other," no matter how much Wren wanted that to be true. Wouldn't Sia have told her that, if it were the case? Could a single dance turn a friendship into a romantic relationship? Wren would have to ask her about that later, if she could work up the nerve.

Sia polished off the rest of the food as she told Nicole a string of lies about everything they'd spent the last few days doing, all of it made up except for how they'd met. Then, just as abruptly as she'd arrived, Sia told Nicole it was very nice meeting her, but she had to go finish packing, because she and Wren were leaving the very next morning. "Bright and early!" she said, and then she was gone, and now it was only a very confused Wren and a talkative Nicole who remained in the clearing.

"That's a pretty big thing to keep from your best friend, dude!" She punched Wren lightly on the arm. "Any other big secrets? Do you have a brand-new magical power, like the ability to spin straw into gold? Or are you a Martian?"

Nicole's two guesses held a grain of truth, as actually, Wren did have a magical ability, or at least she would soon, and she was also from another world. But instead of telling Nicole anything more, she just laughed and put up her hands. "You got me! My alien overlords and I are going to take over Earth and turn everyone gay. Except for you."

"Nah, you can turn me gay if you want, as I just got dumped. Dumb ex-boyfriend, he told me over that fancy meal he took me out for, then had the nerve to ask me if I wanted to make out in his car one last time."

Wren offered her condolences, and they talked about Nicole's upcoming college plans and all the hot guys she'd probably meet there.

Any mention of Wren's future, to her relief, was forgotten for the rest of the afternoon. It had probably been a bad idea, telling Nicole the truth and showing off her wings. Wren could always tell her later, once she'd been given the chance to save Earth. Because if she failed, it wouldn't matter whether she'd told Nicole or not. It was only then that she realized that if she failed, she probably would never see Nicole again. In fact, her best friend might not even survive if she didn't succeed.

Wren's endless cycle of thoughts about the future distracted her from the rest of her visit with Nicole. She only managed to half-listen to her friend's words as they left their picnic spot and walked back to Wren's house. Nicole had to leave then, she told Wren, but she insisted Wren call her from San Francisco, and email her, and send postcards and telegrams while she was at it.

Wren had done her best to hide her fears from Nicole, and it looked as if she'd been successful, because her friend left with a smile on her face. Wren's own smile disappeared as soon as Nicole had jogged away. She knew then that she couldn't make herself accept this being the very last time she saw her closest friend.

So right then, at that moment, Wren decided that she would dedicate everything she had to making sure Earth and everyone on it was kept safe. Who knows, she thought as she shut the front door, maybe it'll even work. Maybe she'd manage the impossible and save everyone. It was a pretty tall order, as she'd told herself again and again. But a tiny spark of belief deep within her had flickered into life the previous night. And if Wren was lucky, its glow would only brighten over time.

She still had the problem of getting her mom out to the clearing, though, a feat that could go wrong in so many ways. As Wren started to clean up from her picnic she wondered if Sia would even let her take her mom with them. Could she trust her new friend, even if she'd just said they were dating? Wren was almost positive she wouldn't be able to step through that portal to Shyon if Sia refused her request, no matter how many people depended on her doing so. She just couldn't leave her mom behind. It was utterly unacceptable, so Sia simply had to agree, she thought with a larger-than-usual touch of conviction. She had to let Wren's mom, who was her true mother in everything but blood, join them in Azyr.

CHAPTER SIXTEEN

W ren had decided that since this would be her last night on Earth, at least for the foreseeable future, she should make tonight's meal special. So she went to the town's best butcher to pick up some organic Cornish game hens. Then it was off to the small grocery store closest to her home to get some fresh rosemary, a lemon, and some garlic, along with several fingerling potatoes. Her last stop was Nancy's Fancies, where she bought an exceptionally expensive flourless chocolate cake. She'd had her eye on it for ages but had never been able to justify its sky-high cost. She was pretty sure that leaving your home planet to save a few billion people did, actually, justify paying thirty dollars for a cake. If *that* didn't make her purchase okay, that cake had no right to exist.

Wren felt her own right to exist emerging, bit by bit. She was finally able to begin adding to the small reservoir of inner strength that had kept her afloat during all these years of challenge and heartache. Now she would be free of every single thing that had held her back; now she was finally ready for a big change. Maybe not one as epic as her near future seemed to hold, but only time would allow her to see if she could handle all this upheaval. She wondered, as she slid the Cornish game hens into the oven, if her mom could handle it, too. She wouldn't even have a day to adjust to this immense change in her life, not like the weeks Wren had been given to adjust to her wings, and to the greater purpose she'd gained upon receiving her dad's letter.

She went into the living room to get her mom as soon as the hens and potatoes were done roasting. Denise was, of course, camped out in front of the TV. When she looked up from the screen, she told Wren how good dinner smelled. Her words were a little slurred, but for the first time in her life, Wren was glad she was drunk. It would make that night all the easier, so she didn't try to talk her mom out of opening a bottle of wine. Nor did she try to stop her from pouring herself a third full glass of it, near the end of the meal.

After dinner, her mom took the remainder of her glass of wine into the living room, and Wren waited until she was settled into her favorite chair to enact the first part of her plan. After turning the heat up to eighty-five, she went upstairs, the rising temperature on the ground floor already making her sweat a little as she reached her bedroom.

She didn't know what to do to fill the hours until the time came to walk away from her house. What did a person normally do when they were going to leave everything familiar behind?

Large parts of what she'd soon be doing didn't allow for "normal" actions. Wren guessed that no one had ever done what she was about to do, leaving Earth for another populated planet. Not just any planet, either, but one full of magic and winged beings, as well as entirely empty of humans. One human would be there in just a few hours, though.

As long as Wren's plan actually worked.

She tried to write in her journal, hoping it might help her maybe manage to process the coming events, but her brain seemed to have turned to mush. All she could write was a jumble of questions and doubts. Just like what was going through her head right then, and sadly, those uncomfortable questions and doubts were the only things she had to keep her company on that night. She was almost certain she wouldn't be able to sleep, but she tried anyway, lying down on the bed she'd slept in for so many years. No matter how familiar it was, this bed was now one she might be using for the last time in her life.

These thoughts didn't provide any comfort. But the heat from the night and the downstairs furnace were reaching out tendrils of exhaustion until Wren was completely entwined. She passed out from the rising heat, barely having the forethought to set her alarm before she sank into her mattress and into sleep.

❖

The alarm that woke Wren from her deep sleep was the least welcome it had been in ages, especially because it had yanked her out of a dream full of delicious food and even more delicious kissing. She slowly came back into wakefulness and the immense reality of the night ahead. As she did, she noticed something at the foot of the bed, something she definitely hadn't put there herself.

On the very end of her bed's covers lay what looked like a robe, and when she got out of bed and picked it up, she saw that it *was* a robe. Furthermore, it was identical to Sia's. She could tell, though, even with only the barest hint of moonlight coming in through her curtains, that unlike Sia's robe, it was pale blue, a blue that would match her wings perfectly.

She smiled at her friend's thoughtfulness, quickly getting over the brief annoyance at both her intrusion into Wren's bedroom and the fact she hadn't woken her to say hello.

She would be seeing Sia soon enough, Wren reminded herself, and besides, she had more important things to think about right now. Like whether her plan for her mom would work. She quickly changed into the robe, leaving her wing-shirt and jeans on the bed, and scanned her bedroom one last time.

Then she went downstairs, where she heard loud snores coming from the living room, snores that told her at least part of her plan had already worked. Her mom was deeply asleep on the living-room couch, and it was no wonder—the ground floor was almost hotter than Wren could stand. Her strong wishes to get out of this feverish room pushed her over to where Denise lay, and Wren began to shake her sleeping mom awake. That took quite a few strong shakes.

"H-huh? 'hat you, W-Wren darrrling? What's…it's hot, so *hot*." Denise looked up at her with only half-open eyes, the heat and her drunkenness clearly making the act of waking up close to impossible. Both of those things were in Wren's favor, for once.

"You're…you're dreaming," Wren told her clearly wasted mother, "and you need to follow me outside. There's a fairy waiting out in the woods, and she's going to grant your wishes, all of them."

Slowly, Wren managed to pull her into an upright position. "Slowly" because her mom felt heavier than a load of metal bricks, which was quite the feat for a woman who couldn't have weighed more than a hundred and ten pounds, soaking wet.

Once her mom was sitting fully upright, or at least leaning upright, Wren got her off the couch, noticing that her mom's hands were damp with sweat. Wren's own forehead was beginning to be drenched as well.

"Ho'kay. Leht's go meet the fairy, dream Wren. I want a mush-huled hunk hoo'll mow my lawn and paint my nails."

Once they were outside in the hot night air, Wren began to lead her mother in the direction of the back fence. Reaching it took longer than ever before, at least five minutes of weaving back and forth while putting up with her mom's strong suggestions that if she were dreaming, the fairy should have sent a chariot to carry them to her.

Wren wouldn't have minded a chariot, but she didn't even have a wagon to carry her mom in, much less the dragon-pulled carriage her mom kept going on about. They didn't exactly reach the clearing in record time, but they did manage to reach it, both of them equally sticky with sweat, from the hot night as well as the struggle it had taken them to reach their destination.

Wren's jaw dropped when they entered the clearing, and she also almost dropped her mom, whose eyes were currently shut from either exhaustion or the effects of alcohol.

Her jaw had gone slack because in front of her stood Sia, her back turned to Wren and her mother. Sia was holding out her portal-making necklace, which had apparently managed to do its job, because a few feet in front of Sia stood one of the most beautiful sights Wren had ever seen, a fast-growing circle of shimmering blue-and-gold opalescence.

She was so awestruck by its beauty that she forgot about everything else, just long enough for her crucial grip on her mom's waist to loosen.

Long enough for her mom to stumble forward.

Long enough for her mom to take three incredibly awkward steps toward the portal, and long enough for her to trip over a root, fall forward, and to dive, headfirst, straight through the shimmering opening.

So what could Wren do but run right past an angry-looking Sia and dive through the portal herself, with absolutely no idea whether she'd reach her mom in time, or any ideas about what else would await her on the other side.

❖

Sia couldn't believe Wren had brought someone with her to the portal. Nor could she believe that this person, whoever she was, had managed to fall straight through the portal that led to Shyon. But she knew what she had to do.

She let out her wings, and just as they were beginning to exit her back, she took two large steps backward and steeled herself for whatever waited for her on the portal's platform above Azyr. It would be good to be home, no matter what, she told herself.

With the small-yet-hopeful thought that at least something might go right, she took off at a run toward the portal's quickly closing opening. She heard it snap shut behind her, just as the last of her left leg left the portal's Earthly side.

CHAPTER SEVENTEEN

Wren now knew what moving at the speed of light felt like: crappy. Her stomach was in knots seconds after she leapt after Denise, and her cramps only tightened and grew as she continued to fall, tumbling end over end. The cramps were quickly joined by nausea, but before both of them had come terror. She was moving so fast she was unable to think anything but "Stop! Stop! Stop!" over and over again.

Wren could just barely see the form of her mom, also tumbling end over end a few feet beneath her, and she could also hear what sounded like someone yelling at her from behind, a voice she finally managed to recognize as Sia's.

After traveling through the dark-blue tunnel for what felt like far too long, things got even worse. Located about a hundred feet below Wren and her mom was what must have been the end of the portal's pathway, and a number of feet below that was a flat, metal circle, lying at what looked to Wren's scattered mind like a very strange angle.

She was finally able to hear what Sia must have been yelling all along: "Put out your wings! And dive, dive for that woman's left arm!" Wren struggled to follow her friend's commands, letting out her wings and righting herself just as she reached the pathway's very end, her head now pointing at its opening. She shot toward her mom, and Sia soon caught up with her. Together, they grabbed her mom's left and right arms seconds before all three of them crashed onto the hard metal surface beneath the portal's end.

Feeling more dazed and confused than she ever had in her entire life, Wren groaned, grateful for the platform's surprising softness. Then she heard Denise moan as well, longer and louder than she had, and her mom mumbled, "B-by God, Wren, y'don't *look* like you're that heavy, but man, are you ever!"

Wren would have been slightly hurt by her mom's words if she hadn't just realized that she'd landed halfway on her mom's chest, her grip on Denise's left arm still strong. She shoved herself off her poor mother, and then she realized that her head was only a few feet from the edge of the platform, and beyond it were only clouds and a star-speckled sky. The moon that hung above them didn't look at all like her own, this one being gold-colored and somewhat oval, with a shining blue halo encircling it.

She got to her feet and stood, grateful to be out of that horrid portal and onto firm ground again. But she soon noticed that this particular "firm ground" lay miles above the actual ground, as, looking over the platform's edge, she saw a large city spread out beneath them. Or at least it seemed to be a city, because many differently colored and various-sized lights were scattered across its expanse.

"Is that...is it..."

It was then that Wren noticed with some surprise a fourth person on the platform, an old woman dressed in a white robe trimmed in gold and blue. Her hair matched the stars, almost glowing in the moonlight, and she couldn't have looked happier to see Wren. She might not have been as pleased with Wren's companion, as the woman directed a quick, annoyed glance at Denise before she turned back to Wren and spoke. "I see you've brought a *friend*. I'm guessing that woman is perhaps your stepmother?"

"Y-yes, and I'm really sorry. I know I shouldn't have brought her. I just couldn't...couldn't leave her, because—"

"Oh, all that can wait, my special Winged Blue sister. It can wait forever for all I care. And it can surely wait until I say what I've been dying to say to you for years. Welcome to Shyon, Wren. Welcome to Azyr."

The elderly woman surprised Wren by taking both of her hands in her palms and bowing her head. Then the woman spoke again, and what she said next brought some unexpected tears to Wren's eyes. "Welcome, our Savior. Welcome home."

PART TWO

Chapter Eighteen

"Wren," Sia said, "this is Nak. She watches over our portal, or at least she does when people are expected to arrive."

"So, you're the welcoming committee?" Wren joked.

"I suppose I am. And since I'm the welcoming committee, I'd like to welcome your travel partner. What's her name?"

"This is Denise. She's my mom…my stepmom."

Denise was standing by this time, but she had been peering nervously over the edge of the floating platform where they all stood. These words caught her attention, though, and turning to Wren, she asked, "You knew? How? And…and where are we? I'm…I'm not still dreaming, am I? Wren, sweetie?"

"I have a lot of explaining to do," Wren told her. She turned back to Sia and Nak, saying, "To all of you, I brought Denise because I had to. I just knew it. I didn't want to leave her behind. For personal reasons." She gave Sia a pointed look, in hopes that she'd understand.

"I get it," Sia said, her face far gentler than it had been when she'd first noticed their unexpected guest. "No explanation necessary. I'll do my best to make sure she enjoys her time here." She turned to Denise, waving at her to draw her attention away from the platform's edge. "I need you to understand something. It's just that, even if you want to go home, you can't. It's not safe for anyone to go through the portal for the time being, at least for a while, so you're stuck here, I'm afraid."

Denise glanced back down at the city beneath them, then looked up at Sia, her eyes wide but not quite as alert as Wren would have been were she suddenly thrown into this startlingly different situation. But her mom was drunk, and probably tired, and well, there were other reasons to cut her some slack, too, Wren supposed. "Stuck here?" Denise asked, then added, "Stuck *where*?"

Wren might have been uncomfortable keeping all her supernatural secrets from her mom, but she couldn't hide them any longer. "That's part of what I need to tell you about." Wren paused. Yep, it was now or never, and "never" wasn't really acceptable at this point in time. "You may have noticed by now that I have wings, Mom?" She fluttered them for emphasis, and her mom took a stumbling step backward. Maybe she hadn't noticed them yet after all.

"Wings?" Denise stuttered. "And this thing we're standing on, and that weird blue tunnel we went through, can you explain all of it to me?"

Sia said, "First, we need to get everyone down to the ground. I'm sure the two of you are almost as tired as I am. We don't want any crash landings, do we?"

Only Wren smiled at her joke, and her mom was looking pretty scared. It also seemed like the shock of being here had sobered her up a bit, and Wren wondered then if the Winged Blue had alcohol down in Azyr. If they didn't, how would her mom react? Detoxing from alcohol wasn't easy, or fun. If the Winged Blue didn't have liquor, maybe her relatives down on Shyon would know some sort of magic to help poor Denise get through the withdrawal period she was likely about to experience.

All of that could or, actually, *had* to wait until they had reached the ground. After a short discussion with Nak and Sia about their options, Wren and the other two Winged concluded that since her mom was so light, Wren and Sia could probably manage getting her down to the city themselves. If they were *careful*, Nak had said, with a sharp glance directed solely at Wren.

She wondered why Nak was singling her out, but only for a moment. Wren knew this was all her idea, and good or bad, they were now stuck with it. She and Sia had Denise wrap one arm around each of their shoulders; Wren had never had her mom hold on to her so tightly in her life.

Not that she could blame her.

Nor could she blame her for yelping each time they hit an updraft, even though the two of them managed to keep a firm grip on Denise the whole way down. Wren barely had the chance to take in the beauty of the city before they reached the ground, landing in the middle of a small square surrounded by blue, one-story houses and dotted with pots of flowering plants. Wren couldn't quite make out the colors of the flowers, but she decided they likely were blue as well.

A bench was located to their left, and Denise begged them to let her rest there for a bit. After she'd sat down, looking very tired and possibly somewhat nauseous, Sia pulled Wren aside. "I don't think she can make it all the way to your dad's," Sia said, her voice soft. "It's at least a fifteen-minute walk, and she looks totally spent. Would you be okay waiting here with her, while I go get my brother? He's a big guy, and I'm pretty sure he could manage carrying her all the way to Torien's. Besides, I don't think we're getting her there any other way."

Both of them turned in Denise's direction. She was looking quite pale as she leaned against the building behind the bench. "You gonna explain now?" Denise said, and Wren took note of the not-so-slight tremble in her voice. Then her mom moaned, leaned over the side of the bench, and threw up.

"You're right," Wren answered Sia. "I don't think we have a choice." She rushed over and sat down next to her mom. "Why don't you lay your head on my lap, and I'll tell you everything I can."

Sia squeezed Wren's shoulder, then took off at a fast walk, which became a run as she reached the corner. Then she was gone.

Shortly after Sia disappeared from the square, Denise slowly leaned over and rested her head on Wren's lap. "So, you know I'm not your real mom, and you have wings, and we're in a weird place that I don't think is on Earth." She groaned, and Wren began to softly stroke her head. "Now, please, sweetheart, tell me the rest."

Her mom's voice was surprisingly full of compassion, despite her nonconsensual transplant to Azyr, which reminded Wren that she was loved, even with the heavy drinking that sometimes had threatened to bury that fact. Denise's loving tone of voice warmed Wren in the cool night air, and she knew then that she had made the right decision.

So Wren told her everything, from the first time her wings appeared to the reason she'd tricked her into coming out to the clearing, as well as the letter from her dad that had started her on this journey. It took far less time to tell her about it than those events had taken to pass, and Wren wondered what would have happened if she'd told Denise sooner. Maybe nothing at all.

Wren apologized after she finished explaining. "I realize you didn't agree to this, and I didn't know you couldn't go home if you didn't like it here, so I want to apologize, as many times as I need to. Please forgive me?"

Denise had probably heard the desperation in Wren's request, because she slowly sat up and tenderly cupped Wren's chin, staring straight into her eyes with a look that could only be described as pure faith: faith in Wren. "My dear, dear daughter. You haven't done anything wrong. You've *never* done anything wrong. It was…it was me, with my drinking and not kicking out your stepdad years ago like I should have. I don't know how I managed to get so lost, but I'm the one who needs forgiveness. Not you. Never, ever you. Can…can you?"

"Of course!" Wren placed her forehead against Denise's and smoothed back her hair. "Of course I can."

Sia returned then, with a sizeable, handsome man following right behind her. Wren was crying, and so was Denise. Sia must have noticed, and she waited quietly a few feet from them. Wren wiped at her eyes and leaned away from Denise, turning toward Sia and the young man.

"Hi, Sia. Hi, Sia's brother."

"Kriss, it's Kriss," he said, approaching her and offering a hand. He hadn't held it out for her to shake, though. Kriss loosely gripped a dark-blue hanky in his giant paw.

"Thank you, Kriss." Wren took the cloth from his hand and dabbed at her eyes, then blew her nose with an embarrassingly loud *honk*. "I'll…I'll get it washed before I return it to you."

"No. I would be honored to own a hanky covered in the Savior's snot. Truly." Kriss's sweet grin showed that he was joking, but only partially. With a small bow, he reached out, and after hesitating a moment, Wren returned the now-damp blue square.

"Thank you," he said, stuffing it back into a pocket in his robe. "Now. I hear you have a mother in need of some assistance?"

"That would be me, young man," Denise said, and she pushed herself up from the bench with a little help from Wren. "Are we headed somewhere with a bed? That would be my preference at the moment."

Kriss scooped her up into his arms as though she weighed less than the hanky. "Of course, miss. We're going to Torien's home, and he has plenty of rooms, including one right next door to your daughter's quarters."

"Torien, huh? I don't know if I'm ready to see him again yet."

She didn't sound like she felt ready, either, so Wren took her hand and gripped it as they began to walk away from the place where they'd first touched down. "I'm not sure if I'm ready either," she told Denise.

"Good. That means we can be unready together."

Despite the fact that Kriss was carrying a somewhat heavy load, he led the way, turning left and right and sometimes going straight for a stretch as they traveled down a number of wide streets. They all contained evenly placed streetlamps, each lamp aglow with a brilliant blue light. The lamplight allowed Wren to see that all of the houses and buildings they walked past were painted blue, but in varied levels of saturation.

It seemed that Wren would be seeing a lot of blue during her visit; she was thankful she liked the color. She was also thankful that, after going up a slight incline, they reached what could only be called a mansion. She saw at least twenty windows scattered across its upper and lower half, and two large doors with stained-glass windows sitting at the building's exact center. Wren paused as Kriss shifted Denise slightly in his arms to open one of the building's double doors.

He'd opened the unlocked door without a second's pause, as if he had every right to enter. And maybe he did. Maybe the Winged Blue were more laid-back than the people in Wren's previous city, where all the houses were locked tight, each requiring one or more keys and sometimes even codes to enter. Wren waited a short while, taking in the gorgeous art contained within the door's stained glass as she did. Each large circle of clear glass contained the image of a Winged Blue, one male, one female. Their hands had met where the doors did while still shut, with their palms almost touching and only divided by the thinnest column of wood.

"Can we go in, Wren, or do you want to keep looking at those doors?" Denise was looking at her, and so were Sia and Kriss.

"Hello, you must be Wren," came a voice to Wren's left.

She jumped a little, then turned in the direction of the voice.

"Good to know I'm still intimidating, but you don't have to be afraid. After all, I'm one of the people who will be watching over you." A statuesque, perfect-looking woman with short-cropped, curly black hair stood in a dimly lit spot on the mansion's small front lawn. The woman's skin was a similar shade to Wren's own, which made her feel she might be able to fit in better here than she had back in her hometown. It also made her feel grateful, even if the woman's looks surpassed her own so far.

Then she noticed two equally tall men, one on the woman's left and one on her right. Both of them looked too similar to the woman to be unrelated. They also looked similar to each other, and Wren realized they must be twins. All three were dressed in the style Wren had come to believe was customary for the Winged Blue, each wearing a long, somewhat loose robe in a matching shade of royal blue.

"Hello," said the twin to the woman's left, raising a hand in greeting. "I'm Quiq."

"And I'm Faest," said the other twin, and he gestured to the woman in between them. "And this is our sister Speyd."

"Very nice to meet you, young lady." Speyd smiled at her, a smile that looked a little more feral than Wren was comfortable with. "You *are* Wren, correct?"

"Um, yes. Nice to meet you, too."

"We'll be your guards for the evening. If you need anything, like someone's butt kicked, just scream," said Faest. Speyd elbowed him in the side, apparently hard enough to make him wince.

"Excuse my brother. It's been too long since he's gotten laid." Speyd winked at Wren as she said this.

"Excuse both my brother *and* my sister," said Quiq. "They're more trouble than they are inches tall. I'm sorry for their rudeness." He also smiled in Wren's direction. Then he smiled at Denise, a slightly wider smile, but not as wide as the one Denise was giving him in return. She also looked a little pink around her cheeks. Was her mother *blushing*?

The statuesque siblings were all attractive, this much was obvious, and Wren wondered if her mom was attracted to the two brothers. They were handsome, she decided, if you were into people with hairy chests and loads of testosterone. Wren wasn't, and she didn't really want to think about her mom finding anyone attractive, either. Not when Torien was here; not when her parents might still stand a chance as a couple.

"I guess we should go inside now?" Wren asked, but it wasn't intended to be a question someone could say no to. Especially not her mom. "I'm pretty tired, and I'm guessing my mom is, too."

"I suppose…um, yes, yes, I am, too." Denise didn't sound tired anymore, and she was still staring at Quiq and still grinning, somewhat like a schoolgirl checking out her first crush.

Wren didn't want to give her mom any further chances to drool over Quiq. It was kind of gross seeing her gawk at a man like that. She turned away from the three Winged relatives and gestured at the open front door. "You ready, Mom?"

"Y-yes. Good night, Quiq. And Speyd, and Faest." Her mom

waved at them, and Wren stepped aside, allowing Kriss to enter first, and then she and Sia followed him inside.

The mansion's interior wasn't nearly as ostentatious as Wren had been expecting. Instead, it had a rustic feel, the high-ceilinged rooms they walked through filled with countless bookcases, a few well-worn sofas, and a large brick fireplace against the far wall of most of the rooms. Each also contained many windows, and the row of them in the fourth room they entered showed a view of a lush, flower-filled garden. It was also filled with what looked like blue fireflies, floating back and forth and lighting up the plants. Wren hoped she would have some time to spend among all those flowers, but she knew her responsibilities here came before any fun or relaxation.

Kriss led the way farther inside that fourth room. As they all reached the back wall, which held a short staircase leading up to a second floor, Wren tried to stifle a yawn. But she failed, and its echo throughout the extremely acoustic room was embarrassingly loud.

"Sounds like I'm not the only one who's ready for bed," her mom told her with a somewhat loopy grin. Denise looked like she might now be the happiest she'd been since she'd arrived. Wren couldn't blame her. Bed was a very welcome prospect, considering all that had happened since she'd gotten out of her usual bed on that night…her bed back on Earth. She knew she was only just beginning to accept that she was somewhere so different, so foreign, but she was also sure her comfort would likely grow with time, and probably quickly, too. It would have to.

Her mom, however, would likely take a while longer to get used to all of this, so Wren made sure to give her an extra long hug when Kriss finally put her down at the top of the stairs. They all continued down a long hallway to the left of the stairs, along which sat vases holding sweet-smelling flowers, each placed on delicate white tables between every one of the hallway's many doors. When they reached the fifth door on their right, Sia stepped forward and turned the knob, and Wren peered around Kriss so she could see. All she could make out in the room's dim light was a medium-sized canopy bed with some sort of quilt on it.

"This can be your room, Denise," Sia told Wren's mom, who looked rather grateful at the young woman's words.

Before she could take in any more of the room that would apparently be Denise's, her mom hugged her again and whispered, "Good night, sweetheart. Sleep well."

Then Denise went inside, and Wren watched as her mom lay down on the bed, fully clothed, and shut her eyes, only managing to pull the quilt halfway over herself before beginning to snore. Wren went into the room and covered her the rest of the way, risking a kiss on her forehead that she hoped wouldn't disturb her mother's well-deserved sleep.

When Wren left her mom's room, softly shutting the door behind her, she saw that they had almost reached the end of the hallway. Just past her mom's room was a large door with a sign on it. The sign brought a smile to Wren's face. Written in elegant, carved cursive were the words WREN'S ROOM. But it wasn't what the sign said that made her smile. It was the fact that she recognized the handwriting that her name was written in, handwriting she'd seen on a regular basis during her first eight years of life. She turned the door's blue-painted knob and opened it, and Sia and Kriss followed her inside, into what was a rather amazing room.

First, Wren noticed it held a canopy bed, like the one in her mom's room. But this one was much bigger and covered in pillows, more of them than Wren could ever possibly need. The large, square pillow in front of the rest had a blue raven embroidered on it, and the words SWEET DREAMS curved out of its open beak. To the left of the bed was a large sitting room, with a comfy-looking sofa and two large, stuffed-to-the-max armchairs, all of them upholstered in cream-colored cloth covered with pale-blue flowers that looked like forget-me-nots. There were also flowers on the two tables on each side of the bed. After taking all of that in, Wren finally noticed the room's very best feature: a full wall of books to her left, all of their spines different hues—every possible shade of the rainbow's various colors. Except, she noticed, not one of them was any shade of red.

Turning her eyes back to the bed, she saw some very comfortable-looking flannel pajamas lying at its foot. They were covered in clouds, as well as moons in gold instead of silver or white, and the letter "Z" with elegant flourishes on each of its tips. The pajamas and the bed were now calling out to her so loudly she could almost hear their voices, so she turned to Sia with one last question to ask before she would thankfully be able to finally get some rest.

"Why isn't my dad here?" It was a question she had been wondering about on and off since she'd landed in Azyr, even with so many other things that could have completely distracted her from his absence. But it was a very important question, especially to her, especially to a daughter who hadn't seen her father for all those years. "He..." Sia said. She cleared her throat, looking a little nervous. "There's a note from him by the bed, he told me." That was apparently all Sia was going to say; she fell silent after telling Wren of the note. So she hugged Sia good night, and Kriss and Sia both wished her a good night's sleep.

But Wren wanted to look around her room a little more first; she'd noticed a large dresser with two tall doors and three wide drawers beneath them. She walked over to it and lifted the wooden hook that held its doors shut. Upon swinging them both open, Wren gasped.

Inside, instead of party dresses or skirts, was a metal breastplate with a dark-blue raven inlaid into its center. It looked as though it might have been glaring at her. Next to it was what seemed to be metal pants, made out of chainmail. Above the breastplate hung a helmet, with a thin piece of shining blue stone dangling down the front that appeared like it would rest on her forehead.

This wasn't something she would have wished to see right before bed, so she quickly shut the doors and turned her back on the cabinet and its frightening contents. With her eyes already half-closed, she trundled over to her bed and changed into her new pajamas, which were even softer than they'd looked. Feeling somewhat more relaxed now, she decided it was time to be brave and read her dad's letter. She sat down on the bed and found a blue envelope with his neat cursive script across the front, lying on the pearlescent-blue bedside table. She smiled as she read the words he'd written: "To my dear daughter." Then she ripped it open and withdrew her second letter from her long-lost dad, and began to read.

Dearest Wrenny,

I'm guessing that you expected to see me at my home as soon as you arrived tonight, but a pressing matter took me away from there: a certain someone's belated Eighteenth Birthday Party (!!!) had some remaining planning to be done. I want to make it the best birthday you've ever had, in hopes that it will at least partially make up for all the ones I've missed. I also have hopes that you will forgive me, at some point, for leaving you behind all those years ago—too many years ago, if you ask me. I plan to do my best to make

*it up to you, to make up for all this sadly lost time we could
have spent together. I send my love, and I look forward, so
very much, to seeing you, finally, again.*

> *Love,*
> *Your dad*

*P.S. Rysha wanted me to add that she's very excited about
meeting my lovely daughter in person.*

Wren couldn't really say the same about Rysha, but the letter did
manage to reassure her about her dad not being there to greet her. The
letter would have to do for now, and she decided that the sooner she
went to sleep, the sooner morning would come, and the sooner she
would see her dad for the first time in, as he had said, too many years.
She got into her bed, its sheets more sumptuous than any she'd ever
slept on, and before she had a chance to think a single thought more,
she was out cold.

CHAPTER NINETEEN

A raven was hammering its giant beak against a giant tree trunk in Wren's dreams. Wren was fairly sure ravens didn't usually do this, but it looked real enough. Then the sound of its loud pecking turned into the sound of loud knocking as she quickly came awake. She heard a muffled male voice through her door, one that she thought she recognized. But until whoever it was spoke again, she wasn't quite sure. "Can I come in, sweetheart? You awake?" the muffled voice said.

"Yes!" Wren shoved herself up into a seated position, her impatience at an all-time high as she waited to see if the person speaking beyond her bedroom door was who she thought it was. After all, it had been years since she'd heard that voice. But when her bedroom door opened, and her dad's curl-covered head peeked through, Wren couldn't hold back her excitement, and all her anger at his disappearance vanished in an instant.

She yelped in joy and shoved back the covers, running straight to him as he opened her bedroom door wide. "Oh, Dad! It's you!" Upon reaching Torien, she flung her arms around his solid, robe-covered chest, the robe a rich, sumptuous brown that brought out the flecks of gold in his smiling eyes. He had a few more crow's feet than the last time she'd seen him, and his almost-black locks held touches of gray at his temples, but it was still obviously him. She hadn't realized exactly how much she'd missed him until she was finally able to touch him again.

"This is the best birthday gift I've gotten in years," she murmured against his chest. Wren was struggling to fight back the tears that were threatening to stream down her cheeks, but it turned out there was no need: her father's voice was also thick with tears when he spoke. "Oh, Wrenny, you have no idea how good it is to see you again. No idea."

He kissed her head and moved a few inches back, brushing some of her typically unruly waves behind her right ear. "You look just the same, and yet, well, very different. Now, do you think we could let everyone else into the room? And what's this I hear about Denise joining you on your travels through our portal?"

"I'm…I'm sorry about that," Wren said bashfully, "but it was completely necessary. I didn't have any other choice. And Dad, I'm almost positive you'd understand if I told you everything."

"I already did, honey," said her mom, and a very unhappy-looking Denise was now entering the room. The dark circles under her eyes made it look as though she'd barely slept, or perhaps she was just experiencing one of her more horrific hangovers. Wren guessed that traveling through a portal to another world might not actually qualify as another one of the many hangover cures her mom had tried over the years. Still, it had to beat drinking raw egg yolks; unlike that particular "cure," it didn't come with the risk of potential food poisoning.

"I understand completely, my dear daughter," her father told her, glancing in her mom's direction as he spoke. "You did the right thing, Wrenny. Denise made this very clear to me."

After her mom and Torien had entered the room, Denise sat down in a chair next to the door, and then Sia entered the room. She was followed by four silver, levitating trays, covered with plates of food and pitchers of orange, pulpy liquid. The fact that the trays were floating didn't even faze Wren, but her mom looked at them with a somewhat suspicious glare. After the trays had settled onto the table between the chairs and sofa, one last person entered the room and shut the door behind her.

She happened to be someone Wren didn't want anywhere near her, or her dad. She almost would have preferred a Winged Red to the woman who stood in front of her. "Welcome to Azyr," the woman said, her smiling, long-lashed eyes staring in Wren's direction.

She seemed to sincerely mean those words, but that didn't even come close to winning her any space in Wren's heart. "Hi, Rysha." Wren had ordered her voice to be completely empty of the pain Rysha's presence caused her.

By the time her words had hung in the air for a few seconds, Wren had become pretty certain her tone had held at least a hint of her distress and distrust. But when her father's current partner—her stepmother's replacement—spread her arms wide to offer Wren a hug, she decided it would make her look bad if she refused to respond "appropriately" to the woman's gesture.

Still, she kept the hug as short as possible and tried to ignore the way Rysha smelled a little like her dad, a scent that she in no way had earned the right to carry.

After that short-but-still-too-long hug, Rysha joined her father on the wide couch, placing her hand in his. She looked far more relaxed than she had any right to be, Wren thought. "You look so like him, Wren," Rysha said in her silky-smooth voice, "especially your eyes. Those almost deadly, long-lashed eyes. I practically swooned when I first saw them."

"Yep, she always has looked a lot like Torien," Denise added, and Wren was surprised when she didn't detect any sign of pain in her mother's words. Wren had expected a fair amount of hurt in her mom's eyes when she first saw her ex-partner with her romantic replacement. However, Denise was smiling when she voiced her agreement, and it didn't look like she was forcing her lips to curve upward.

Not the way Wren had to whenever Rysha looked her way throughout breakfast. In the end, the delicious food managed to distract her from her animosity. There were waffles covered in blue and green berries and something that tasted like yummier crème fraîche, potatoes flecked with herbs and garlic, and juice that reminded her of orange juice but was much better. Even the coffee was perfect, so she allowed the delicious food to carry her worries away.

At least for the time being.

Throughout the meal, her dad dropped teasing hints about her party that night, and these mysterious hints managed to keep most of Wren's attention off her dad's girlfriend. She still had to fight to keep the occasional rude jibe from leaving her mouth, each one threatening to escape her lips whenever Rysha touched her dad.

What she wanted more than anything was to kick Rysha out of her room. And her life. However, she didn't want to ruin everyone's good mood, so she kept all of her thoughts about the woman's many-leveled encroachment to herself.

Toward the end of the meal, Wren started to wonder how she would have felt if this were her biological mother sitting beside her dad, if it were *her* hand draped casually across his knee, but she found she didn't have a clue about how it might make her feel. She didn't even know if that woman was still alive, or if she'd possibly be glad to see her daughter again, if she were. Maybe she'd even stayed behind here on purpose.

But that was a ridiculous thought, Wren decided, so she turned and smiled at her dad, allowing her joy at finally seeing him in front of her to wash away every stain of anguish it was able to reach.

"Now, Wren, we have a gift waiting for you downstairs, the first one for your birthday, and the most important. If you'll just join us there, you can open it." Rysha rose from the couch, and Wren followed her out her bedroom door, with her father, Denise, and Sia right behind them.

Downstairs, after going back into the hallway, they entered a room that contained an incredibly long glass-topped table surrounded by too many chairs to count in one quick glance. It had only been a quick glance because Wren's eyes had instantly been drawn to the item that lay near the edge of the ornate table. There, a few feet away from Wren, sat a large, long, rectangular box, a velvet ribbon wrapped around its middle. Wren approached it and reached out, tearing off the ribbon and lifting the lid. She'd had no way to tell what the box might have contained, but her gift wasn't even close to what any of her guesses might have been.

Within it lay a bow and a quiver of arrows, all of them made of blond wood with delicate threads of blue scattered across their surface. The bow's string was also blue, thick enough to make it seem like pulling it back would take the abilities of a goddess. The quiver had dark, lapis-like stones running down its front and back, and each of the fifteen arrows Wren counted was tipped with multi-colored feathers that had likely come from the Winged Blue's raven forms.

"That's what's known as a 'self bow,' and the quiver is a 'back quiver.'" Rysha pointed to the bow and then the quiver as she spoke. Like Wren needed any help telling the difference between a bow and a quiver! "Quiq, Speyd, and Faest will help you learn more about it later, sometime tomorrow, as we want your first day to be relaxing and fun. It wouldn't be much of a welcome, to start your first day here with training!" Rysha chuckled, but laughter was the last thing on Wren's mind as she took in the intimidating weapon that lay before her: the weapon that was now hers, to wield and, perhaps, to kill with.

She didn't like a single bit of that train of thought, so she mumbled a quick "Thank you" and turned away from her gift.

"I hope you like it, Wrenny," her dad said. "One of our most skilled weapon-crafters made it, a good friend of mine named Brynn.

And if you don't truly like it, she can make you another." Her father looked concerned, and Wren guessed he might have noticed that she wasn't exactly thrilled with her gift.

"No, no, it's totally beautiful," she assured him. "I'm just... just nervous about learning how to use it. It looks like it might be challenging." That was only part of the truth, but Torien looked as though her words had smoothed over any doubts he'd had about his gift.

"Piru, our land's most skilled seer, is certain you will have amazing ability with the bow. And don't worry, sweetie. The triplets are great teachers. All three are incredibly skilled with any sort of weapon."

As if his words had made the triplets materialize out of thin air, Speyd entered the room, followed by Quiq and Faest. Speyd was carrying a large platter with a silver lid, and Quiq and Faest each held one end of a thick roll of blue-and-gold fabric. They all greeted Wren and then her father, but just as he was about to leave the room with his end of the fabric, Quiq paused at the propped-open doors to the garden. He was silent for a moment, and then he looked in her mom's direction, and said, "Hello, Denise. I hope you slept well?"

"Yes, yes, I did, very well. It's nice to see you again, Quiq." This time her mom's grin wasn't aided by alcohol, and it looked even more genuine than it had the night before. Yep, her mom definitely seemed to have eyes for Quiq, and he didn't appear all that unhappy to be looking at her, either, a large, off-kilter grin directed toward her mom's equally goofy-looking face. Wren still wasn't happy to see her mom flirting, especially with someone who wasn't her dad. It made her uncomfortable in more ways than she could count, and she sighed as Quiq finally went outside.

"You okay, Wren?" Denise asked, her brow knitting together as she touched Wren's cheek. "Didn't you sleep well?"

It had obviously been Denise who hadn't slept well, yet she was looking the most awake she had since she'd entered Wren's bedroom. "I'm fine, Mom, totally fine." Wren tried to hide the annoyance she was feeling with her mom, and she must have been convincing, because Denise just smiled wider and kissed her forehead.

CHAPTER TWENTY

After breakfast, Sia told Wren the five of them were supposed to go to the open-air market in town. Denise attempted to beg off, but a bit of pleading from Wren and Torien managed to convince her to come along.

"After all," Torien said to Denise, "how often do you get the chance to explore an unfamiliar planet on such a lovely day?"

The weather spoke of summer when they got outside, the air fresh and warm and free of certain human-caused things Wren had barely registered on Earth. Like the smell of car exhaust, and honking, as well as technology's not-so-subtle markings: no one's face in the Winged Blue's city was staring at a screen of some sort. Instead, the people were actually interacting with each other, smiling and greeting and hugging. After all, Wren thought, who would want technology when you could have the ability to fly, and who would need it if everyone in town had their own fantastic magical power?

Wren couldn't wait to discover what hers would be, but the sight of the colorful market a few streets away from the mansion thoroughly distracted her from thoughts of anything else. The breeze carried many different scents as she came closer, and not one of them was unpleasant to Wren's pleased nostrils.

Here, also, was the racial diversity her town had always lacked, people of so many ethnicities scattered among the stands it almost took Wren's breath away. She entered the crowd of many-colored robes and diverse peoples and began to excitedly look around.

Sia explained while they walked how their society operated. Most things were free, but the market involved a barter system—you traded the use of your particular magical power for something from a person's stand, and these trades were apparently going on all over the place as Wren walked around. She took in the varied aromas from a spice vendor's stand, all the heaps of spices looking like they would make quite a mess were the wind to pick up. Next to that was a booth full of mind-bogglingly beautiful flowers, with many familiar types and a fair number she'd never seen before, probably native to the Winged Blue's world. It was interesting to Wren to see the "cross-pollination" between the humans' world and the Wingeds'. She had assumed the worlds would be very different, and in some ways they were, but thankfully, there was enough familiarity here to keep Wren feeling right at home.

More at home than she'd ever felt back on Earth, she realized as they reached a stand full of jewelry, each piece dangling from small, copper-colored trees with tiny, dark green leaves on their branches. Wren jumped a little when one of the branches reached out in her direction, brushing against her arm in a gentle caress.

"It's saying it likes you, miss." The woman who spoke had a long, blue-black braid down her back, and a small, Egyptian-looking eye was painted in the middle of her forehead. Wren almost jumped again when the eye blinked, but the woman's sweet, welcoming smile helped to reassure her enough to smile back. "I see you're here with my sister-in-law, so might you be Wren? I'm Kriss's wife, Yhen. He told me about meeting you last night. Seems he really liked you."

"That's nice. Thanks for telling me, Yhen," Wren said. She allowed her eyes to wander away from the pretty woman's face and back to the jewelry. One piece in particular caught her eye, a delicate female figure made of blue-painted metal, her arms stretched out about a centimeter from her robe-covered sides.

The woman must have noticed Wren looking at it, because she said, "She's yours, if you'd like. Kriss and I wanted to give you a gift from our stand, a welcome-and-Happy-Birthday one. Here, let me show you something." Yhen reached down and picked up the delicate silver chain, its pendant twinkling in the sunlight falling over Yhen's stand. Then she placed her fingers on the pendant's arms, pushing them down, in tandem, three times in a row. When they popped back up the third time, glowing, transparent wings appeared at her back, slowly flapping up and down as the pendant swung forward and back.

"That's awesome!" Wren exclaimed. "I love it. And thank you, very much," she added with much gratitude as Yhen handed it over to her.

"Here, let me help put it on you," Sia said.

Wren, delighted at her crush's offer, quickly turned around, and the magical little woman was soon hanging a few inches beneath her robe's neckline. The feel of Sia's hands against the back of her neck as she fastened the chain in place stole the show from her lovely gift, but it didn't make her appreciate it any less. She thanked Yhen again, who smiled shyly and said, "Anything for our Savior."

Wren was getting a little sick of being referred to with that particular word, including a mild touch of entirely physical sickness from the nerves it caused to tumble around in her stomach. But she chose to ignore as best she could the anxiety those words seemed to cause in her.

"What's next?" she asked her dad, whose arm was resting on Rysha's narrow shoulders.

"Next is a trip to Piru's, for lunch and knowledge," Torien said. "And a swim, if you'd like."

"I'd *more* than 'like'!" So Wren followed her father and Rysha down the long pathway through the rest of the market, trying to pay attention to the stands and their wares instead of the way Rysha's hand was holding on to the far side of her dad's waist. She was starting to think she would just have to get used to Rysha being around; it was obvious that her dad felt just as much affection for this woman as Rysha felt for him. Did her mom stand a chance with him, anyway? And did she even *want* to get him back?

Wren was also starting to think she shouldn't try to meddle in her parents' lives. Especially with the way her mom had been looking at Quiq only the second time they'd seen him, when they had encountered the triplets downstairs. She hadn't looked that way at Wren's dad once since they'd arrived. Maybe she'd fully moved on by now, and maybe Wren would just have to accept that fact.

All this didn't mean that liking Rysha would be easy for her, but maybe with time it would become a bit easier. Rysha hadn't really given Wren any reason to dislike her, after all, other than the fact that she'd replaced her mom at her father's side.

But Denise didn't seem to be paying the least bit of attention to Torien's affection toward his girlfriend, so Wren chose to do the same and to just enjoy her walk through the city's winding streets and past all of its diverse, winged people.

After about twenty minutes of walking, with Torien and Rysha leading the way and a tired-looking Denise taking up the rear, their path began to go a little uphill. At the top of the small hill sat a house the color of the summer sky, with open-shuttered windows and an also-open front door. Out on its porch sat an older-looking gentleman wearing wire-rimmed glasses and a robe with a golden tree woven over his chest.

"Wow, nice robe," was the first thing Wren thought to say to him, and she almost slapped herself after those dumb words escaped her lips.

"I do quite like this one, and so did my wife. You have good taste!" He rose from his rocking chair, looking surprisingly spry for a man with so many wrinkles decorating his tanned skin. "Would you like to come inside, Wren? And Denise, how have you been liking your stay so far?"

Both Denise and Sia spoke at the same time, Sia with an annoyed, "Grandpa, you knew and you didn't tell me?" and Denise told him, "It's amazing here, beyond anything I ever could have imagined. I love it."

"Well, may I be one of many to welcome you here, and to let you know you're never going to wear out said 'welcome.'"

"Thank you." It wasn't Denise who said this, but Wren, because she finally felt certain she'd made the right choice in bringing her mom to Shyon and the city of Azyr. Hopefully the Winged Red wouldn't make her regret her decision.

"So, are you all ready for lunch, or do we have time to talk first?" Piru might have been asking all of them, but his intelligent-looking eyes were trained on Wren.

"I'm up for talking, if everyone else is," she told him. Sounds and nods of assent came from the other four people. But first, Wren's strong curiosity led her to ask Piru a question before she could feel ready to enter his house. "What will we be talking about?"

"You, Wren, you and your future. I would wager that you'd like to know all you can!"

"Yes, I really would." Her words couldn't have been more true. The fact that she knew so little of what would come to pass had been weighing heavily on Wren for days.

"Then come inside, and I'll fill you in once we're all seated." Piru placed his hand on her upper back and gestured to the front door. He turned his head away seconds after his hand met her robe. It seemed he might have been trying to hide his face from her, but he didn't move fast enough: Wren could see him beginning to wince just as his thumb first pressed against her bare neck.

"What is it, Piru? Are you okay?"

Piru turned back to Wren, and then she could see that his pain wasn't coming from himself: it was coming from her, and only with the lightest touch of his skin to hers. "Oh, my dear, dear girl. Yes, I am fine. You…I…if you could just please go inside, I'll let you know anything you want." So she did as he asked, entering his home after he gestured toward his front door for the second time.

Piru's living room held a large, unlit fireplace, two long tan couches, and a rocking chair. The six of them sat down on the couches, with Wren seated between Sia and Piru on the one farthest from the door. Denise, Torien, and Rysha sat opposite them. Between the couches was a pale wooden table laden with trays of sandwiches, a bowl full of sliced fruit, and two pitchers containing something that looked a lot like iced tea.

"I apologize for touching you without asking first," Piru said once everyone was settled. He was turned in Wren's direction, his left hand resting a few inches away from her thigh but not touching it. Wren was glad of this, because while she hadn't minded him placing his hand on her back at first, the sign that he might have gotten a glimpse into her mind had troubled her a fair deal. Wren decided then that she didn't want him looking inside her brain without asking first, ever again.

"Apology accepted, as long as you…as long as you don't do that again without getting my permission. Please," Wren added, because Piru seemed nice enough, despite his intrusion into her head.

"I didn't even intend to read your thoughts, I promise. I would hold my power back if I could, I swear." His look of contrition was more than believable, so Wren took him at his word. "Now, before we eat, would you allow me to touch you again? It will tell me, and everyone else who's here, much more than I've been able to foresee for you before now. And it will likely help you with your lack of knowledge about what is to come. Would that be all right?"

She paused to think for a moment. Would it be? It seemed it was probably entirely necessary, so she answered, "I think so. Yes, I definitely think so, because I really do want to know more, as much more as you can tell me. This not knowing anything about my future, when so much seems to depend on me, well, it's really kind of scary."

"I can't blame you for feeling that way, so, with luck, gaining some knowledge about your future will help to lessen your fears. But in order to help you, I need to touch you again. Would you be kind enough to give me your definite permission, Wren?"

"Yes, you have my permission."

Piru took her hand after she'd spoken. He ever-so-gently turned it upside down and rested his thumb on her palm. Then he shut his eyes.

It was almost completely silent in the house for the next few minutes, only the occasional sound of birdsong from outside interrupting the quiet. Then Piru began to speak.

"I see you becoming a very skilled archer in almost no time at all, but you already knew that, of course. I see…I see that Torien's power will not be passed down, but you will be gaining your own power soon, a very strong one, a very mighty one, and it will cause you pain, until it finally…until it finally changes everything for you. Permanently. The power is…the power…I can't see what it will be. That part of your path, for whatever reason, is blocked to me."

Piru's eyes opened again, and he blinked a few times. His unfocused gaze wandered back and forth across the room. Then it rested on a large, shiny blue cloth hanging from the ceiling in the far corner of the room. "That's all for now." Piru's voice sounded distant, but then he seemed to come fully back into the present, back from wherever he'd been. "Thank you, Wren, that was very helpful." He rubbed his hands together swiftly, then spread them in a gesture that was directed at the food and drinks scattered across the table. "Now, would everyone like to eat? And after we're done, I have a gift for you, Wren, over in the corner, by the fireplace."

Wren hadn't noticed it before, but a small gray box sat on the hearth. "Thank you, for whatever it is. You really didn't have to."

"That's the point of a gift, my dear—that you don't really have to give it." Piru lifted one of the pitchers off of the table and pointed to the glass in front of Wren. "I hope you like iced tea?"

Once everyone had eaten almost all of the sandwiches and a large amount of the fruit salad, Wren retrieved the box and opened it. Inside was a two-piece bathing suit, with ivory-colored vines winding across its chocolate-brown background. It consisted of a pair of shorts and a sports-bra-like top, with delicate, lacy strips of cloth crisscrossing the back of its top half, which gave it a subtle touch of femininity. "It's beautiful," Wren told Piru. She kept silent about the fact that she in no way had the figure for the suit.

"I think you'll look great in it," Sia told her, and Wren turned away from her and toward Piru, to hide both her delight at Sia's words along with the doubt that they could possibly be true.

She couldn't wait to try it on. "Where's your bathroom?" Wren asked him.

As soon as she'd changed, everyone else stripped down to their suits, and Sia looked Wren up and down, then said, "Yep, I was right."

Wren turned away from Sia again, this time to hide her reddening cheeks and her grin. She couldn't fully accept that Sia had meant it, but a small voice in her head told her that maybe it actually was Sia's honest opinion.

Everyone went outside, into the bright, warm backyard. The temperature was perfect for a swim, and the waters of the impossibly clear pond beyond a richly green spread of lawn beckoned to them. In the water, bright-colored fish swam beneath Sia and Wren, and a teasing remark from Sia led to a lengthy splash-fight between the two of them.

Wren couldn't remember the last time she'd had this much fun or felt this free. It had to have been before her dad left. But now, wonderfully, he was back in her life, sending a smile in her direction every few minutes.

After a long swim, everyone went up to the shore to dry off. Piru brought out more iced tea and some rich, buttery cookies to go with it. Wren didn't even care that after eating three of them in a row she had become completely coated in crumbs. Any chance of embarrassment was washed away with the pure happiness she felt at this time spent with both loved ones and new friends. Besides, another dip into the water washed away the crumbs.

For once, though, she didn't need water to wash away any worries. Just then, in the pond's cool waters, under Shyon's hot summer sun, Wren didn't have a single one.

CHAPTER TWENTY-ONE

When Wren took note of the location of the lowering sun, she guessed it was around six by the time everyone was done swimming and sunbathing, and she left the waters behind with a touch of regret. But she knew she could come back there any time she wanted, as Sia's grandfather had said as much. After everyone had changed into dry clothes, they began the trek back to Torien's home, arriving there just as the sun was starting to dip below the city's surrounding hills. Piru had come with them, and he'd told Wren he wasn't willing to miss the festivities that night. "After all," he'd said, "your father throws the best parties in the whole city. I'm guessing that will be especially true with this one, considering it's in the honor of his incredibly missed, well-loved daughter."

It felt great to Wren, hearing those words secondhand, even though it was more than clear that her father was elated to have her in his life again. Wren shared those strong feelings, which were refreshed and strengthened every time he glanced in her direction on the walk back to her new home, always with a beaming smile.

Once they'd arrived at Torien's door, he suggested that Wren go upstairs and change clothes. "Something's waiting for you on the bed, something special to wear to your party. Then I want you to meet me at the foot of the stairs, and I'll lead you there. Blindfolded, of course."

"Of course?" But instead of waiting for a single word more from her father, Wren rushed upstairs to her room. Laid out on her bed were robes even more beautiful than Piru's. They were every shade of blue possible, and the fabric even held a few colors Wren had never seen before. The sleeves contained an even vaster array of blues, and all these blues were made up of small, downy raven feathers, every single one of them iridescent and incredibly soft against her fingers as she ran a hand reverently across them.

When Wren had almost reached the bottom of the stairs, dressed in what was now her new favorite outfit, her father sighed softly and took her hand as he helped her down the final two steps. "You should know that those feathers came from every single Winged Blue I invited to your party, and all of them were given with great respect to you. Do you like your robe?"

"I more than like it. Much more. It's the most beautiful thing I've ever worn." Wren didn't add that it was also the most beautiful thing she'd ever owned.

"And you do it complete and utter justice, my dearest girl. Happy Birthday."

The robe was so incredibly beautiful Wren wasn't sure her dad was right, but she chose to believe that he meant his words, even if she couldn't completely agree with him. She stood at the bottom of the steps while he tied a strip of black fabric around her eyes, placed his hand on her back, and slowly led her forward, then left and right a few times. He might have been trying to confuse her, and the thought made her smile.

Soon, she guessed she was outside. She could feel the warm breath of early night, and the unfamiliar, yet still-soothing sound of Azyrian crickets echoed through the space where she now stood. She could also hear sounds that implied she and her father were no longer alone. Torien took off her blindfold, and possibly upward of one hundred Winged Blue, with Denise standing in the very front, all yelled, "Happy Birthday, Wren!" A single tear rolled down her cheek after all those happy-looking people called out their welcome, but an almost impossibly wide grin joined it.

"Let the festivities begin!" Torien shouted.

And begin they did. Two Winged Blue walked on stilts, breathing out blue and silver flames in the shapes of various birds Wren had never seen before. Three huge tables were so weighed down with delicious-looking food and drink that Wren half-expected them to collapse. A band played unfamiliar instruments but familiar music, an old jazz tune Wren recognized but couldn't name. And many, many Winged all looked in her direction with an abnormal amount of appreciation, considering that they'd never met before. It was probably because of her "Savior" status, though. That has to be it, she thought.

After receiving hugs from her mom, Sia, and then Rysha, Wren filled a plate with food and got a mug of sweet-and-spicy scented punch. She found a seat at one of the tables and was joined by Sia, her mom and dad, Rysha, Kriss, and Yhen. She didn't mind being around Rysha for the first time since she'd met her, and it didn't hurt when Torien told Wren that Rysha had come up with all the ideas for her robe.

"I just thought it would be a nice way for all of us to welcome you here," Rysha said, her humbleness helping to tip Wren's opinion of her a little further into the positive.

After almost too many people had shaken her hand and she'd eaten more than her fill of food, Wren decided she needed a break. She told everyone around her that she wanted to explore the garden. She wandered through the flowers, amazed at both the garden's beauty and its size, and found her way down the hill the garden grew upon; the party grew farther and farther away until the distance between her and the festivities eclipsed both its sounds and the sight of them.

Wren sat down on a bench at the bottom of the hill, a tall hedge with jasmine-like flowers at her back. She shut her eyes to rest them for a while, but they stayed closed for only a short moment. Just after she'd shut them, a female voice interrupted the tranquil quiet. "You're Wren, aren't you?" the voice asked, and Wren opened her eyes.

She'd seen many beautiful people in her life, but this young-looking woman outshone them all. Her wavy auburn hair was shorter than Wren usually liked, but somehow the intensity of her features—her high, sharp cheekbones, her narrow, full-lipped mouth, her golden skin that almost glowed, and her large, aquamarine eyes—managed to make Wren ignore this fact. Instead, she found herself deciding that short hair was better than long, and always had been, and this graceful, flawless woman was the proof that it was so.

"Um, yes, I'm Wren. And who are you?" She realized instantly how rude her question's wording was, but instead of saying anything about it, the woman glided into the space next to Wren and put her hand on Wren's knee.

Normally such an assuming physical gesture would have bothered her, but the woman's looks made it welcome somehow, and Wren just smiled, feeling stupefied and awestruck, as she listened to the woman's answer.

"I'm Elle. And I'm here to help you. Do you trust me?"

Wren answered in the affirmative with a quick, emphatic nod.

"Good. I'm going to assist you with your archery lesson tomorrow, and all you have to do is picture me. Does that sound easy enough?"

Elle's lips turned up into a smile that looked almost lascivious to Wren. She decided she hoped it was, even if the idea of a woman this attractive finding *her* attractive struck her as way past impossible. But when the woman asked a fourth question, it became abundantly clear to Wren that it wasn't impossible, not at all. "You look beautiful in that dress, Wren. May I kiss you? I know that's forward of—"

Wren couldn't get herself to wait for the end of Elle's statement before she uttered a loud, insistent, "Yes!" And before she could say anything else, the woman's luscious, soft lips were upon hers, tasting of cinnamon and sugar. It wasn't the deliciousness of whatever Elle was wearing on her mouth that made Wren lose herself in her first kiss. It was the fact that it was obvious to her, even as someone who had never kissed anyone in her life, that Elle was a world-class kisser.

Their kiss felt like it lasted for hours, but when Elle removed her lips from Wren's, it also felt like it had lasted far too short a time. "That's all for now, I'm afraid," she said in her low, supple voice. "I have to go. But remember to think of me tomorrow, and your arrows will easily meet their marks. I will see you soon, though, I promise, and I can't wait for that moment." Elle winked and then rose from the bench, but instead of her walking away, a cloud of blue mist began to spread from her feet, slowly twining its way up her body. As the mist reached her head, she said one final thing to Wren. "Promise me you won't tell anyone about this, or all will be lost."

"I promise!" The second after Wren spoke, the mist swirled up around Elle's head, and then it began to dissipate, until it was quite clear that Elle and her lovely lips were gone.

Wren sluggishly adjusted to the woman's sudden disappearance, deciding that the kiss had definitely been too brief, and so had the time she'd just spent with Elle. As Wren slowly found her way back up the hill and to the party, she thought about that wonderful kiss. But how would merely thinking of Elle help with her first time using a bow?

The sight of a large, four-tiered cake sitting in the middle of the partygoers momentarily distracted her from thoughts of the woman she'd just met, and kissed, but only until the cake had been cut and she'd blown out the candles. The memory of the woman and that passionate kiss kept reappearing in her mind, interrupting any chance of Wren staying in the present.

Despite her mental absence, the party still continued, and the cake was soon served. The first slice, which went to Wren, was decorated with an elegant gold-and-silver orchid, made out of mousse-like, delicately sweet frosting. The rest of the night passed in a blur, although she was sure when the night finally drew to a close that she'd had a huge amount of fun.

As Wren got ready for bed, her thoughts were filled with pictures and sounds of the party, but those memories were mixed with thoughts of Elle. She had trouble falling asleep that night—that first kiss kept playing and replaying in her head, every second of it perfectly recorded in Wren's mind. The rest of the night had been wonderful, too, but the kiss stood out—the kiss, and Elle's face.

They floated around in Wren's head, rushing to the forefront of her mind again and again until, finally, sleep took over, and Wren became lost in that night's dreams instead of Elle's lips.

❖

Wren was still asleep when the mirror in her bedroom began to change. Instead of showing her sleeping in her bed, a red haze had begun to swirl around beneath the mirror's glass surface, until it was filled with crimson clouds and not a single inch of Wren's bedroom could still be seen.

"Look at how much Wren has grown since she was last in this world," came a voice from the mirror.

"Only you would know that," a younger, haughtier voice replied. "I hope she will follow the advice of our Seer, as you and I have planned. I still don't know if you've done everything necessary though. I feel like we need to do more, or at least that *you* need to do more."

"Everything will work just fine. I've completed every step I can, for the time being. As you well know, part of it depends on *you*, my friend. And remember, you are still only second-in-command to me, young woman."

"I know, you don't need to remind me." The younger woman sounded annoyed at what likely were words she'd heard before from her older superior.

"Wren will follow what the Red Seer has planned for her, what *we* have planned for her. Is everything in place with the Blue's Seer, though?"

"Of course. He's been blocked from witnessing everything we don't want him to see, but our Seer is also unable to see everything, as you're already aware."

"Yes, of course I am." The older raven's voice held a hint of anger, but it was unclear whether it was directed at the younger raven or the knowledge they shared of their Seer. "And it's quite maddening, to be blocked from what may be some incredibly important facts about young Wren's future. I'm sure everything will work out in the end, though. We have everything planned perfectly. We will not fail."

"We *can't* fail, either."

"Well, we'll know whether we will succeed…or fail…in only a few short days and nights."

Then the mirror's surface began to clear, until Wren's sleeping form underneath her blankets was once again all that was reflected in its surface. The mirror couldn't show Wren's suddenly troubled dreams, though. Nor could it reflect the anxious furrows in her forehead that were covered by her hair, their creases appearing as soon as the mirror had begun to turn red.

CHAPTER TWENTY-TWO

The next morning, the triplets joined Wren, Denise, and Torien for breakfast at the large dining table. Denise didn't even come close to hiding her glee when Quiq sat next to her, and he looked equally happy to see her. The two soon lost themselves in a private conversation about the previous night's party, and Wren remembered seeing her mom spend most of the night by his side, laughing and flirting more than Wren had thought appropriate for public. She also noted that Quiq was still wearing what he'd worn the previous night, which led her to believe he hadn't left the mansion's grounds or, potentially, her mom's side.

The thought of what this meant almost spoiled her appetite completely, so she ate more lightly that morning than the previous one, this despite the fact that the spread laid out before them was just as tasty as all the food in Azyr had been so far, more delicious than anything she'd ever had on Earth.

While Wren was chewing her final bite of coffee cake, Quiq spoke to her for the first time since he'd wished her a good morning. "Your mom tells me you're a really good cook."

"The best!" Denise said, sending a short, sweet grin in Wren's direction before she returned to ogling Quiq (as she had been during all of breakfast).

"I guess I'm okay at it," Wren answered, taking a swallow of coffee so she wouldn't have to say anything else.

"Oh, she's far better than just okay, aren't you, Wren? Be honest." Denise looked in her direction again, with a clear expression of pride joined by an expectant stare.

Did her mom really believe she would ever answer in the

affirmative to such a statement? Wren supposed Denise did, so she did something she'd never done before, saying, "Yeah, I guess I am."

Where the hell did that *come from?* Wren thought she might die of embarrassment and halfway hoped she would, but no one looked at her in the way she expected them to: doubtfully or disgustedly. And no one said, "How *dare* Wren give herself a compliment?" either. Instead, everything stayed calm and pleasant as the meal wrapped up, and there wasn't a single trace of fallout from Wren's statement about her abilities.

That fact made it seem like it might not have been wrong for her to do so. Not even slightly wrong.

After breakfast, the triplets led Wren out of the mansion and through an intimidating iron gate, where her bow and quiver were leaning against a high brick wall. In front of the wall, about one hundred feet away from it, was a row of targets, with concentric black circles all leading toward the place Wren knew she would never hit: the red bull's-eye. The fact that a *red* bull's-eye might have a different meaning in this world didn't escape her.

"So," said Speyd, "you ready to start heading away from sucking horribly with that bow? I bet it won't be long at all until you only half-suck."

"My dear sister," Quiq said, pulling her a few feet away from Wren, "I think you could find better ways to motivate the girl. But you're the best with the bow, so how about you leave the pep talks to me, and you take care of teaching her how to hold it?"

"Sure, Quiq, sure, if you say so. That type of motivation always worked fine on me, though," Speyd grumbled as she went over to where Wren's weapon sat. She picked up the bow and a single arrow and brought them over to Wren. "You'll get the next arrow in just a few minutes, just as soon as you've missed…I mean, fired at your first target."

Wren took the bow and arrow from Speyd, who then led her to a line of white chalk parallel to the targets. The female triplet stood behind Wren then, helping her find where to place her hand on the bow and how to set up the arrow so it would, as Speyd said, "fly true." Wren tried to ignore it when Speyd added that it would fly like a falsehood for her at first, but she wasn't able to lessen the slight shake in her arms as she finally held the bow and arrow in her hands alone. She lined up the arrow the way Speyd had taught her, squinting at the target that seemed miles in front of her, and prepared to let go.

"Wait," Speyd said with a laugh. "Not everything is set up correctly yet."

Wren watched with no small amount of apprehension as, to her left, Faest wrote something in the dirt with a silver rod. *What on Earth... on Shyon is he doing?*

Everything was made clear when the row of targets began to wobble and then float upward, until they were about ten feet off the ground. Wren groaned, but she knew this training was necessary, and she was easily able to figure out the need for the targets to be in the air. That would probably be where she would be during the battle as well, so she might as well get used to it in less stressful circumstances. She released her wings and flew up until she was level with the targets, careful not to go past the white line.

Flying while wielding a bow was challenging for a beginning flyer like her, but more challenging was firing the arrow. Wren did her best, letting it go when the bowstring was as tight as she could pull it, but the arrow didn't fly true, not at all. It reached the top of its awkward arc only about halfway to the target, hitting the ground softly and only bringing up a small cloud of dust.

Her next four arrows didn't do much better, even despite helpful pointers from each of the triplets. Quiq was the most patient of the three, but she managed to get her following arrow to travel only a few extra feet after his lengthy lesson. This was like learning to fly all over again, she thought as her eighth arrow missed yet again.

She wanted to give up after fifteen arrows and fifteen failures, but Quiq suggested she just take a short break, close her eyes, and take a few deep breaths. Wren figured that couldn't hurt, so she did as he suggested.

It was then that she thought again of the woman she'd met the night before and what she had said: to think of her when she was doing her target practice, and that doing so would help Wren succeed in hitting the target. Or something like that...

So Wren closed her eyes, floating above the ground and holding her bow loosely in one hand, an arrow in her other. She pictured Elle's face, every bit of it almost perfectly memorized from only their brief meeting. Then the thought of Elle turned into a fantasy, one where Elle was leading her onto a dance floor in a crowded club.

A heavy bass line thumped throughout the room, matching itself to the beat of Wren's heart. All around them, women in low-cut shirts and short skirts or skintight jeans moved in rhythm to the music, their skin dewy with sweat.

Elle led Wren by her hand, until they stood in the center of the floor, with flashing lights all around them, going on and off to the beat of the music. When they were off, she felt Elle place her hands on her hips, and when the lights turned back on, Elle began to dance with her, the heavy pulse of the song's drums leading Wren to dance as well.

Elle leaned forward, as the lights flashed and the women around them danced, and then she brought her lips to Wren's ear. "Fire the arrow. Now!"

Wren heard a loud *whiz* go shooting away from her, and she slowly opened her eyes. By the time she had them open fully, her arrow had already reached the other side of the target area, and it had also reached the red center of the target that lay ahead of her. Wren whooped and did a little dance, one that wasn't nearly as hot as the one Elle had done in her fantasy, one that in fact was downright silly-looking, she was sure. But the triplets didn't seem to think so, Speyd and Faest patting her on the back when she landed and Quiq drawing her into a tight half-hug at his side.

"You did good," he told her. "Great, actually. Your mom and Torien will be really proud. Why don't we break for lunch, and then we can come out here and you can be amazingly awesome again."

"Bet you can't do that twice," Faest told her with a slightly rough elbow to her side. It was clear that he had been impressed with her triumph, at least at first, but it was also clear he wouldn't stay that way for long. She'd just have to see if she could repeat her success.

It annoyed her a little that she hadn't succeeded without help—though how that fantasy had helped her, she had no clue. The power of her fantasy would have to be explained later, whenever she met Elle again. Wren didn't know when that would be, but she didn't possess the patience to wait very long until she saw the gorgeous woman once more. Yes, she realized, she could hardly wait until she had the chance to kiss Elle's soft, welcoming lips for the second time.

CHAPTER TWENTY-THREE

That night, Wren awoke to a loud sound. After listening a moment further, she realized it had been a thunderclap, echoing through her room and entering through the open bedroom window. Rain was pouring down outside, fast and heavy, and then an almost blinding flash of lightning followed the sound that had woken her.

It was an epic storm; its size and power drew her to her bedroom's partway-open main window to watch the rain fall and lightning strike outside. Strangely, the rain almost looked red. Was that just a trick of the light?

But something else was happening, something far more interesting than a simple summer thunderstorm: a red raven was flying straight toward her, then alighted on her windowsill, just as Sia had, back on Earth.

The fact that it was a red raven frightened Wren almost into backing away. She only just managed to hold her ground, calling out to the raven, "What are you doing here?" The storm almost drowned out her trembling yell, and she barely heard the raven's reply.

"I will see you soon, Wren," it said. A woman's voice came from its large, crimson beak. Then it flew off. And Wren, despite the shock of seeing one of the Winged Red in the Blue's land, was surprised to find herself crossing her bedroom once more and climbing back into bed.

When morning came, the memory of the storm and the visit of a red female raven had faded only slightly. A glance out her open window showed no sign of a storm having occurred during the night. The sky outside didn't contain a single cloud, and the grass and bushes were completely dry. She decided it had just been a bad dream as she dressed in an amber robe and went downstairs for breakfast.

Only her father was at the breakfast table, reading a cloth-covered book and eating a piece of jam-smothered toast. He looked up when Wren entered the room. "Good to see you, Wrenny, and good morning. I hope you slept well?"

"Yeah, except for a bad dream."

"Oh? What was it about?" Torien marked his place in the book and put it down next to his half-finished plate of food.

"A storm." Wren kept the rest to herself. Maybe she would tell her dad later, but first she wanted a chance to get some food into her stomach, along with some much-needed coffee.

"Afraid of storms still, huh?" He pushed a large dish of toast and eggs closer to where a second place had been set for breakfast.

Wren sat down and loaded up her plate with eggs, toast, and some sort of meat; it looked like bacon but was the color of well-done steak. She decided to call it "steacon," especially after taking a bite that tasted like a wonderful mixture of the two.

"So, it's just you and me today. Denise is eating outside with Quiq, and Faest and Speyd are sparring. Rysha is at home taking care of something, can't remember what. And Sia's at home with her family. She said to say 'hi' when I ran into her in the marketplace this morning." Torien took another bite of toast, the loud sound of his teeth crunching through the bread almost making Wren jump.

What the hell was going on with her? She had no reason to be nervous, so she pushed her tension down and turned her attention back to breakfast and her father's company. "That's nice of her," she told him in answer. She might have been more excited to get a "hello" from Sia if it hadn't been for meeting Elle. She still liked Sia, of course, but Elle had completely replaced her in the category of love interests. Sure, Sia was attractive, and Wren enjoyed being around her, but she didn't draw Wren to her, not the way Elle did; she didn't constantly haunt her thoughts.

After Wren had eaten her fill, she pushed away her plate and wiped some crumbs off her mouth. She had decided with her last few bites of breakfast that she needed to tell her dad about the previous night, even if it had probably just been a dream. "So, Dad? There was more to my dream. The rain, it looked like it might have been red, and a red raven landed on my windowsill. It said it would see me soon, and then it left, and I went back to bed."

"Sometimes, Wren, the especially powerful Winged have visions."

"You think that's what it was?" She didn't want it to be a vision. A vision meant that whoever that red raven was had been telling her the truth.

"Or maybe it was just a dream. As you can see by looking through the open doors behind us, there are no carnelian-colored puddles outside. Or any puddles at all."

Her father was right, at least about the lack of puddles, and nothing outside was red, either, not even the flowers within her range of vision. "I'm pretty sure it was just a dream, then," she told her dad. She didn't tell him the fact that the dream, or whatever it had been, hadn't felt like it had come from her. Instead, it felt almost as though someone else had placed it inside her head…almost like they had forced the dream into her mind.

"You could be right, and you may just be worried about the days ahead of us," he said. "I won't judge you at all if you are, but I'm very confident in your abilities, especially after I heard about your target practice yesterday. Now we just have to wait for your power to pop into place, and then you'll be fully ready for whatever is next."

Wren gave her dad a quick hug, hiding her nervousness behind a faked smile. "I'm going outside for some more target practice. I want to make sure my abilities yesterday weren't just a fluke."

"Oh, I doubt they were, but that sounds wise of you, all the same. Even the best can still get better. It's important to remember that we all always have room to grow and change," Torien advised her, and his strong, stable voice told her all she needed to know about whether her father meant the words he'd just spoken.

Feeling slightly reassured by her father's positivity, Wren left the room. She found her bow and a full quiver propped up against the door that led to the outdoor practice area. She hung the quiver over her right shoulder and picked up the bow, stepping outside to the place where she'd made her first bull's-eye. Wren wished she'd hit it without anyone's support but her own. But if she'd had to have some help, at least it was Elle who had provided the necessary assistance.

After she'd taken note that the targets were already floating, she flew into the air and drew back her bowstring, an arrow in place and aimed straight at the target in front of her. She did just what she'd done the day before, picturing Elle dancing with her, and her arrows found the bull's-eye again and again. Hours later, and thoroughly worn out, she noticed that the sun had moved a fair distance across the sky; it was likely sometime around noon or one. A growl from her stomach told her that no matter what time it was, her body was insisting it was time for lunch.

Back inside, she replaced her weapon and quiver by the same door and headed to the dining room, where yet another large spread of delectable food awaited her and her quietly growly stomach on numerous white, porcelain platters. Sia also happened to be there, and she looked in Wren's direction and grinned when Wren entered the room. She was still glad to see Sia, even if she didn't hold Wren's interest the way she had in the past.

She realized then, with slowly growing certainty, that Sia was just meant to be her friend. Which was just fine, because she was really good company. Wren found herself laughing again and again as they ate, and she was almost sad when the meal was over and Sia said she was leaving.

"My parents want to invite you over for dinner tonight," Sia said after Wren had walked her to the front door. "That sound good to you?"

"It sounds great. What time would you like me to show up?"

"Around five thirty."

Wren hadn't noticed a single clock while she'd been staying with her dad, but she'd also had a lot on her mind since her arrival. She decided her number-one goal after Sia left would be to get a better feel for her dad's house and whatever the Winged Blue possessed in terms of time-telling technology.

Sia gave her a hug good-bye, and Wren set off in search of timepieces. She was hopeful she would be lucky enough to find one before five thirty came and went.

CHAPTER TWENTY-FOUR

Wren managed to find a clock after only about ten minutes of wandering the halls of her dad's home. Seated in a comfy armchair in middle of the cheerily lit library, she happily passed the hours between lunch and when she would have to leave for dinner by reading a book of short stories she'd found in her dad's library. It was about various young women on Earth, and she kept laughing at all the details the obviously non-Earthling writer got wrong.

Sia had given her directions to her parents' house before she'd left, and so at about five fifteen, Wren set out, looking forward to spending time with Kriss, Sia, and Yhen, as well as meeting Sia's parents.

After flying for a number of minutes, she reached the road that led to Sia's. But halfway down it, she paused in mid-flight when she heard a woman's voice, coming from a street to her left. "Psst, Wren. Come here..."

Wren recognized the voice instantly, and so she landed on the ground, hurrying off her prior path and down that street. A much more run-down group of buildings than any she'd seen so far lined it; if Azyr contained a bad section of the city, this must have been where it started. A short way down the street, she heard the familiar voice again, coming from an alley. "Wren, I'm in here..." the voice said. So Wren turned into the dimly lit alley, and partway down it stood Elle, wearing a black robe that was far more low-cut than any she'd seen since she arrived. Not that Wren was about to complain.

She did her best to keep her eyes on Elle's face, and it wasn't exactly painful to stare into her almost glowing, sea-colored eyes. They made Wren think of tropical waters, which made her think of Elle in a bikini, and she had trouble drawing her attention away from the delightful thought of rubbing sunscreen into Elle's likely perfect shoulders.

When Elle spoke again, her incredibly sensual voice managed to pull Wren back to reality only a few seconds later. "I have something important to tell you and something equally important to give you." She held out an envelope, and Wren didn't hesitate at all, taking it from Elle's hand and placing it inside her robe's left pocket. It didn't hurt that taking it from her allowed their hands to touch, a spark of wanting traveling from where Elle's hand touched hers and rushing straight to Wren's chest.

"I need you to open this envelope tomorrow night. Its contents will lead you to where you need to go. Your mother's life depends on you doing as I say." Then she pulled Wren into a tight embrace, pressing her lips against Wren's for the second time, and this kiss was no less arousing than their first.

This time, Elle didn't even remove her lips from Wren's before she disappeared in a cloud of mist. But to Wren's very confused eyes, the mist that had appeared this second time almost looked like it might have been red. Though if it had been, it only was that color for a very brief moment. After that, all Wren could see were the very last vestiges of a cloud of blue, fading quickly before her eyes.

Only when the mist was completely gone was Wren able think clearly again. That had been some kiss! As her mind cleared further, her plans for that night slowly returned to her head, and guessing that she might already be late, she rushed out of the alley and headed back toward Sia's home. If she did happen to be late, which seemed likely by the time Sia's house came into view, at least it was for a very good reason. If Elle had been telling the truth, about her mom's safety…her *real* mom…then it had been worth ducking into that alley and hearing what she had to say. Besides, there had been that kiss, that amazing kiss, the feel of its heat still warming Wren's lips as she reached Sia's front door and knocked.

❖

The dinner's high point was some sort of fatty, roasted bird that tasted somewhat like duck, coated in rings of lemon and sage. Halfway through the meal, Wren had decided that Sia's parents were charming, both of them just as funny as Sia, if not more so. Wren had a very enjoyable time during the meal, even if a not-exactly-small portion of her mind was still occupied with thoughts of Elle.

As Wren wiped her mouth on a soft cloth napkin at the end of the meal, she started to wonder what her new acquaintance had meant. Would her mother really be in danger if she didn't do as Elle requested? It didn't seem she had a choice about following her instructions, even if something about them didn't seem quite right. But that was probably just nerves, nerves from finally getting to meet her birth mother. And, likely enough, from the chance to spend more time around Elle.

That particular part seemed as if it held more appeal than meeting her own mom, even if it meant she'd be learning why Passea had been gone for all these years. For Wren's whole life, practically. She hoped that her birth mom would have a really good explanation for her lengthy disappearance. Passea had missed far more events in her life than even Wren's dad had. She'd missed almost everything…except for her birth.

Once the plates and leftovers were cleared and dessert had been served, Wren finally managed to pull her attention back to the room she was in and the people in it. Sia's mom Zyr was telling a story about Sia's first time going swimming, and Wren did her best to concentrate on what the charming woman was saying. She was mostly able to, and no one seemed to notice that she'd checked out completely for a few minutes.

After everyone had finished dessert, Wren thanked her hosts and rose to leave, heading for the entryway and the walk back home. Sia accompanied her to the front door, but before Wren could go outside, Sia asked her if she wanted to go up to her room and hang out for a bit.

"Sorry, it's just that I'm really tired. Thanks, though." Wren knew the truth was that she didn't want to because of Elle. She had no interest in going into Sia's room, even if it would lead to more than just talking. Elle had stolen the final remnants of Wren's attraction to Sia with that last kiss, and so with a hug and a quickly spoken, "Good night, Sia," Wren left and started her walk home.

She was still buzzing slightly from her meeting with Elle when she got back to her dad's house. What would he think, if she were to tell him about her mom still being alive? Would he tell her not to go? Wren decided it wasn't worth the risk of a bad reaction from him, so she kept it all to herself, just as Elle had told her to.

Instead, she agreed to play a game of cards with Torien before she went to bed. No secrets left her lips while they played, but a smile danced across them because of those secrets, a smile she hoped Torien would think was directed at him. Then she chugged down the last of the now-lukewarm cinnamon-and-honey-flavored milk he'd made for her, gave him a light peck good night, and sleepily headed upstairs. Her tiredness was tempered with excitement, because Wren couldn't wait for morning to come, as that would mean that the next night—when she would see Elle and finally meet her true mom—was that much closer to arriving.

Chapter Twenty-five

Sia hid the reason for her bad mood from her family as they talked and read before bed that night, but it seemed her mother had noticed her unusually sullen affect anyway. Zyr pulled her aside before Sia went upstairs.

"Is something wrong, honey?" she asked her, a gentle hand resting on each of Sia's shoulders as she spoke.

"Nothing really, just…I guess I misunderstood a situation. But it's fine. It shouldn't exist in the first place. It's better this way." Sia hugged her mom. Then she said good night and headed up to her room, but she didn't turn away soon enough to miss the doubting expression on her mom's face.

Up in her room, her own doubts rose to the surface. She really liked Wren, despite the fact that her still-growing attraction to Wren was such a bad idea, and she'd thought Wren liked her back. As she sat in front of her mirror brushing her hair, she tried to clear away the thought of Wren's sweet smile and of her sweet lips, lips that Sia had wanted to kiss for ages. It seemed that would never happen, though, so she resolved to do her best to get over this unhealthy crush and turned her focus to getting out the last stubborn tangles in her long hair.

Just as she was placing the hairbrush back in its spot, her mirror stopped reflecting her bedroom. Instead, she saw the image of a woman sitting at a table. She looked slightly older than Sia and went far beyond being slightly more attractive. She was tucking some of her short, reddish-brown hair behind one of her ears, a wolfish grin directed at whomever she was talking to. Then the vision shifted, and Sia saw the other side of the table, where Wren sat behind a plate that held the remains of what looked to be breakfast. Then the visual began to move away from Wren, panning until it reached a woman with a dark, wavy mane of hair, staring lovingly in Wren's direction. Her look of compassion didn't match the tone of her voice, though. She sounded downright angry as she spoke, although for some reason Sia wasn't actually able to make out what she was saying.

The vision ended before Sia could make any sense of the woman's words, and she decided that she had to talk to Piru as soon as possible. She would set out for his house first thing in the morning, but first she'd have to somehow manage to get to sleep. It wouldn't be easy, she knew, not after the shocking discovery she'd just made, because that woman had borne a striking resemblance to Wren and to the way Passea had been described to her by Torien and other Winged Blue.

Was it true, though? Had that woman been Wren's missing mother? And what the heck had this vision been trying to tell her? Maybe it had something to do with the fact that all the walls surrounding the three seated women had been a color you almost never saw in the Winged Blue's land. So had everything else in the room, down to the robes Wren was dressed in. Did that mean that Wren was in the land of the Winged Red?

And did that mean Passea was not a Winged Blue?

❖

In the morning, Sia didn't even eat breakfast before she set out for Piru's. She was sure he'd have something around that she could eat, and even if he didn't, this was too important to wait. Even if, now that she was dressed and downstairs, an inhalation told her some sort of sweet-smelling pastry was baking in the kitchen. Had that been a hint of almond she'd smelled? Could her brother be trying a new recipe?

But before her steps could veer into the kitchen so she could find out, and perhaps be the first judge of whatever that delicious smell was coming from, she forced herself away from the sunlit kitchen and went outside. She had much more vital things to take care of than merely enjoying another one of her brother's creations, even though her mouth was watering at the thought of tasting the carrier of that delectable scent.

The flight to her grandfather's house took more time than it normally did due to some strong winds, but Sia made it there as fast as she could. She was a little out of breath when she reached up to knock on his door, but as usual, it opened before her fist could even hit the wood once.

"You took longer than I expected. Welcome, granddaughter. Come in, please, come in. I have some pastries and coffee waiting, although they aren't as fresh as whatever your brother might be baking this morning."

"What, you can't tell what it is this time?" Sia said, her question coming out harsher than she might have liked. She blamed her grouchiness on the early hour, the lack of caffeine, and the fact that she hadn't gotten to try her brother's latest baked concoction. But she still apologized, an apology Piru waved off and told her was completely unnecessary.

"I know how you are when you have to get up too early. I also know whatever it is you've come here to tell me is important, so let's get some coffee into you and sit down, and then you can fill me in."

Sia was surprised that her grandfather didn't already know what she'd seen in the mirror the previous night, but she was always forgetting that he couldn't see everything. Some of the most important parts of the future were always hidden to him, no matter how hard he tried to learn of what was to come. That had been a problem with the prophecy for Wren, but that was mainly due to the gaps in the Winged Blue's book of prophecies. If even a book that powerful was missing such information, it was, of course, impossible that Piru would be able to fill in the book's missing sections.

Sia couldn't wait to inform her grandfather of the prior night's vision, or whatever it had been, so before he'd even poured her coffee, she began to tell him all about it. "I'm not even sure if it was a vision," she said, "but if it was, I really need to know what to do about it."

"I'm almost positive it wasn't a vision. I think...let me see," Piru said, and he took her hand in his. "I think you were dreaming, and that it wasn't prophetic, but just a symbol of your fears for our future. I will give you some special juice, from a tree I grow out back. It will help you with any future bad dreams. You do need your sleep to be restful, after all, and not filled with scary nonsense like what you just described."

Sia had trouble believing that it had been only a dream, but her grandfather always knew what he was talking about, or at least he had up until this moment, so she couldn't find any reason not to believe him now. She finished her breakfast and told him she wanted to return home to lie down, and after Piru handed her a corked glass bottle full of dark-purple juice and she gave him a quick hug good-bye, she headed home.

CHAPTER TWENTY-SIX

After breakfast and more target practice, Wren sat in the library with her stepmom for a bit, her mind still a flurry of questions about her biological mother and the possibility of seeing her again. Before she could stop herself, she tapped Denise on the shoulder.

"Just a minute," Denise said, and she marked her place in the book she'd been in the middle of.

"It's really nice to see you reading, Mom," Wren told her.

"There are no TVs around here to watch, so I decided I might as well pick up a new hobby. Thanks to what that Winged woman gave me, I've been lucky enough to avoid any ill effects from not drinking any more alcohol, but I have been going through a bit of *Earth*-based withdrawal. So, was there something you wanted to ask me, Wren?"

"Just…well, this is hypothetical, but what chance do you think I have of seeing my birth mom here? And what do you think I should do if she were to contact me, tell me she wanted to meet me?" Wren was counting on Denise not catching on to the fact that these questions weren't hypothetical in the least.

"I'm sorry, Wren, but I doubt that your mom will get in touch with you here. After all, no one has heard from her in many years. But… but if you were to hear from her, I would tell you to definitely take her up on the offer of seeing her again. After all, she owes you some explanations and some affection from all those wonderful years she missed out on with you." Denise paused, and she looked as though she might have a question for Wren now. It turned out that she did. "Wren, hon, can I ask you something now?"

"Sure, Mom, anything."

Denise chewed on her lower lip for a second, her hesitancy at asking whatever it was as clear as could be. "Are you…are you mad, at your dad and me, for keeping the fact from you that I'm not your biological mother? I really hope you aren't, but I also really wouldn't blame you if it had made you angry, or disappointed in us, or anything like—"

"Of course not, Mom!" Wren was quick to answer. "You're... you're more of a real mom to me than she'll ever be, and I guess I kind of understand Dad keeping the truth from me. After all, I might have tried to contact her, if I had found out, and that would have maybe opened me up to asking a whole bunch of questions before Torien was ready to answer them."

"That's great to hear, Wren. A very big relief, to be sure. Now, would you mind if I return to my book? It's at a particularly exciting part right now—the queen is just about to find out who was trying to do away with her husband."

"Maybe I'll read that book after you're done with it, if you're enjoying it that much. It's great to see you so hooked on a novel, you know. But I think I'll go to Piru's now. I have some things to ask him about, things only he might know."

"Of course, Wren, go ahead." But Denise sounded as though she was already miles away, and Wren smiled to herself at the new but comforting vision before her, her mom totally lost within the pages of a book.

On the way over to Piru's, she began to worry that he might not appreciate her showing up like this, uninvited. But when she arrived at his doorstep, he was already out on the porch, a pitcher of red, seed-filled juice next to two tall, ice-filled glasses on a small table. Today's robe had a blue raven surrounded by a blue-and-black ouroboros, even prettier than the last one Wren had seen him wear.

"Pull up a chair, Wren," he said, gesturing to the empty chair on the other side of the table with a welcoming smile. "Despite the fact that I was expecting to see you today, I actually don't know why you've come. So I would love it if you would fill me in and share a glass of strawberry juice with me."

"I'm glad it's all right that I'm here, and I'll be more than happy to fill you in, because I really need some answers." Wren sat down in one of the table's matching wicker chairs and waited only long enough for Piru to pour her a glass of juice before she began. "I met someone at my birthday party, a woman, and she found me again last night. She told me that my birth mom, Passea, is in trouble, and that her life depends on my following this woman's instructions. I don't know what to do, so

I came here to get some help from you in deciding how I should handle this. I want to help her, I really do, but I just don't know if it's a good idea."

"Oh, Wren, I think you already know, despite what you may be thinking. Forgive me for being so forward, but I think you've spent almost your entire life doubting what your gut is telling you, and I think in this case, it's telling you to help your mom. It's what I would do, anyway, and I know you're good-hearted enough to do the right thing. No wonder I couldn't see this coming, though, as it's a pretty darned big deal!" Piru chuckled, and Wren smiled for the first time since she'd arrived. She wondered for a moment why he hadn't been able to foresee it, but apparently he couldn't see everything. It was amazing enough to Wren that he could see as much of the future as he could.

"You really think I should go to her? I guess that's what I think I should do, too."

"I'm positive. Wait, let me take a moment to see if I can see anything of your future that involves your mom, now that you've told me." Piru closed his eyes and fell silent. Then he began to speak, a slight smile on his lips. "I see you…saving your mother. Yes, you will save her, and by doing so, well, the Blue's safety depends on it…on you. You will rescue her, and she will be so, so happy to see you again." Piru reopened his eyes, grinning at Wren. "I know you should do as this woman asked. I don't have a single doubt in my mind. Now, do you already have plans for lunch?"

"I should probably get home, actually. I don't want anyone to think anything is up before I leave to join that woman tonight."

"Of course you don't!"

"I'm not supposed to tell anyone about this, by the way, but I figured I could trust you with it. I can, right?"

"Of course, of course. I won't tell a single Winged soul. Promise."

❖

Right after Wren had left, Piru went back inside. As soon as she'd disappeared from his sight, his eyes had begun to change color. By the time he'd gone over to the corner of his living room, they had turned entirely crimson.

In that particular corner of the room, a blue cloth cloaked a large, rectangular object. Removing the cloth, Piru revealed the mirror that had been hidden behind it. The sound of flapping wings came from beneath the mirror's surface, and then a red raven alighted on a table within the mirror's now non-reflective glass. "Have you done as you've been told?" the raven asked him.

"Yes, I have," he answered. Piru's voice sounded distant, and though his eyes were staring straight into the mirror, it was almost as if he were looking beyond it, to another time or place.

"She will be following Ember's request and the directions in the envelope?"

"Yes, she will."

"Good. You will continue to tell us everything, everything the Winged Blue have planned, correct?"

"Correct. I will do as you tell me, always."

"You may return to your day's activities now, but I expect frequent reports from you as to your people's plans."

Then the mirror became a mirror again, and Piru covered it back up with the opaque cloth, blinking a few times as they returned to their normal pale-blue color. He went outside and picked up the pitcher in one hand and the glasses in the other, carrying them back inside. Halfway to the kitchen, one of the glasses slipped out of his hand, spilling bright-red juice across the hardwood floor. "Oh my, gosh darn it." Piru went into the kitchen and moistened a dishrag, humming to himself as he walked into the living room again and starting mopping up the mess.

CHAPTER TWENTY-SEVEN

Night arrived faster than Wren expected it to, considering what she thought it might hold for her. As the sun slowly set, the anticipation she'd been feeling during the rest of the day had grown so intense, she felt as if she could taste it on her tongue: a sour taste with a touch of potential sweetness. It held two possibilities for that night: the chance that this reunion would be wonderful and everything would go well, or that she would completely fail to save her birth mother. Even though she wanted to meet Passea, and had wanted to ever since she'd discovered Denise wasn't really her mom, she still felt immense love for her stepmother, love that seemed as if it might not be replicated with her actual mother.

But all of it would be revealed soon enough. Everyone had now gone to bed, and Wren, with the envelope from Elle in her pocket, had begun to sneak out of the house. Halfway down the stairs, she heard voices, voices that sounded like the triplets. So she tiptoed to the far side of the door the voices seemed to be traveling through. She planned to ignore whatever they were saying as she left, but then she heard one of them say her name. As quietly as possible, she found her way to the edge of the doorway and cupped her ear to listen.

First she heard Speyd, who was saying, "…dumb girl. I can't believe she fell for it, for her father's lies. For everyone's lies. What an idiot!"

"Yeah," said Faest, "I can't believe she fell for all of it, either. And so quickly, too!"

Then it was Quiq who spoke, and his words hurt Wren the most. "I can't believe it, either. To think that she imagines she matters to us in the least! I've even convinced Denise that I have feelings for her! So, do you think Torien's plan will work, to manipulate Wren into helping us conquer the Winged Red?"

She'd heard enough. As tears began sliding down her cheeks, Wren left the triplet's cruelty behind and made her way to the mansion's front door. Then she was outside and away from those ugly words. She didn't want to think about what the triplets had said, what the truth really was about all of the Winged Blue. She didn't want to accept that none of them cared for her, not even her father. It seemed certain now that she was making the right decision, and she hoped her mother would be different than the rest of the Blue, and that she and Elle would be enough to help Wren heal her now-shattered heart.

About a block away from the house, she opened the envelope from Elle. It contained a square of pale-beige paper, with words she didn't recognize written on it in elegant, curving handwriting. She heard sounds coming from the paper, as if it were whispering, and then it began to pull at her arm, and so she followed its lead, letting it guide her in a familiar direction, until she found herself in front of the alley where she'd seen Elle the previous night.

The magical paper pulled her into the alley, and then it felt as if the paper were heating up, its temperature rising quickly. As it got warmer, it changed from the color of parchment to a glowing red. Soon it was too hot to hold. Wren dropped it, the paper falling straight to the ground as if made of stone. Then mist, like the one Elle had disappeared into each time, began to flow from the paper, but this mist was most definitely not blue. The red haze spread before Wren could escape it, until it was all she could see, and then it began to dissipate as quickly as it had appeared.

When it had faded from her vision completely, Wren no longer stood in the alley. Instead, she was in an opulently decorated hall. In its center sat a long, garnet-colored table, and red-velvet curtains lined the walls. Two women, dressed in form-fitting, red robes, stood only a few feet from where Wren had suddenly appeared. One she recognized as Elle. The other was an older woman she had never seen before, although something about her still struck Wren as familiar.

"I'm afraid I've lied to you," Elle said, looking very happy to see Wren. "My name isn't Elle. It's Ember."

"And mine is Passea," the woman said. "Welcome to Kremsin, Wren, the home of the Winged Red. Welcome home."

CHAPTER TWENTY-EIGHT

If it hadn't been for what she'd overheard the triplets saying, Wren would have tried to outrun Passea and Ember. Instead, she just tried to stay calm and waited for an explanation.

Apparently, there wouldn't be one. "We will explain everything in the morning, Wren, darling," Passea told her with a kind smile, "but I think for now, you should head to your bedroom. After all, you need to rest, because we have much to accomplish in the next few days. Ember will lead you to your quarters, which I hope will meet your approval. I tried to make them as lavish as I possibly could. May I give you a hug good night?"

Wren didn't know how she felt about getting a hug from a woman who had kidnapped her, even if she happened to be Wren's close relation. She gave in, though, with a quick nod, and Passea pulled her into a warm embrace. Then she kissed Wren on the cheek. "Off to bed with you, now, young lady. Sweet dreams."

Feeling very tired, not to mention completely confused, Wren followed Ember down a dimly lit hallway that began to the left of the large table. When they reached a set of double doors, Ember opened the one on the right. Ember led her through it by the hand, taking Wren's in hers without asking first. This bothered Wren only slightly, because the room they'd just entered actually managed to take her breath away.

It was almost as huge as the room she'd first arrived in, with a high, domed ceiling that held revolving, glimmering stars and a moon that was smoothly flowing through all of its phases. In the center of the room lay a bed with red ribbons winding around the bars of its wooden headboard, ribbons that somehow were dancing in the room's still air. One of the room's large walls was lined with floor-to-ceiling bookshelves, and the opposite one held a tall, wide terrarium, inside of which were salamanders and frogs, all various shades of red, some with black or purple markings scattered across their skin.

"Do you like it?" Ember asked, her tone implying that she already knew Wren's answer.

"Yes, oh yes, very much. It's amazing."

"I picked out the amphibians myself, and they're all trained to be held. So, I guess should let you get some sleep now, but remember that your mom will explain everything in the morning, with a nice, big breakfast as an added bonus. Our chef is the best in all the land, so bring your appetite. Now, come here." She held out her hand, and Wren could find no reason to hesitate, so she let Ember draw her into her arms, her embrace soon joined by a kiss, long and deep. Many others, with the occasional dart of Ember's long tongue into Wren's mouth, followed this first kiss.

"Sleep well, Wren." Ember let go of her and left Wren alone in her room to wonder about what the next day would bring. Would she even be able to sleep, with all these abrupt discoveries and all of the immense changes in the past few hours?

A set of silk, crimson pajamas lay on the table to the left of her bed. Wren changed into them, more than ready to get some rest. As she climbed into the soft, comfortable bed, though, she realized that Ember had lied to her: her mother's life *hadn't* been in danger. Had all of Ember's words been just a ruse to lure her here? But she also realized then that she wanted to stay, despite the large untruth Ember had told to get her here.

Yes, Wren decided: she belonged here, because now she knew the Winged Blue's secret, the one they'd hidden from her so very well up until this night. She could no longer trust the Blue, not after what she'd overheard today.

❖

A flock of red ravens was throwing Wren a party. They all wore glittery party hats, and bright, silver confetti fell as Wren dug into her chocolate cake. Then the ravens began to caw, their warning sounds echoing through the hall where Wren sat. She looked outside past the wall of tall windows and saw that beyond their wrought-iron frames, clouds were filling the sky, clouds that were a dark, cobalt blue. Then large droplets of rain began to fall, hammering against the windows, and one by one, the windows all shattered. Along with the rain, raven after raven, all different shades of blue, began flying into the room. The red ravens rose up from the table, and each red raven began a battle with a blue one, clawing and pecking at each other with far more violence than Wren had ever wanted to see in person. Dark blue and red droplets began to flood into the rain, all of them falling from the ravens' wounded flesh.

Two ravens were still on the table, Wren noticed now, and they began to chant four words, over and over, louder and louder, until Wren cried out and covered her ears against the awful uproar of chaos.

❖

The ravens' words were still echoing in Wren's mind when she woke in the morning, and it was almost as though she could still hear them in the large, sunlit bedroom.

You'll have to choose.

Wren knew which side she would choose, if it came down to it. She couldn't trust a single Winged Blue, not after she'd learned of their deception. So, after wiping the sleep out of her eyes along with the last vestiges of her dream, she climbed out of bed.

She changed into the red, scoop-necked robe that had apparently been placed in a chair by her bed while she slept. It was more tightly fitted than the Blue's robes had been, a fact that Wren didn't think came from a nationwide shortage of material. It still fit her okay, although she didn't feel entirely comfortable wearing something that hugged her curves so closely. But a glance in the room's large mirror told her that she didn't actually look all that bad in the robe, its tailoring seeming custom-made for her more ample figure. She almost looked good in it, actually.

Wren left her bedroom and found her way back to the hall where she'd first arrived in Kremsin. When she reached it, she saw that Ember and Passea were already seated at the table. On its surface were a few artfully arranged platters of food, including herb-flecked mini-quiches. Beside them sat a platter almost brimming over with cubed, red-skinned potatoes covered in some sort of creamy, white sauce, and what looked and smelled like coffee filled two narrow glass pitchers. Ember's appreciative stare when Wren entered the room told her she might possibly look more than merely okay in her robe. A wink followed Ember's skimming of Wren's body, and she felt herself begin to blush.

"Good morning, Wren. I hope you slept well?" Passea looked better rested than Wren felt, her face glowing and her smile cheery.

"Mostly." Wren pulled out a chair and sat down, making sure her first move was to pour herself a large mug of liquid from one of the pitchers. Yes, thankfully, it was coffee they contained. Delightfully strong coffee, and also some of the best she'd ever had.

As she ate her meal, the two other women ate mostly in silence. Wren echoed their quietness. She wasn't quite ready to start sharing things like her dream with Passea and Ember, even if the dream was somewhat more than just a dream. Wren was pretty sure that it was, but instead of telling her two tablemates about it, she just complimented the breakfast and waited as patiently as she could for Passea to tell her the whole truth. She could barely handle the suspense, so when Passea put down her napkin, her breakfast plate now empty, Wren directed all of her attention to her birth mother's spot at the table, awaiting what she hoped would be the entire story of the Winged Red's side of things.

"I suppose you'd like me to tell you everything now, then?" Passea asked.

"Absolutely. I mean, yes, please, if you don't mind." Wren quickly put down the big forkful of potato she'd been about to shovel into her mouth. Eating the last of her delicious meal could wait.

"Later today, Ember is going to take you to our Seer, Myuss, who will be able to fill you in far better than I possibly could, I promise. She's quite knowledgeable in 'everything Wren.' But first, I have a gift for you."

Wren had failed to notice the sizeable black box at her mom's side of the table, which Passea was now gently pushing in her direction. "Go ahead, open it," she told Wren, sounding rather excited, and so Wren took the box and removed its long, rectangular lid, placing it on the floor. Contained within the box were a bow and a quiver, the quiver embroidered with red ravens and a face on each side of it that resembled hers. Beneath the quiver was a bow, even more beautiful that the one her father had given her, this one ruby red and slightly transparent, almost as if it had actually been carved from a single, enormous ruby. The bowstring was red as well, and Wren pulled it back just a bit, taking note of its heft and texture for future reference.

"I can't wait to use it, Passea! Will I be doing some target practice today?" she asked her birth mom, who nodded.

"Once you're done eating, Ember will lead you to our practice field, and you can spend as much or as little time there as you want. Your invitation to Myuss's is for any time today that you choose. Although, if you'd like, we can get there in time for lunch. She has a fantastic meal planned for you, should you be there in time."

"Lunch at her house sounds great." Wren ate her last bite of food, followed it with the last of her coffee, and rose from the table. "Now, where's your practice area?"

Ember led her out to a field quite similar to the one in Azyr. Wren was more than ready to show off and, if she were lucky, to impress Ember as well. But not a single arrow met the target, not even when she tried picturing the two of them, even though it had always worked in the past.

"You'll get better with time, I promise," Ember told her, and kissed her on the cheek.

Wren wanted to tell her how she already *was* better, that she was great, to be completely honest, but there was clearly no proof of it in her botched attempts to hit the mark. "Should we go to Myuss's now, I guess?" she said, unable to stop herself from sighing quietly at the end of her sentence.

Either Ember didn't notice Wren's disappointment or she didn't want Wren to know she'd noticed, because she grinned at Wren and said, "That sounds great. We can get there through our marketplace, where I'll buy you a terrific new robe, if you'd like. Or a dozen of them!" Ember laughed and grabbed Wren's hands, twirling her around in a circle. Wren squealed, and despite the unsteadiness she felt when they stopped spinning, she didn't regret a second of it.

They told Passea they were off, and she wished them a good day, after informing them that she had much to accomplish in preparing for the Blue's arrival, so she wouldn't be able to join them. Wren was still shell-shocked from the sudden twist in her reality, and she realized then that she hadn't quite accepted the evil of the Winged Blue, not fully, even though it was obviously the truth.

Ember led her through a large, crowded marketplace full of Winged Red, all of them bustling about and shopping. Most of the Winged Red seemed happy enough, but some of their haggling seemed to show some displeasure at how those particular Winged were doing in their deal-making. The two of them reached a stand full of robes, each one fancier than the last, and Ember helped her to pick out three, all varying shades of red. The stout female shopkeeper told them she would send them to Passea's later, all of it free of charge. "Anything for our wonderful leader," the shopkeeper told them with a slight bow of her head.

As they were reaching the last of the stalls at the far edge of the market, Ember put out a hand to stop Wren and turned to face her. "Why don't you let out your wings?" she suggested, and Wren decided she might as well, even though she was uncertain what the Winged Red would think of her *not*-red wings. She let them out of her back, and then, reflected in the window that stood behind Ember, she saw something surprising: her blue wings were almost half-red, with their central line of feathers slowly fading from red to blue.

"They didn't used to look like that," she told Ember, turning left and right to get a better view of her now-multi-colored wings.

"I think they're quite becoming, Wren. Much better than only blue, of course, and I do prefer the red. Maybe if you're lucky, they'll change all the way to red before the Winged Blue arrive. That way you can state with your wings alone whose side you're on."

"Yours, of course," Wren told her. She didn't need her wings to be fully red in order to let everyone know who she thought was to be trusted. She just hoped that none of the Winged Red would be bothered by the fact that they were bi-colored. Kind of like her biracialism, which had definitely caused problems for her back on Earth. She wondered if the Winged Red would be more forgiving than those jerks in her hometown, and she mentally crossed her fingers as Ember took her hand and led her the rest of the way out of the market. She took one last glance at her new, different wings and decided that even if her gorgeous romantic interest wasn't totally happy with them, she was. At least for the time being.

She had to know the truth about something, though, something she was surprised that neither Passea nor Ember had told her. "How was Passea able to hide the fact from my father that she wasn't Winged Blue for all those years?"

"Ah, that would have to do with her special power. You see, Passea is able to disguise herself, any part of herself, as either a Winged Red or a Winged Blue. She was even able to hide her power from Piru. Pretty impressive, if you ask me, as he's not *entirely* hopeless when it comes to seeing into people's heads. Does that explain it well enough to you?"

"Yes, I think it does." It was a believable explanation for Wren's multicolored wings, for one thing. Would she gain her birth mother's power, then? Being reminded that Passea was her birth mother made Wren remember the woman she'd thought was her mom all those years, for the first time since she'd arrived in Kremsin. She felt rather worried about leaving Denise behind. Before she could ask Ember about how they could make sure her stepmom was safe, her new friend let out her own wings and told Wren to follow her, as Myuss's house was still a few miles away. "Bet you your new wings will work better than the old ones," she called over her shoulder with a smirk, and then she took off.

Wren quickly discovered that she could barely keep up. Nope, her new wings weren't any more functional than her old ones. She finally managed to catch up to Ember just as they reached a forest slightly beyond town, with a two-story, black-and-bloodred cabin sitting a few hundred feet away from where the trees started. A large, circular swimming pool sat to its left, filled with bright-blue water, the first blue Wren had seen since she'd arrived in Kremsin. She figured a pool full of red water would be kind of creepy, so it made sense that the water was left its natural color, even if it looked rather out of place here. The cabin and its surrounding grass-covered grounds were spotted with dots of red, dots that turned out to be ravens as Wren drew closer. A few of the birds cried out greetings to her as they flew closer. "Welcome, Wren!" one after another yelled as she and Ember flew closer to the building.

"This is it!" Ember yelled to Wren, and she began to descend toward the ground at a rapid pace. Wren followed her down, landing a few feet away from Ember. She could now see a middle-aged woman waiting for them outside. She wore the shortest robe Wren had seen here, with bell-shaped sleeves and lace around its V-neckline. Her hair was the same colors as the house, and it curled and tumbled down her shoulders and back. Wren found her surprisingly attractive, since she must have been at least thirty years Wren's senior.

"Hello, Ember," the woman said in a husky voice. "And you're Wren—I recognize you from my visions. You're just in time for an early lunch. I had it catered by one of Kremsin's best restaurants. I hope you like what's served, but if you don't, I can have them deliver something else right away."

"I'm sure it'll be fine, whatever you're serving. I'm not picky," Wren told her.

"You're allowed to be picky here in Kremsin, Wren. You are our honored guest, after all. Now, please, come in, and I will begin your meal with some high-quality, ice-cold hard cider. It's one of Kremsin's specialties."

Inside the cabin, both the colors of its outer walls and Myuss's hair were echoed in the decor, everything either black or the intense, saturated red of the Seer's curls. The room contained two antique-looking sofas, with richly black wood used for their arms and feet, and a black-and-red lacquered table sat between them. In the corner of the room lay something tall and rectangular covered by a dark-black cloth. As Wren looked at it for a bit longer, she thought she might have detected something blue through the cloth's ripples and folds.

Before she could get a closer look, Myuss spoke, interrupting her curiosity about what was hidden behind the fabric. "Please have a seat, Wren, and as I said, I can send everything back if you aren't happy with it."

Wren didn't plan to send anything back, even if it was disgusting. After all, based on the amount of food and the elegance of what each white porcelain platter held, she knew at once that the chefs had gone to a great amount of effort to prepare everything she saw.

She sat down on one of the sofas, her eyes settling on a pint glass that held a golden, fizzing liquid. That must have been the hard cider. Wren didn't know how she felt about drinking something alcoholic, especially after the problems her mom had experienced with the stuff. But she didn't want to be rude, so she limited herself to a few small sips of what the glass held and tried to ignore how thirsty all the food was making her. Lunch consisted of many different canapés and miniature treats, which included small burgers with some sort of sharp, smoky cheese melted over the meat, and salmon, dill cream cheese, and caviar-covered circles of flatbread. Everything was wonderful, if a bit too salty, at least without any water. But it was all so good that Wren had trouble stopping, and she felt positively stuffed by the time she quit eating.

The two women had kept her busy talking, with questions about Azyr and the Blue. Myuss had told her that her visions only revealed so much. After everyone was done with their food, Myuss rose and walked to the far end of the couch Wren was sitting on. Once there, she picked up an ancient-looking, red-leather-bound book that rested on the far end of the couch. She carried it over to Wren and placed in it her lap. "Go ahead, open it. You'll find everything you want to know inside its covers. I bet the Blue's Seer didn't let you see *their* book of prophecy, did he?"

"No, not even once." Wren was more than a little miffed at this realization, but it was obvious why Piru hadn't shown her, now that she knew that the Blue had been plotting against her all along.

"Well, Wren, sweetie, why don't you go ahead and take a look?" Myuss gestured at the book, and she almost appeared as though she could have been feeling impatient as she stared pointedly in Wren's direction.

With the pressure of Myuss's gentle nudging pushing her into action, Wren lifted the book's cover and opened it to its first page, revealing words written in a beautiful, curling script. She couldn't tell what they said, though, because before she could begin to read, the words began to move, swirling around the page, faster and faster. Then one of them started to tumble toward her hand, just where her fingers met the page, and it began to travel onto her skin, not stopping until it had shot up her arm. It was followed by a second word, then another, and Wren practically dropped the book, letting go of the cover and its pages as fast as she could. But the words still found their way onto her body, and then the pages in the book began to turn, speeding up more and more until it appeared as if every page in the book was now blank.

Wren looked down at her arms, then pushed up her sleeves, but somehow all the words seemed to have faded away, her skin back to its usual pale brown. The two women looked just as shocked as Wren was, if not more so, and Myuss cleared her throat before saying, "Any chance you can return those words to the book, dear? I don't exactly have them memorized, so it would be really great if you could."

"I…I don't even know how they managed to *leave* the book in the first place. I didn't do anything to get them to do that, Myuss. I swear." Wren noticed then that her arms had started shaking slightly, and Myuss seemed to notice too; she reached toward Wren and began to rub slow, calming circles in the center of her back.

"I believe you, Wren, but if you can manage to return them to the book, it would be most appreciated. Maybe you could think it over during the next few days? For me? For the Winged Red?" Myuss's voice held more concern than her facial expression let on, and Wren couldn't blame her. She hadn't meant to remove the words from the book, and she felt rather alarmed that she didn't know how to put them back, either. She just had to hope that the Winged Red could win the upcoming battle without their prophecy's help.

"I promise I'll make sure Wren tries her hardest to figure out a way to return the words to the book, Myuss," Ember said, and Wren thought she noticed Ember's face harden a little with those words. But she must have imagined it, because when Ember turned back in Wren's direction, she showed no sign of anything but joy to be spending time with Wren. "And on that note, I think we should head out now. I have a great place in mind for us for dessert, as one of our best bakeries is nearby," Ember told her, rising from the sofa in her usual graceful manner.

Wren wished she could move with such elegance, but she doubted she'd ever be able to glide through the world so sensually. She simply had to believe that Ember was happy with her just the way she was. Which had seemed to be the case so far. Except, perhaps, for the part of her wings that were made up of the wrong color of feathers. Could Ember ever fully accept Wren's blue feathers?

Wren said good-bye and thanked Myuss, then followed Ember out the door. She hoped the bakery's pastries would be tasty enough to take her mind off her wings and their lower, imperfect, still-blue half.

CHAPTER TWENTY-NINE

I can't believe there's still no sign of Wren!" Torien's voice held just as much worry as it had when he'd first discovered her missing, if not a good deal more.

Sia's mother Zyr placed a caring hand on his back, but Sia wondered if it would make a single bit of difference to Wren's clearly distraught father.

Wren had been missing at breakfast that morning. Sia, who had been invited over for the meal, had gone upstairs to investigate. After knocking on her friend's bedroom door for almost five minutes, Sia called out, "I hope you're decent!" through the door, unwilling to admit to herself that a small, embarrassing part of her hoped that Wren *wasn't*.

But decent or not, there was no Wren in her bedroom, or in the bathroom, or, after an hour or so of searching, anywhere on the mansion's grounds, inside or out. So search parties had been formed, and Sia had joined her mom and Torien, a trio she regretted ending up in as soon as she saw the terrified look on Wren's father's face. It wasn't that she didn't care that Wren was missing, not even close to it, but the upsetting level of torment Torien was clearly experiencing was almost too painful for her to see. It had only grown worse the longer they'd searched.

Now they were near Sia and Zyr's home, and Sia began wondering what her brother might have baked recently. A loud rumble from her stomach told her why Kriss's foodstuffs had come floating into her mind. She should have been concentrating entirely on finding Wren, but she knew she wouldn't last much longer if she didn't eat, and Torien needed to keep up his strength as well. "Why don't you try to pick up her scent one more time?" Sia asked her mom. "Then we should probably get something to eat, the three of us, at our house. Before we pass out and lose our ability to keep looking," she added, hoping her joke might bring a smile to Torien's face.

A pitiful-looking half-smirk appeared on his lips, but it was gone as soon as it had shown up, and he nodded dejectedly. "I suppose you're right, Sia." He sighed one of the most mournful sighs Sia had ever heard and then said, "So yes, we'll kindly ask your mother to try one last time, and then we'll just have to give in and fill our bellies, loath as I am to stop searching for my poor Wrenny." Torien sighed again, then said, "And I suppose I can go ahead and start up to your home, so Zyr can focus fully."

In addition to her impressive talents with potions and charms, Zyr also had the magical ability to shape-shift into the form of a small, pale-blue cat with wings. She had this power in place of being able to take birdform. As a result of her unusual ability's benefits, she might possibly be able to track Wren down. Her sense of smell was always heightened when in catform. Sia had brought along one of Wren's worn and unlaundered robes so her mom could familiarize herself with the person she was trying to scent.

"Should we start from here?" Sia asked her mom after Torien had disappeared around the street's bend. She waited as Zyr did the necessary shifting into her smaller, furrier catform, and Sia picked up her mom's now-the-wrong-size robe and folded it, draping it over her arm as she waited for the final tufts of fur to appear on her mother's pointy ears.

"I'm good to go now," her mom said, and Sia watched as Zyr's small nostrils flared, her shoulders bending down as she started to sniff the ground in front of her. "Let's try heading back toward Torien's. Maybe there's some path we haven't tried yet."

"Yeah, that sounds like a good idea. After all, Wren isn't familiar with our city, so maybe she was out on her own and got lost, or something like that?" Sia didn't really believe what she was saying and watched doubtfully as her mom nodded her cathead and began walking away from their house, moving her head back and forth across the ground with long, audible inhalations.

"Why don't we go down that way?" Sia gestured toward Nectar Avenue, and her mom nodded again, turning left onto a narrow street lined with old, blue-brick buildings. No one had lived in this area of town for a while, and there was talk of tearing the dilapidated houses down and putting up a community garden and perhaps a playground in their place. Sia didn't like how this part of the city was making her feel. She wished she hadn't suggested they try their luck on this particular street. When they arrived at an alley after they'd passed by a few houses, Zyr paused, her left front paw dangling a few inches above the uneven cobblestones.

"What is it, Mom? Do you...do you smell something? Do you smell her scent?"

"Yes, yes, I think Wren was here, right at this alley's opening. Follow me, Sia!" Her mom darted into the dark alley, and Sia followed her. She found herself in a short, narrow space between two of the street's more shabby-looking homes. A few broken wooden boxes sat in one corner of the alley, and Sia saw a rat run off and take cover behind them, clearly familiar with the scent of cat that her mom must have been giving off. Not that it was in any danger. Zyr never ate rats: even as a cat, she preferred the food of the Winged Blue, as the rest of their people did when in their ravenform.

"So?" Sia didn't bother hiding the nervous anticipation in her tone; she knew her mom would be able to smell her nervousness anyway.

She had to wait, though, while her mom gave the whole alley a thorough and vigorous nose-tour. "So," Zyr finally answered, turning to look up at Sia, "she was definitely here. But she disappeared, somewhere around the far corner, where that rat is hiding from me, silly thing. And...and it gets worse."

"Worse? *How* does it get worse?"

"I can smell something else in here, something that doesn't smell like anything from the Winged Blue."

"Could it be that a Winged Red was in here with her? Do you think she got kidnapped?" If Sia had been the type to wring her hands, she would have started then, but instead, she steeled herself for the chance that her mom would state what she had already decided was the truth.

"That's one possibility, yes, a very likely one. Only...I don't think this scent of Winged Red came from a person. It smells more like... more like magic, I think. And not our magic," she concluded grimly.

"Well, fuck." Sia knew her mom didn't like it when she swore, but she also knew she probably wouldn't mind this time, considering the current unpleasant circumstances.

"Yes, my dear, 'fuck' indeed."

"I think we should use one of your transportation potions to travel to the Winged Red's world. I'll go, and you, and Tor—"

"No, that's not a good idea." Zyr shook her head as she spoke, as if her intensely emphatic tone hadn't been clear enough on its own. "Sia, please put my robe on the ground and turn around so I can change back, and then we'll take this news to Torien and formulate a plan. One that couldn't possibly lead to my only daughter getting killed."

After her mom was in both her Winged form and her robe again, they hurried back to their house with the news. Torien seemed even more upset now that he knew more of what had probably happened to Wren, and Sia couldn't blame him. There was no way Wren would be safe there, in the Winged Red's world, all by herself. That was why, as soon as her mom had told her she couldn't go try to rescue Wren, Sia had decided to do exactly that.

After a quick lunch of sandwiches and a small glass of wine for Torien's nerves, everyone returned to Torien's except for Sia. She had to take the draught her grandfather had given her, as it had already come to be many hours past when she'd last been supposed to take a dose.

Sia hurried up the stairs in the now-silent house, hoping to get back to Torien's before the whole plan had been decided upon—and before she was left out of it entirely. But just as she reached for the bottle beside her bed, a vision hit her, and every inch of her bedroom was washed away as it took over her completely.

She saw Wren lying in an unfamiliar, red-blanketed bed, and someone equally unfamiliar was kissing her. Except that Sia had seen her before, she realized, seated across the table from Wren in a red-walled room. She flinched as this vision became clearer, because it now had revealed exactly how gorgeous the young woman kissing Wren was. Worse still was the fact that the woman's wings weren't blue, their shiny feathers the color of freshly spilled blood.

Sia wanted it to end, but apparently whatever was making her watch all of this thought she needed to see more. Her magical vision continued with the sight of the woman with dark, wavy hair, from the last time she'd seen the future, standing on a balcony. The woman raised her fist into the air, and she shook it as she screamed out the words, "...and we will be victorious!" Her yell was followed by a loud roar, both applause and menacing yells coming from the hordes of armored Winged Red that filled the streets below the balcony where the woman stood.

The vision seemed adamant on showing Sia one more thing before it ended; the last portion of it contained Piru. He was staring, glassy-eyed, into a mirror in the corner of his living room. The young woman who had been kissing Wren was looking at him haughtily through the mirror's surface. "You are to stay out of our way when we reach Azyr, Piru. That is an order."

"Yes, mistress, I will do as you say. I will do whatever it takes to help you, once you arrive."

"I'm sure some pathetic little part of you would like to do otherwise. That's half the fun for me, just so you know, Piru."

"Anything for you, mistress. Anything." Piru sank down on one knee and bowed his head, and the beautiful, red-winged woman just tilted her head to the side and grinned, a small, assured chuckle escaping her ruby-painted lips as her smile grew wider and wider still. But Piru didn't fight back, only bowing his head deeper and lower, until his forehead rested on the floor.

It was then that, finally, the vicious stream of images ended. They'd left Sia so weak that it took the last of her remaining strength to find her way up from the floor and into her bed, where a deep, dreamless sleep dragged her down into its depths.

CHAPTER THIRTY

It could have been either minutes or hours later when Sia awoke, but she didn't need her usual large dose of strong coffee to keep her eyes wide open. No, that vision had done more than enough to give her the energy to get out of her bed, no matter how late the night sky told her it still happened to be. The moon's golden beams painted her bedroom in its warm glow, the moonlight coming in between the curtains she hadn't had the chance to close.

Yep, that vision had hit her hard, but not hard enough to keep her down for long. And it had given her the knowledge she needed to decide what she had to do next—she had to rescue Wren, and she certainly wasn't waiting around for Torien and the rest to continue making up their own minds about what to do.

She was as quiet as possible as she sneaked down the hallway, and a quick listen against her parents' bedroom door told her they were both still fast asleep. Good. That would make the rest of her plan all the easier. Past their bedroom was the closet-sized room where her mom brewed all her potions, which was where Sia was headed. She slowly opened the small door, hoping to silence the creaking sound it had made for years, ever since the race she and her brother had undertaken down the long hallway that had ended in tears for him and stitches for her. The door still bore a small crack near the lower left hinge, and her hairline still had the scar the door had given her in return.

The door might have still groaned when she opened it, but she inched it open, so it was barely louder than a mouse might have been, and she knew there was no way it would wake her parents or her brother and sister-in-law, who slept farther down the hall.

She waited until the door was fully shut to reach for the table lamp, and in the room's complete darkness she bashed her shin into a chair. "Shit!" She just barely managed to catch the chair before it fell over, and she knew then that this room still had it in for her, even if her damaging its door had happened a good eleven years back. Spell rooms usually held grudges, or at least *this* particular one did. "I'd like to apologize again, Spell Room," Sia said as she felt around in the pitch-black chamber for the lamp. The floorboards creaked, sounding somewhat like a sigh of annoyance under her feet as she found and then flicked the switch. "I know, I know, we've never gotten along, and I promise I'll be out of here soon enough," she grumbled softly.

The heavy-based lamp barely brightened the room, but Sia could still make out the labels on her mom's wall of potions well enough. "Now, where are you two hiding?" she said aloud. After a few minutes of rearranging the bottles, and one near-catastrophe when a container of Instant River almost fell off the shelf, she found what she was looking for.

One bottle had a shimmering circle of blue on it, with the vivid images of many different locations flashing and alternating within the circle's center. The other showed a woman fading in and out of visibility, dancing as she did so. "Thanks, Spell Room. All done in here. I'm leaving now." The floorboards creaked again as she left, but this time their noises were more akin to the sound of someone rudely mocking another. Sia believed the humans called that a "raspberry." I'm glad I'm leaving now too, you annoying, poorly built hovel of a room, she thought with a fair bit of irritation. She didn't dare speak her thought aloud, though: who knew what the room might come up with, to get even for such a slight?

Safely back in the hallway, Sia then crept down the stairs, her stomach aflutter with the worries her head alone couldn't contain. Would she be able to return Wren home safely? Would she even survive her trip into the land of the Winged Red? Was she up for this immense challenge in the least?

Her worries only multiplied as she walked down the empty, moonlit streets, until she was joined by a whole jeering crowd of anxious thoughts by the time she reached the alley where her mother had scented Wren.

This was her first attempt at invoking a portal spell. She knew that all the Winged Blue's magic, even from someone as powerful as her mom, could sometimes be quite iffy. And these were two rather powerful potions she had "borrowed," so who could guess just how badly things would end up if something were to go wrong?

But she couldn't abandon Wren to the enemies of the Winged Blue. So she pulled out the stopper from the first bottle and lifted it to her lips, swallowing a few drops of the contents. Next, she unstoppered the second bottle and tipped out half of its shimmery, blue liquid onto the ground just in front of her. She didn't wait for the first to take full effect, although she would have loved to. No, the portal potion had its own plans for her, perhaps plans that the unfriendly spell room had helped to construct: a swirling vortex of bright-blue smoke quickly encircled her and pulled her forward, just as she noticed that her arms were almost fully invisible.

Well, at least the invisibility potion seemed to work, she was relieved to discover. Now she just had to pray that the portal potion would function correctly, too. She shut her eyes and filled her thoughts with pictures of Wren, from all the lovely time she'd spent with her. Moments later, she felt her feet gently make contact with what she fretfully hoped was the floor of Wren's bedroom.

Thankfully, the first potion had seemed to do the trick: she couldn't see a single bit of her body. It was surprisingly challenging to put the stoppers back into the now-invisible bottles, but somehow she managed, and she gently placed them in her robe's equally invisible left pocket.

And it was very lucky that the invisibility potion had worked, because she now heard footsteps coming down the hallway. She barely had time to rush over to the far corner of the ostentatiously decorated bedroom before its door swung open.

The first person to walk through the doorway was Wren, wearing a revealing, body-hugging red robe. It wasn't the robe that made Sia delighted to see her friend standing there intact, but she couldn't help enjoying the sight of Wren in such a flattering outfit, even if it happened to be the wrong color. Blue suited her better, Sia thought, and she frowned as she realized that Wren was probably wearing the robe willingly. She looked pretty happy, actually, and not bespelled in the least, her eyes clear and bright as she smiled at the next person to enter the room.

And then Sia had to just stand there, as silently as possible. The untrustworthy young woman from her vision had just entered the room, and now Sia had to watch her touch Wren in person, as the impossibly beautiful woman cupped Wren's chin and pulled it slightly upward. Sia's sudden burst of anger only grew as she was forced to watch Wren kiss someone other than her. Sure, it was fine if Wren kissed someone else, she told herself, but it was *not* fine if it was someone this evil, a clearly deceptive member of the Winged Red who had somehow won her poor friend over, won her over completely, it seemed. Sia knew she couldn't do anything, though, at least not yet, and so she just clenched her fists and waited until the auburn-haired temptress finally pulled away from Wren's lips.

"I have to take care of something, but I'll be back in about an hour, if you'd like," she told Wren. It was obvious that she was expecting Wren to reply in the affirmative, her face empty of any doubt. Or any respect.

But Wren clearly couldn't see that, her face also free of doubt as she answered, "I would like that, Ember. Come back whenever you're ready."

"Okay, see you soon." The woman—Ember—paused before she let go of Wren, then pulled her back into her arms for one last kiss. Even worse than the last few, this final kiss seemed to involve some tongue. There was no way Sia's mouth would ever feel clean again if that woman's tongue had been in *her* mouth.

Then the woman left, shutting the door behind herself, and it was just invisible Sia and Wren in the room, exactly as Sia wanted it. Well, minus the invisibility and the fact that they were in the land of the Winged Red, completely alone, without even the certainty that Wren would trust her after all that Sia had seen.

But Sia knew she had no other choice. "Hi, Wren," she said, and Wren spun in her direction toward the sound.

CHAPTER THIRTY-ONE

"Who the hell is in here?" Wren growled. She didn't sound all that scared, which surprised Sia. Wren's apparent bravery caused some pride to well up in Sia's currently invisible chest.

"It's…it's me, Sia. I have something important to tell you, and—"

"I don't care." Wren planted her hands on her hips and narrowed her eyes, then turned in just the right direction to make eye contact, had Sia not been invisible. "I don't trust any of the Winged Blue anymore, not after what I overheard the triplets saying."

Wren's face showed quite clearly that she not even remotely happy to see…well, to *hear,* Sia. What *had* she overheard the triplets say? Sia wondered. What could they possibly have said that would make her distrust the Winged Blue so completely? It didn't sound as if there was a shred of doubt in Wren's mind that the Blue were now officially on the "bad guys" list, but Sia knew she had to convince Wren to trust her again. Just a little, just enough to get her to follow Sia down the hallway to wherever the two women in her vision were located. Because maybe, if she were lucky, they would overhear some part of the Winged Red's plans that would clear things up for Wren…so she could once again trust the right group of Wingeds.

"Whatever you overheard, I swear, I…it's not true. And also, I need to tell you about my vision." The words rushed out of Sia's mouth almost without help, and she allowed them to continue tumbling out into the air of the red-colored room and into Wren's ears. She knew she didn't have much time, either to save Wren or to save the Winged Blue. *And the humans, as well.* "So, I need you to know that a while back," Sia said, "I started having visions, just like my grandfather. Then they stopped, I think because of a potion he gave me. I'm pretty sure, based on my last vision, one of the Winged Red has somehow taken over his mind. The one who was just kissing you. And in that vision, I saw a woman, with dark, wavy hair, who was standing above far too many Winged Red and who was about to lead them into battle. Oh, and she looked something like you and has a mole right above her left eyebrow. It's in the shape of a heart, which is kind of cool, but she clearly isn't. Cool, that is. I think that we should sneak down the hallway and find her, and that other young woman, the one you were…the one you were *kissing*, so we might overhear part of their plan."

Sia took a deep breath, and as she was exhaling, Wren's answer came. "You may be able to describe that woman because you actually saw her in that vision you just told me about, but you could have figured that out some other way, like from spying on her, and on me and on Ember. Which you kind of already did, when you appeared in my new bedroom. Why…why should I trust you?"

"I don't know…I don't know how to convince you, other than by having you hear it directly from her, her and your new buddy…but what do you have to lose?" Sia knew it wasn't that simple, because if the woman in her vision *was* Wren's mom, Wren actually did have something to lose. Something big.

"What do I have to *lose*?" Wren said quietly, a look of furrowed concentration on her attractive face making it seem as though she were actually considering Sia's words. Wren bit her lip, which somehow managed to make her even more attractive to Sia. But she had to ignore her baser instincts right now, Sia reminded herself. She had to resist doing what she was picturing right then—sweeping Wren up in her arms and kissing her, and somehow managing to prove to Wren that better kissers than that horrible Ember bit…woman existed. Better kissers, and less-evil ones, too.

"I just…I have a lot to lose either way," Wren finally said. "But I'd rather know for sure that Passea can be trusted, and Ember, too, so as long as you don't switch the invisibility magic with one that'll turn me into a Winged toad, I'm willing to trust you…at least enough to not turn me into a feathery amphibian."

"I promise, you stay just as attrac…I mean, uh, you'll stay yourself. Completely." Sia tried to ignore Wren's cute smirk, which appeared in the middle of that butchered sentence. Damn it, Wren had caught her little slip. She had other things to worry about right then, though, and decided to just be happy about the fact that Wren couldn't see her blushing. She walked over to Wren and, taking Wren's hand in hers, opened it, pressing the invisible half-empty bottle of potion into her hand.

It was visible once again the very second Sia let go of it, and Wren lifted it up to her face, examining it. "Looks like it's at least marked appropriately. Here goes nothing," she said, and she uncorked the small bottle and downed what was left of it. "Or, here goes something, I guess," she added. Wren sounded surprised, but she was smiling by the time she'd looked down and seen her hands starting to fade. "This is pretty awesome," said a now-invisible Wren. "Now what?"

"Now, we tiptoe into the hallway and go in whatever direction you suggest and try to hunt down Ember and Passea. Any idea where they'll be?"

"None," Wren told her, "but let's just try going past my room, because I think I saw what looked like more sleeping quarters down that way."

Sia began to walk forward, but Wren crashed into her before she could get very far. "Ouch! Wren, that was my foot. Watch out...please."

"Fine," came Wren's voice, from slightly to Sia's left. "I'll go first. Stay where you are and follow me. Except...here, take the potion. And my hand. I don't want you to fall behind."

Sia felt Wren's hand moving down her left arm, and then she could sense the pressure of the potion bottle in her left hand, followed by the warmth of Wren's fingers and palm. She tried to ignore how good Wren's hand felt in hers. In place of that thought, she redirected her attention to the pull from Wren's hand that now traveled up her left arm, letting Wren lead her out of the room and down the hallway to their right.

The size of the hallway indicated that, unlike Torien's home, this was more a palace than a mansion, and it was much more richly appointed, too. The walls were all constructed out of large, jewel-like stones, and their particular shade of red looked more like that of rubies than garnets. Sia didn't have much time to wonder whether they were real or bespelled; nor did she have a chance to wonder what kind of person would build a palace out of such rare stones. Instead, she had no choice but to concentrate on keeping her footsteps as quiet as possible and also on not stumbling. It seemed clear that Wren wanted to find out if Sia was telling the truth, based on her quick and mostly silent pace.

After passing four or five doors to their right, Sia heard what she thought were women's voices coming from a pair of large golden doors at the end of the hallway. Wren stopped there for a second, and then her movements became much quieter, only the final gentle tug on Sia's arm letting her know Wren had moved closer to the door.

Sia joined Wren there, still holding her hand, and placed her ear against the door, hoping the voices would be loud enough for her to hear.

Sia was relieved to learn that she could hear them perfectly. At first she noticed that neither of the women who were talking sounded happy in the least. Nor did they sound like they were trying all that hard to keep their voices down, which made spying on them pretty darn easy. Sia would have been grateful for this if it hadn't been for the way Wren's grip on her hand fell slack at the first words they both overheard. She hadn't thought till then that learning the truth about Passea might break Wren's heart, hadn't thought through what it might do to her. What kind of friend was she to Wren, if she hadn't realized instantly how much this might hurt her?

"So, Piru is still acting under our orders, correct?" These were the first words they heard, from a voice that sounded old enough to be Wren's mother. And Ember's reply turned Sia's guess into a certainty.

"Yes, Passea, he is." Ember sounded somewhat bored, a fact that didn't manage to surprise Sia in the least. "He will continued to mislead the Blue until the last moment possible, I promise you. My magic has always been pretty fucking powerful, as you know, and I topped myself off when I swallowed some of your daughter's blood."

"You weren't supposed to do that!"

Passea sounded truly angry, but Ember didn't seem intimidated in the least. "Aw, you know she wouldn't notice. She's too love-struck by me right now to think I'm capable of the slightest misdeed, the dumb little kitten."

"My *daughter* isn't *dumb*."

"Sure she isn't, Passea. But back to more important things. Do I still get to keep a human as a personal slave once we take over Earth?"

"Do whatever you want with them once we arrive, Ember. You know that lesser species are too stupid to even understand enslavement. They'll probably be grateful to us for taking charge of all their decision-making."

Now Sia wanted to stop the Winged Red more than ever, the quickly whirling pool of anger within her head almost causing her to slam that closed door open and tell Passea off. Her time spent on Earth with the humans and from getting to know Denise had taught her quite well that the humans would mind. However, she just might be okay with Ember taking Wren's stepdad for her personal slave. That would be a good way to get even with *both* of them. But all those other humans? No way in *hell* would she let the Winged Red's plan come to pass.

"And of course I'll still be taking care of Wren, just to remind you. That'll be fun!" Ember cackled at the end of her sentence—it wasn't a pleasant laugh, that was for sure. No, it didn't hold even a shred of anything sweet or good.

"Yes, you will. But remember, Ember, you aren't allowed to harm her. You'll just have to take out all that aggression on any of the Blue that get in your way."

"Yeah, that'll be fun, too, but remember, the prophecy was vague about Wren and her part in this. Whatever dumbass wrote that prophecy didn't seem to want to make it clear enough to actually be understood completely. And now, thanks to Wren, we don't even have access to it."

Now *that* was good news.

But what Ember said next definitely wasn't. "So, I'll keep Wren safe, as long as she doesn't get in my way. Or annoy me."

"Ember..." Sia could hear the unspoken warning in Passea's voice, clear as anything, and she hoped Ember had heard it, too. But now that Wren had to believe her, she could get her back to Shyon, safe and sound. And they wouldn't have to worry about Wren getting hurt by that bitch Ember anymore. Unless the battle with the Winged Red didn't go well. Which there was still a chance of, Sia admitted to herself, the unpleasant thought triggering a sudden jolt of pain in the middle of her chest.

Just then, she heard Wren rush toward the wall to the right of the double doors. She realized that between her immense anger and her growing list of worries, she hadn't heard the sound of Ember walking to the doors; only a moment later, one of them began to open.

"I'm looking forward to all of it, especially seeing the shocked look on Wren's face when she discovers it all was a lie." Sia could see Ember's face now, her expression of self-satisfied pride souring Sia's mood even further.

"I'm afraid that I'm not looking forward to that part, no matter how necessary it is. At least I won't be here to see it," came Passea's somewhat gentler voice from beyond the now-open door. "And remember," she said, her voice regaining all of its previous harshness and then some, "you are not to lay a finger on her. She may be the Winged Blue's only chance of winning, but she's still my daughter."

"Sure, whatever you say, Passea." Ember shut the door behind her, muttering the word "Idiot" as she began to walk down the hallway and away from the closed golden doors.

Sia felt Wren begin to move, leading Sia forward once more with her still-invisible hand. They crept almost soundlessly down the hallway, following Ember. Then she opened a door to their left and disappeared inside. But before she shut the door, Sia overheard her say, "Like I'd actually keep her stupid daughter safe. She'll make a delightful plaything before I—" Sia was somewhat grateful when Ember shut the door, cutting off a sentence whose ending was best left unheard. "Come on!" she whispered to Wren. "We've got to get back to your room, and then we've *got* to get you home."

"You're right," came Wren's answer in a muted, defeated-sounding tone.

Sia took over leading, and soon enough, they reached Wren's room, where the invisibility potion started to wear off. "Good timing on that!" Sia said, the tightness in her limbs beginning to loosen now that she could return to speaking at a normal volume. "Now, how'd you like to get out of here?"

"I'd like nothing more than...than..."

But before Wren could finish her sentence, she began to shake, shuddering violently, and her face started to disappear. First her mouth, then nose, and then, finally, her bright, beautiful eyes faded away.

Sia didn't take time to think. She just unstoppered the portal-making bottle, poured out a little more of the liquid, and shouted, "My house!" Then she grabbed Wren's hand and dragged her through the portal, not looking back for a single instant.

CHAPTER THIRTY-TWO

The journey through the portal from the land of the Winged Red to Sia's home seemed like it was over in a second, and perhaps it was. Or maybe Sia had been completely distracted by her current worries about what was happening to Wren. What had all that shaking been about? And her face disappearing had been equally alarming to Sia.

They had landed in a heap on the kitchen floor of Sia's home, where her mother and her brother sat eating what looked to be a midnight snack. She would have asked for some of the fruit and bread for herself, if it hadn't been for the fact that she had now noticed that Wren's face was no longer blank. But it clearly wasn't Wren who had traveled through the portal with her, because underneath her lay the last person in the world she wanted to be lying on top of: Ember, whose red wings were out for all the room's inhabitants to see.

"Where are we?" Ember asked, and Sia couldn't get off her fast enough.

"What have you done with Wren?" Sia asked in return.

"Who's that?" Zyr looked from Ember to Sia as Sia took a few steps back for safety's sake. "What have you done, bringing a Winged Red back to our world?"

"*That*," Sia answered, jabbing an accusing, angry finger in Ember's direction, "is a young woman who is officially my biggest enemy, number one on my crap list."

"I think you mean 'shit list'?" Ember appeared nervous as she said this, but she clearly wasn't as panicked as she looked, or she wouldn't have bothered to correct Sia. "And what do you mean, I'm your biggest enemy? I thought you were still trying to convince me I could trust you again. I mean, now I do, but I'm confused, and—"

"Stop with this horse-shit innocent act, Ember. I can't believe you had me fooled all along. But how you managed to be in two places at once and disguise yourself as poor Wren, I don't know. I'm sure it'll all come out in time. Too bad we Winged Blue are above torturing people, unlike you jerkholes!"

"Language, Sia. And keep it down. Your father's sleeping. I told him to try to get some more rest while I waited for a potion to finish melding, one I'd forgotten about until it was my own daughter who had disappeared. And apparently I woke Kriss when I left my bedroom to make it. Now it looks like I won't need that potion after all." Zyr leveled a fierce glare at Sia, but it was clear to her that Zyr was more relieved than angry. At least, Sia hoped that was the case. "You had us worried, very worried!" Zyr said. "And now you've brought this young woman through the portal instead of Wren?"

"I didn't mean to, I swear." Sia raised her hands in a Winged Blue gesture of innocence, one that she believed the humans used sometimes, too. "I thought she *was* Wren," she explained, lowering her hands with a frustrated *thump* on her thighs. "But she's Ember, one of the highest-ranking Winged Red, as you can see, and she and Wren's mother are assembling forces to attack us. Very soon."

"I'm not Ember, Sia. Please, you've got to believe me!" Ember sounded convincingly pained, but it was obviously an act, Sia thought; somebody *that* evil was definitely capable of such convincing theatrics.

"Prove it!" Sia yanked Ember up from the floor and dropped her into one of the kitchen table's empty chairs. Then she flipped the nearest chair around and sat opposite her.

"How's she supposed to do that?" Kriss asked, and Sia knew him well enough to know she hadn't imagined that hint of a smile at the end of his sentence.

It was a fair question, but Sia didn't care. She wanted to watch Ember squirm, even if she was only doing it for show. It would be satisfying either way. "Go ahead, try to prove it, just *try*."

"O...okay. Remember all that stuff I told you about my stepdad, when we were sitting on that rock in my favorite clearing?"

"You could have gotten that information out of Wren while you had her in captivity."

"But...I...if you don't believe me, if you don't trust me, how on Earth am I supposed to convince you?"

Zyr rose from the table, wiped her mouth with a cloth napkin, and pushed her half-empty plate in Sia's direction. "Go ahead and finish my fruit and bread. You look hungry. I'm going upstairs to get one of my experimental potions. I'm not sure it'll work, but it may get us some honesty out of this young lady. Either she's telling the truth, or we'll be able to drag some of the Winged Red's plans out of her in the event she isn't."

"I'll drink anything you want." Ember looked like she meant it, which surprised Sia. Wouldn't she want to put up a fight, try to avoid letting them learn anything about the Winged Red's battle schemes?

"Why? Why would you?" Sia took a small bite of the slice of purple peach that sat on her mom's small, flowered plate. Zyr had been right—she was hungry; apparently all that stress had helped her work up an appetite. She would have assumed that her fear in the land of the Winged Red would have done the opposite. Her stomach had felt like it contained a cloud of fanged butterflies the whole time she'd been in the Winged Red's land. But apparently, now that she was safely back in her homeland, and with Ember as their captive to boot, her stomach had decided to settle itself. And then some.

While they waited for Zyr to return, Sia keeping a very careful watch over Ember, Sia noticed the girl's facial features were beginning to fade. Just like they had when she'd looked like Wren…and her body began to shake again, too. This time, Sia only allowed herself to be mildly worried, because what did it matter if Ember looked terrified as the last of *her* face faded into blankness?

Sia wasn't too happy when Ember stopped shaking, because now it seemed she was once again disguised as Wren. She didn't manage to pull off her disguise completely, though, because instead of Wren's purely blue wings, these were about half red.

"Guess your powers are weaker here, huh?" Sia didn't let Ember's reversion to looking like Wren again fool her this time. She didn't let it kill her appetite, either.

Instead, she gobbled down the rest of the fruit and bread, and was halfway thinking of getting a second serving of the bread, and maybe some cheese, when her mom came back through the door. The top of a glass bottle was peeking out of her left hand. Zyr walked until she was facing Wren, who was starting to shake again. Soon enough, she once more looked like Ember. Strangely, throughout this third change, Zyr's lips were slightly turned up, and the way she looked at "Wren" was soft, almost like she felt concern for her.

Of course, that couldn't possibly be the case. Her mom was a really kind person, but it wasn't reasonable for her to act this friendly with one of their biggest enemies. Especially an enemy who Sia knew was an absolutely horrible person. So she crossed her arms and stared Ember down, hoping the peach hadn't left its usual purple splotches around her scowling mouth.

"So, Ember, or Wren, you're really willing to drink this?" As Zyr placed the black, square bottle on the table, she didn't look the least bit angry. That was all right; Sia knew her own expression was intimidating enough for the two of them. But a quick glance at her older brother showed that he didn't look mad, either, just cautious and, perhaps, a bit curious.

"Yes, of course, Zyr. Anything to prove my innocence." Before Sia could scoff aloud at this ridiculous statement, Ember popped out the potion's stopper and downed all the liquid in a few loud swallows.

Zyr's mouth fell open the second the bottle became empty. "You, uh, aren't supposed to drink the whole thing," Zyr told her with raised brows. "It isn't perfected yet. There might be side effects…"

The only side effect at first was the small burp that came from Ember, followed by a slightly embarrassed sounding "Excuse me." She put the bottle back on the table, looking a little green. "That wasn't…I mean, no offense, but you might want to work on the flavor. It tasted kind of fishy."

"Well, at least we know it's made you honest enough to be rude," Sia grumbled. "Although you probably would have said that anyway."

She continued glaring at Ember but found her frown softening when Ember said, "Could you please stop looking so angry, Sia? It's kind of scaring me. So's the fact that I look like Ember, but maybe now you'll actually believe me when I tell you I'm not. And also, I really don't like looking like her, or sounding like her, and I have no clue why I do."

"My *goodness*." Now Zyr was grinning, of all things. "So that's your mother's power! Quite a good one, if you ask me."

"You mean…you mean not only is this *really* Wren, but she's finally gotten her power?" Sia was just beginning to adjust to the fact that Ember, or Wren, actually, had been telling the truth all along.

"What power? You mean, the fact that I can look like Ember? Not really a power I want to have, to be honest. Can I trade it in for another?"

"Wren, dear, you wouldn't want to, nor would you be able to. But this is one of the best powers possible. It means more than that you can shapeshift to look like other Winged. It means something else, too, but I believe we'll have to ask Piru to research that, as it has been many years since we've had a Winged Changer. Well, at least since your mother, I suppose."

"M-my mother." It seemed like the stress of the night had caught up to Wren all at once, because now she began to sob.

"Wren?" Sia didn't like this latest turn of events, even if it meant she was now certain this was Wren, not Ember. No evil villainess could cry that convincingly. "Oh, Wren, I'm so sorry. Do you...do you want a hug?"

In reply, Wren-in-Ember-form grabbed Sia and pulled her in close, practically crushing her in her tight embrace. Sia decided against mentioning it, instead just enjoying having Wren hug her, even if she didn't look like herself. But she was acting like herself, because these clearly weren't Komodo-dragon tears. Or was it alligator? It didn't matter. All that mattered was that she wanted to help Wren feel better, and if that meant having her own breathing be mildly impaired, she would gladly put up with a slight lack of oxygen.

"Should we take you to your dad?" Sia asked, her words coming out a little choked. This brought on another bout of sobbing from Wren. God, couldn't she say anything right? First she'd proved to Wren that her mother wasn't to be trusted, and then that the young woman she'd just recently been kissing was an evil bitch. And to top it all off, she hadn't trusted Wren in her Ember form.

"Yes!" Wren cried out in answer, loudly, and right by Sia's left ear. Now Sia had a slight headache along with her current challenge with getting enough air. It was still a fair trade, since it seemed like the choking hug was probably helping Wren. And the fact that Wren was clinging tightly to her, Wren's body pressed against hers, well, that felt like it was all the payment she needed for giving Wren whatever comfort the hug could provide. Not that Wren owed her anything. No, Sia owed Wren something, a debt she would do almost anything to repay. But before Sia could start brainstorming ways to make it up to her, Wren slowly let go, her own familiar, beautiful, and currently tear-covered face coming into view.

"So, what's with your red-and-blue wings, Wren?" This was only the second time Kriss had spoken, but it was definitely a question worth voicing.

"Her mom, Passea, is a Winged Red," Sia told him, worried that her words would bring on a new bout of tears. Luckily, they didn't seem to. Wren was even smiling a bit. "After all," she said, turning in

Kriss's direction, "Wren had to get this power from somewhere, and apparently her mom was able to hide the true color of her wings. And of her soul," Sia couldn't help adding. Wren looked like she was just about to start crying again at those words, so Sia quickly added, "But Wren is clearly nothing like her. She obviously takes after her dad. And Passea did say that she doesn't want Wren hurt. Although thankfully," and Sia shot a very happy grin in Wren's direction, "we don't have to worry about Ember hurting her now anymore, either. You're safe now, Wren. Isn't that great?"

"What would be even greater is if I could see my dad. Do you think…do you think it's too late at night for us to go now? I don't want to bother him or anything."

"Oh my, Wren! Bother him?" Zyr shook her head back and forth, and Sia noticed a few seconds later that she was echoing the gesture. How could Wren have possibly thought her safe return would be a "bother"?

"Let's head straight there," Sia suggested. "Torien will be incredibly relieved to see you're home now, and unharmed."

Wren rose from the table. She seemed ready to leave, until a worried look appeared on her face. "Do you think…I mean, I overheard the triplets talking before we left, and…are you sure we can trust my dad? They were saying things that made it sound like he couldn't be, and…I'm just afraid what they said might have been true."

"Or maybe the Winged Red found some way to make them say those things, or…wait, I have an idea. Mom?" Sia asked, standing up and looking at Zyr. "Do you have any more of that potion? I'm sure Torien would be happy to drink it, and the triplets, too. That would convince you, wouldn't it, Wren?"

"Yeah, I think it would."

"You two start over to Torien's, then," Zyr said. "I want to tell your father that Wren is back, Sia, and then I'll grab the potion and follow you two."

Sia was surprised when Zyr began to look startled. Turning, she saw that Wren no longer looked like Wren, but like the woman from her vision, the one who apparently was Passea, Wren's mom. She realized that Wren had sensed something was wrong when Wren-with-Passea's-face said, "What is it, Si…oh, God, do I look like my mom now? After all, I sound just like her. Well, even if my dad can be trusted, now *he* won't trust *me*!"

Her lower lip began to quiver. Sia wanted nothing more than to reassure her, so she looked into Wren's eyes and said, "It'll all work out, I'm sure of it. Now, let's get going. I know for certain that your dad will want to see you as soon as possible. In fact, maybe we could fly over there. And just maybe your mom is better at flying than you. Want to attempt some loop-de-loops? Or instead, we could try to scare some night-pigeons?"

That got a small laugh out of Wren, who apparently looked like Passea right then, and who also sounded just like her when she giggled at Sia's joke. This would definitely take some getting used to.

"You ready to go then?" Sia gestured toward the hallway. "I'm guessing you'd like to get to bed soon, anyway, seeing as it's pretty late, so why don't we get the hopefully-not-too-tearful reunion out of the way so you can hit the grass?"

"Grass? Do you mean hay?"

"Something like that, yeah. I still have a lot of trouble with all the human slang," Sia told her as they headed down the hallway.

Outside, it proved to be a slightly chilly but clear-skied night. The golden moon was almost full. When they took off a few paces away from Sia's front door, she glanced at Wren, who still looked like Passea. Sia wondered if Wren's half-blue, half-red wings were here to stay. They just might be, considering her blood was half-Blue and half-Red, too.

Wren-with-Passea's-face looked happy, although Sia would have preferred to see that smile on Wren's face instead of the face of their shared enemy. Still, even if she looked nothing like herself, there was still some sort of Wren-like essence to Passea's features, almost as though Sia could see who really lay hidden beneath the full-body mask.

But just as the land Torien's mansion sat upon began to come into view beneath them, Sia heard a sharp gasp from Wren's direction. A quick look showed her that Wren's face was beginning to disappear yet again, and this time her non-Wren face changed much faster than before, her body altering shape and size as well, until she looked like herself again. Only seconds after that, she began to transform again, back into Passea, and it was then that she began to fall, her wings suddenly gone.

Sia dove after her. About ten feet above the ground, she *just* managed to grab Wren, stopping her from hitting the hard cobblestone street that had been uncomfortably close to Wren's head. But she couldn't keep them both in the air, and so with as much grace as she could manage, she landed and placed Wren on the street, kneeling beside her. She might have become unconscious when she began to fall, but at least she looked like herself once again.

Luckily, Wren was just barely light enough for Sia to carry her the rest of the way to Torien's, at least while walking on the ground. His mansion was only about twenty of Sia's footsteps away from where they'd almost crash-landed. Upon reaching the front door, Sia kicked it twice with her foot, almost falling over in the process.

An exhausted-appearing Torien answered the door, but he looked like he'd had a double shot of adrenaline the second he laid his eyes on who Sia was holding. "You found Wren? Where was she? Oh, I'm so glad she's safe. Come in, Sia, and here, let me take over." The relief showed clearly in his voice, but he also seemed to have held on to some of his anxiety about his daughter. Sia couldn't blame him, either, since he had no idea why Wren had passed out. And admittedly, neither did Sia.

She was grateful to hand Wren over, because despite the pleasure that came from holding her so close, Sia's arms were starting to ache. She took turns rubbing some life back into each aching arm as she followed a Wren-laden Torien into the large sitting room, where he laid his daughter on one of the couches. Sia sat down opposite her, and she took a deep breath in preparation of explaining everything to Torien. She figured the wings coming out of Wren's back at that moment might help explain the story at least a little, because their vibrant combination of red and blue feathers told a story of their own.

CHAPTER THIRTY-THREE

The first thing Wren saw when she opened her eyes was what must have been the ceiling in her dad's large living room. No one else she knew had a fresco of ravens performing what might have been Shakespeare on their ceiling, much less one as well-rendered and realistic looking as this. For some reason, the painting was striking her as funny right then, and she let out a high-pitched peal of laughter.

Had her laugh always sounded so strange? Or was this just what it would sound like now that she'd learned she was the daughter of a mother she couldn't trust? And a father who might soon be joining her as equally untrustworthy? Those thoughts cut her laughter short, but not before someone in the room had taken note of it.

"Glad to see you're feeling well enough to laugh, sweetheart," Torien said. She turned toward his voice and saw her father staring down at her. The way he was looking at her was confusing at first. But soon, she decided it was because he seemed equally concerned and relieved, if such an incongruous combination could be held on one person's face. And now she had to wonder: were those his true feelings, or were they just an act, just something to keep her thinking that he was worth trusting?

To his left stood Piru, who looked almost as if he *wasn't* glad to see her, glancing quickly from her face to his feet and back again. Standing in a group behind the second-largest sofa in the room—she seemed to be lying on the biggest one—stood Faest, Speyd, and then Quiq, whose expressions of concern intensified in the same order they stood. Quiq even went so far as to be wringing his hands, not something she'd seen too many men do before that moment. His tightly knit brow and pursed lips almost made his caring expression look believable. But she was guessing it wasn't, and so she followed that guess with another: that it was meant to look the most extreme because he and her stepmom were obviously both still buddy-buddy. Denise was standing so close to him, they were almost touching. Buddy-buddy, or, more accurately, kissy-kissy.

"Ew," Wren said with a grimace. Not the most impressive statement to open with, but now it was too late to say something more intelligent, like, "How could you betray me, you dastardly, loutish threesome?" Instead, she slowly pushed herself upright, because she didn't think lying on her side was the best pose if she needed to defend herself against any of them. "Hi, Dad. Hi, *triplets*. Fooled any unsuspecting teenagers lately?" These words did nothing to lessen her pronounced scowl, and their accompanying thoughts only increased her hopefully obvious distaste at sharing the room with those three bastards.

"Come again?" Speyd asked with a slightly stupefied expression.

"Yeah, why aren't you happy to see us?" Faest asked, an equally intense scowl now directed right back at Wren.

Quiq didn't frown or sound even slightly as irritated as Speyd had. Instead, his mouth had fallen open a little at Wren's words, as if he were genuinely surprised at her accusation. "What do you mean, Wren?" he finally said. "What do you think we've done?"

"Nothing much, just worked side by side with my dad to pull the wool over my eyes. It's bad enough that Passea can't be trusted, and now there's this brand-new power I've received, which I have pretty much no control over, not that that fact concerns you guys in the least. I just need to know if there's anyone, anyone at all I can even begin to trust in this world."

Just as she finished speaking, Zyr entered the room, striding quickly over to where the six Winged Blue stood around Wren. She realized then that she was the only person who wasn't standing; while she'd rather stay seated, it wasn't exactly a position of power in this situation. Wren stood up, quicker than she probably should have, as a slight floaty feeling in her head made her grab for the table beside the couch.

"Wren, you look like you might be a little dizzy," Zyr said. She was the first person whose worried expression Wren decided she could trust at the moment. "Here, I brought the potion. Why don't you fill everyone in, Sia? And Wren, I think you should sit back down, considering how much you've just been through."

Wren allowed Zyr to help her back onto the couch, its support helping her head to feel more stable. Standing or not, fainting probably wouldn't make her look as though she could hold her own against the triplets and her father. But as Sia told them the whole story, starting with her visions, continuing with her trip to the Winged Red's land, and ending with Wren finally gaining her power, the "honesty potion" (as Wren had taken to thinking of it) was passed to Torien and then each of the triplets. All of them willingly drank from it without any sign of hesitation. And when each of them told Wren the truth, that they could be trusted, she decided she didn't need to put up any sort of front; she relaxed enough to let herself sink into a slight slouch against the sofa's soft, plush pillows.

It came out that two of the triplets hadn't even been home the night Wren had been sneaking out of the mansion. Instead, Speyd told her they had been out with a group of friends until three in the morning, which earned a stern look from Torien. "You were supposed to be guarding Wren's room as planned," he said gruffly. Despite how she felt about being protected without her knowledge (not all that happy!), Wren was too tired to complain. Besides, it was slightly touching, even if it would've been less patronizing if her dad had asked her permission first.

"I was here, actually," Quiq told them, and Wren wondered why he was suddenly blushing.

"But you weren't outside Wren's room, were you, you dog?" Speyd nudged her brother in the ribs, and then she raised her hand in the air, looking like she wanted to give him a high five.

"Please, sister, not with Wren in the room." Quiq seemed to be seeing if he could get his cheeks to turn a brighter color than Wren's red feathers.

Before Wren's tired mind could figure out why Quiq was looking so embarrassed, Piru finally spoke. "I...I should..."

"Wait," Sia said before he could finish. "Piru, Grandfather, I hate to do this to you, but I want you to drink some of the truth potion."

"Why should that matter?" Piru spoke so quickly that Wren was startled out of her half-asleep haze. "Isn't it clear that Wren was wrong, and we're all now to be trusted?"

"Not really," Sia answered slowly in return. She looked somewhat ashamed as she said, "I don't want to distrust you, Piru, but, you see, I've had a vision, with you in it, and—"

Piru didn't allow her to finish her sentence. "Shut up, Sia!" he shouted. Everyone in the room turned to look at him, and they all must have seen the startling change in Piru's normally kind face. A feral snarl had replaced his usual gentle smile, and this was the first time Wren had thought him even slightly capable of anger. With one last furious glance in Torien's direction, Piru changed into his ravenform and flew out of the room. Wren was sure she wasn't the only one to notice the fast-growing cloud of red that had surrounded his feathered body. She probably wasn't the only one who had been startled, either, but unlike her, some of the room's other occupants were quick to respond to this new and unpleasant knowledge.

After only a moment's pause, Sia yelled out an order. "Follow him!" But even before the second word had left her lips, the triplets were already at the door Piru had left through, with Quiq quite obviously in the lead.

"I guess in the end, Piru was the only one who couldn't be trusted," Wren said. A few moments ago she'd been about to yawn, but with this latest surprise, she'd found a surprising amount of energy had come back into her body. After a brief stretch of her arms and a wiggle of her back muscles to relax her shoulders, she turned to Torien. "What should we do now? About Piru?"

"I think we should follow the triplets. Yes, it's obvious that a trip to Piru's is in order."

"Damn right it is!" Sia didn't look nearly as certain as her choice of words might have implied, and Wren couldn't blame her. It was bad enough that Wren had her own heartbreak from discovering the lies of her birth mother and Ember. Why did Sia have to suffer the same pain Wren had just been forced to experience? "We'll get through this, Sia, I promise," Wren told her, getting up from the couch with some effort and walking over to her. "At least we can still trust each other, right?"

These words seemed to brighten Sia's mood, at least a little. She turned to Wren with a weak smile, but her voice had regained some strength. "We absolutely can." Sia rolled back her shoulders and released her wings. "Okay, Wren, are you up for another midnight flight?"

"Totally. Let's get to the bottom of this. I'm sure Piru is innocent, no matter what it looked like." Wren started striding toward the mansion's front door.

"I hope so." Sia sounded rather doubtful, but Wren just chalked it up to shock. She was carrying plenty of that herself, but it wouldn't do to let it take over, not now. Not with their problem with Piru still to solve.

And not with the battle that would be arriving on their doorstep in far too little time.

CHAPTER THIRTY-FOUR

Wren hoped that this next journey through the night would pass less eventfully than the last, even if things were likely to be a little too exciting once everyone had landed at Piru's. She couldn't help but enjoy the feel of Sia's hand in hers, who had insisted that she needed to hold on to Wren in order to help her if she shifted too quickly again and started to fall.

Wren's frustration with herself was pretty deep by the time Sia first took her hand mid-air, and she wondered while they flew what she had ever seen in Ember. Maybe it was just that she was young and able to be manipulated by someone's good looks, rather than led to like them by their good heart.

Like the one Sia happened to have.

On the way to Piru's, Sia told everyone all about her vision. She added her theory that while Piru was obviously not in his right mind, if they could get him back to his normal self somehow, maybe he could still help them.

"I'm worried we might be too late for that, but someone will need to help us with my daughter's impressive new power, and I don't know who that could be, other than Piru," Torien replied with a slight frown.

"Impressive?" Wren asked quietly. Then an idea came to her, just as Piru's home was coming into view. "I wonder if we need Piru's help at all. If we can find the prophecy book, maybe something in it could help us instead?"

"Possibly." Torien nodded slowly. "Yes, I think that's a damn good idea, Wrenny. Good thinking!" Her father's compliment struck her as surprising, considering how much "bad thinking" she'd practiced in the past few days. But it seemed her father might have already forgiven her. Or at least she hoped he had.

A moment later, Wren, Zyr, Sia, and Torien landed next to Piru's front porch. Just as Zyr, the last of them to land, touched down, the triplets came out of Piru's house, one by one.

"He's gone," Speyd told them, and Wren could clearly see that she was worried, appearing almost scared. Wren couldn't have imagined this strong-looking Amazon looking scared before now, but apparently the tough-seeming Speyd was capable of fear after all.

Quiq turned to Speyd, rubbing her back for a second. "You okay, sis?"

"Obviously!" Her angry tone held notes of the same ferocious emotions Wren saw on her face, and she guessed then that this was bravado, just there to cover up what Speyd was really feeling.

"You should come inside," Faest told them, sounding none too pleased with Piru's disappearance. Wren wasn't all that happy about it, either.

The foursome followed the triplets into Piru's house. The first thing Wren noticed was how startlingly hot the living room was.

"Bit warm for a fire," Torien said, and Wren instantly agreed with her father. Why would Piru build a fire on a warm night like this? And why would the fire glow blue, instead of orange? Unless...

"The book!" she cried out, and she ran over to the fireplace as quickly as she could. Lying partway out of the roaring fire was a thick, blue-covered book. Wren grabbed it, dropping it almost instantly on the rug a few feet away from the fire. Flames still danced across its cover and pages, but not for long: a blanket brought over by Sia landed on top of it, and she and Wren frantically worked at smothering the burning book until all that remained of the burning parts was acrid, blue smoke that made everyone in the room cough.

Zyr and Torien busied themselves with opening all the windows and doors in the room, and soon the air was clear once more. "Well?" Sia asked Wren. She sounded a far way beyond mere impatience. "Aren't you going to open it?"

"Of course." Wren lifted the blanket off the book, its cover and the edges of the pages scorched black. She was surprised that it was already completely cool to the touch. Wren lowered herself to the rug, and Sia sat down next to her. Torien and Zyr walked over to them and stood on each side of Wren's back, and even the triplets seemed to think that it was worth more attention than the missing Piru, as they went to stand behind Wren and Sia as well. Now that everyone was gathered round and able to see, she picked up the book and lifted open its cover.

The first two-thirds of the book were undamaged, thankfully, but that didn't seem to matter, because they were completely blank. Page after page was empty, and she found herself increasingly losing hope as she looked at each following blank page.

"This isn't doing us any good," Wren said, allowing her hands to flop onto the pages the book was open to.

Then Wren's luck with the book abruptly began to change. First, a single word appeared on her left hand, moving too fast for her to make it out as it traveled down her fingers and onto the page on her left. Then a second word, a third, and then more and more, until her wrists and hands were completely black, as word after word traveled from her skin and across each of the two pages. After a few minutes of this startling event, the book rose, floating into the air in front of her. Unsure why, exactly, she was doing this, Wren lifted both hands off the pages.

The words continued to travel from her skin to the book. Now its pages were turning, but slowly, almost as if the book was worried it would get something wrong if this magic worked too quickly. At last, a final word flowed from Wren's left thumb and landed on the last remaining blank page. The fire had made the rest of the book entirely black. With the final word now in place, the book landed with a quiet, happy sigh in Wren's lap, almost as though it were coming home.

Now the prophecy book's pages were once again full of words for them to read. Wren began to thumb through the book's pages, noting that the cover was now red *and* blue. Its text was also varying shades of blue and red, some paragraphs entirely printed in hues of red, while others were completely blue, and some were both. A fair number of the words were even half of each color. "No wonder the Winged Red couldn't make sense of most of it," Wren said softly.

She stopped going through the book when she reached the beginning of the book's undamaged pages, and there, on the page on the left, slightly burned around the edges, a penned drawing caused her to pause and stare.

Sketched in the same ink that made up the words on each page was a picture of a girl, one who she realized might be her: she was dressed in a robe that looked strikingly similar to the one Wren had worn her first day in Azyr. She looked a good bit like Wren, too. The final clue that it *was* Wren were her wings, identical to the bi-colored ones that she now possessed. But, as useful as the drawing made this part of the book seem to her, that was where its helpfulness ended. The words on the facing page were in a language Wren had never seen before.

"Can any of you read this?" she asked, looking at Sia and then Zyr. Glancing at her father's face, she saw his brow was furrowed. His slightly squinting eyes made it seem as if he was trying to figure out the book's strange-looking symbols, and his next words made it clear that this was true.

"I can understand only one paragraph, this one that's entirely blue," Torien said, placing his finger right next to the words. "It may take me a while, though. I'm a little rusty in this, our oldest written language."

"Please try your best, Torien," Zyr pleaded, "You know how important this is."

"Yes, of course I do." Wren's father cleared his throat, then began to speak. "'She...she will be...of both lands. She will be able to...shift into becoming anyone, and this will be her blessing but will also be tied to her greatest pain.'" Torien paused, seeming to ponder what the words said. "'Her greatest pain'? That doesn't sound very...I mean, I should continue reading before I make any guesses as to what it means. 'The full moon will turn from blue to red, and the young shifter must learn to use her...her ultimate power by the time the Winged Red have come. And...and then she will have to give all of herself to succeed, and then she will be gone.'"

But that was where Torien had to stop, because the book's words began to flow back onto Wren's arms before her father could continue reading. She tried to will the words to stay where they were, but this magic wasn't under her control. Just like her shifting abilities, it seemed that someone or something else believed she didn't deserve power over either these words or her own flesh. That thought made her even more upset than the loss of the book's knowledge. And what was this "ultimate power"? Would she even be able to come close to controlling it, when she couldn't even control her emotions?

Because her tears were just now threatening to fall for the second time in mere hours, it took all the fight Wren had within her to not let them escape her weary eyes again.

CHAPTER THIRTY-FIVE

It was time now for Passea's next task. It had been one of the parts she hadn't looked forward to, because it required that she leave Wren with Ember, and she was already starting to wonder how much she could trust the young woman; she hadn't felt all that great about tricking her daughter in the first place. All those years she'd spent away from Wren, merely watching her daughter through her mirror as often as she could, had taken their toll. She already felt almost unbearably raw from all her lies to Wren.

Now that Wren was apparently back in the land of the Winged Blue, probably thinking that her mother was no good and didn't love her, well, that had made Passea's limbs ache and her chest clench painfully for hours. It had been part of the necessary plan, but still: it hurt.

She didn't want Ember and Myuss to discover exactly how much pain this had caused her, deceiving her daughter, nor did she want her troops to know of this hidden weakness of hers. It wouldn't do for them to all go into battle knowing that their leader was not completely empty of fear, of softness of heart, of caring for any of the Winged Blue. The humans, yes, she held no love for any of those lowly creatures. Myuss had told her many stories of the humans' stupidity as they'd grown up together, stories that Myuss told her proved that it was the Winged Red's duty to overtake those lesser beings.

She hadn't planned to have any feelings for the daughter she and Torien had made together, the daughter she had borne out of duty instead of the craving for a child she'd lied about to the Winged Blue's male leader. She hadn't wanted to feel guilty about abandoning her daughter: it had been planned, and the prophecy had foretold of this, too. She certainly hadn't wanted her guilt to grow, bit by bit, as she helplessly watched all that happened to her daughter when the girl's stepmother remarried. Even having a Winged Blue for a father was an improvement over *that* monster.

She'd had to stay strong, though. If she went to the Winged Blue's land, gave in, told Torien everything, it wouldn't have helped matters. She'd had no other choice. Books of prophecy didn't lie, and as Myuss had told her, if she didn't listen to what she, the Seer, had told Passea about the book's knowledge, things would only grow worse for Wren. Maybe it had been a mistake, all of those years of pain from watching her daughter grow up from afar. Maybe. But it only would have hurt more if she hadn't. It only would have made the hole in her life from abandoning Wren even larger and emptier.

So yes, now it was time for the next part of the plan: the plan the prophecy had for her, and for the rest of the Winged Red. At least she was convinced it would work, as Myuss had assured her time and time again. And at least once she had conquered the Winged Blue, she and Wren could finally be together. As they were meant to be.

Passea, already in her underthings, went over to the bed to study the robes Wren had arrived in, robes of a color that had no place in Passea's beautiful city. As she studied the blue cloth, she wondered: maybe their horrible blueness wasn't quite as repulsive as she'd previously thought. Wren's blue wings had struck her as nothing other than intensely beautiful, starting at the first time she'd seen them. The blue feathers paired with the now-red ones had looked striking, too, and not at all unpleasant.

At least to her. She'd known that Ember felt very differently, but maybe with the right words from Passea, her second-in-command would change her mind. Passea just hoped Wren would change hers, too—and that she might be as quick to forgive Passea as she had always hoped.

After she'd changed—in both the necessary ways—Passea turned toward her mirror, where she now saw her daughter's lovely face, Wren's sweet smile tinged with sadness at the moment. Not Wren's sadness, but there might be an echo of this smile when Wren found herself back in the land of the Winged Red. If there even *were* a smile on her face, once she woke to find herself in Passea's bedroom.

At least her daughter's accommodations would be pleasant enough. Passea had done her best to make Wren's bedroom in her soon-to-be-home as inviting as she possibly could. It was the only way she could think to show her daughter how much she had missed being in her life. The words would come eventually, she thought, to tell her daughter the truth—a truth Wren would accept, given enough time.

She had to.

Passea glanced around her bedroom one last time. She wouldn't be seeing it again until the battle was over, but that fact didn't matter to her. Home wasn't home without family. And since the Winged Red's victory would be quick to come, she could soon return home and relax fully—for the first time in almost twenty years.

With less enthusiasm than she would have liked, she walked over to her dresser, where she selected and uncorked the bottle she needed, then poured out its contents onto the floor. A few moments later, a knock came on her bedroom door. "You may enter, Ember," she answered. "I'm just about to leave." Her voice startled her: she hadn't remembered that, for the time being, she would hear her own daughter's voice whenever she spoke.

Her second-in-command came into the room, looking a lot calmer than Passea felt. The young woman always seemed so confident, so cocky; it was starting to seem possible that Passea might need to have her step down, once the battle had been won. But Ember had assured Passea she wouldn't do anything to Wren, and Passea's good friend Myuss had promised she would also be there to keep a watchful eye on Ember.

"You don't have to worry," Ember had reassured Passea the last time they'd spoken, and Myuss had smiled kindly at her younger friend and told her, "Everything will work out just as it's supposed to. Wren will be in good hands."

It was a struggle to come back from the past, but ruminating on risks wouldn't help her with her next actions. She needed to stay in the right frame of mind, and so all her doubts would somehow have to be left behind. "I guess it's time for me to go," Passea announced, and she wondered if she was saying it more to Ember or herself.

"Yep, sure is. Safe travels, and like I said, Wren will be fine. She probably will sleep through at least half the battle, according to what Myuss said the prophecy stated."

"It seems that our prophecy is surprisingly precise."

"Yeah, and isn't that nice?" Ember smirked, and Passea tried to ignore the thought that it had sounded like there was something else behind her words. But then the girl's smile sweetened, and she winked at Passea, saying, "Good luck," and followed her words with a jaunty salute.

Time to go. Passea took a final look around her bedroom, then turned toward the red mist that would guide her to her daughter. She shut her eyes for a moment, took a deep breath, then spoke. "To my daughter's bedroom in the land of the Winged Blue." Then she stepped into the mist and, minutes later, into her daughter's bedroom.

Wren lay sleeping in her bed, looking peaceful and relaxed. Good, Passea thought, I haven't disturbed her. The mist had formed a portal right next to where Wren lay in the bed, Passea noted, so thankfully it wouldn't be too challenging to get her daughter through it.

Passea paused for a moment, staring down at her daughter's familiar face. A face belonging to an amazing young girl, one who would finally be with her in person from now on, a fact Passea was exceptionally grateful for. "Sleep well, darling," she whispered, then pulled back the bed's covers and lifted Wren's sleeping body, passing her through the red mist and into the land where she truly belonged. "I'll see you in a short while."

As long as everything goes according to plan.

The annoying Winged Blue girl crashed down on the floor a short distance away from Ember and Myuss's feet. But she wasn't in Passea's bedroom, as their "leader" had planned. No, instead, she was in a cell deep in the depths of the castle, the cell that would be her well-deserved home for the time being. Until she didn't need any home but a hole in the ground.

"Looks like everything's going according to my plan," Myuss cackled, taking a few steps forward. "I told you it would work, back when we were watching that idiot Sia sleep in the humans' world."

"I guess you were right. At least so far. Now we just need to wait until the battle is won. You said it was inevitable, after all," the girl said, but her words held little if any reverence directed at the Seer. Yet Ember would come to see the truth in time. Oh, would she *ever*.

Myuss glanced at the ground, careful not to let Ember view the truth written on her face. It wouldn't do to allow Ember to see how many of her words about the prophecy had been lies. It had been the only way to get Passea and Ember to follow her directions, though.

And it had worked. That was all that mattered in the end. And soon, she would be able to take her rightful place, the top-ranking position in the Winged Red, once they had won the battle. And once that useless Winged Blue girl—the one in that nasty cell, the one who was now waking up—was dead.

Which wouldn't exactly be a huge loss, Myuss thought with a grin. One more dead Winged Blue to add to the pile they'd be leaving in their wake, and what did it matter that she was Passea's daughter or that Passea loved her? Wren's mother would be the last of the Winged to fall, after all. Maybe their stupid leader's broken heart, upon finding her daughter dead, would take care of things for Myuss. She grinned even wider at that delightful thought.

"Where am I? What's happened?" Soon the girl was fully awake, her eyes widening with fear as she took in first her cell and then Myuss and Ember. She rose on slightly shaking legs, almost stumbling as she made her way over to the cell's bars where the two stood watching her. "Ember? Myuss? Who put me here? Please, let me out. Please!"

"Fat chance," Myuss told her. It might have been a phrase she'd heard from those pathetic humans on Earth, but it seemed almost perfect for this particular moment.

CHAPTER THIRTY-SIX

When Passea woke after a night of dark dreams, it took a few moments for her to remember why her surroundings weren't as familiar as they should have been. Wren's room at Torien's wasn't too bad, even if it was the wrong color scheme. But the room she'd provided for her daughter, in her soon-to-be permanent home, was so much lovelier. Passea found herself smiling at that thought, a smile that lasted as she changed into one of Wren's unpleasantly blue robes.

Her smile faded the instant she heard an unexpected knock on the bedroom's door.

"Wren? You up? And decent?" The voice was female and sounded like someone about the age of her daughter. She chided herself then for her momentary lapse in concentration: she had work to do, and she wasn't here in Azyr on vacation.

"Come...come in."

A younger woman entered Wren's bedroom, and Passea saw that her visitor was indeed close to Wren's age. She wore a sleeveless robe of a similar blue to Passea's, along with a grin. "Good morning, Wren! Ready to have breakfast? Torien invited me over, and then I was hoping you could come to my house later, to blow off some steam. After all, who knows how much time you'll have left to do so until the Winged Red arrive."

"Yes, who knows?" Passea stood there for a few moments, lost in thought about exactly how much she knew about the Wingeds' shared future, compared to this oblivious Winged Blue girl.

"So, um, breakfast? Downstairs? And what about lunch?" The young woman gestured toward the open bedroom door, an expectant quirk of her lips showing Passea she'd waited too long to answer.

So Passea cleared her throat and squared her shoulders. "Oh, yes, let's. And sure, I guess I can come to lunch at your house, as long as you come meet me here first." She tried to keep her voice passive, the way she expected Wren's to sound, but the girl looked disappointed with her answer. Had she said it wrong? Did she...or, rather, did Wren and this person have more affection for one another than she had assumed? Passea realized that this girl looked happier to see Wren than she would have were she a mere friend or acquaintance of Wren's.

Maybe she could use that knowledge to her advantage.

Downstairs, the shock of seeing Torien in person after all these years hit her harder than she would have liked, or expected. She paused at the entrance to the room where her husband sat, his chair near the middle of the far side of a large, wooden table. He had touches of gray in his hair and a few more lines on his face, but otherwise he looked just as handsome as when they'd first met. It hadn't been hard to look at him when they'd had sex or when she'd sat across from him at mealtimes. No, it had just been hard to listen to him, because all his actions and words had been lies, lies and deceptions. He wasn't the good man both his words and actions had implied. Myuss had made that very clear to her all those years ago, before Passea had taken off for the land of the Winged Blue.

Torien's right arm was currently draped over the shoulders of a rather attractive woman with straight, black hair and an obvious attachment to him, based on the adoring look she was sending in his direction. A woman she did recognize sat to the right of Torien's companion—Denise, Wren's pathetic stepmom, the one who had failed to protect Wren from that monster of a stepfather. She would never forgive this woman for how greatly she had failed her daughter, and she could barely fight back the angry glare that threatened to accompany those thoughts. Denise was smiling at her, though, and so she forced an equally happy grin onto her face and took a seat opposite the black-haired woman.

"Good morning, Wrenny. And welcome home, again, from all of us here. We're so very happy to have you back here in Azyr, and safe. But I'm guessing you don't want to think about the past few days, when you were...gone. So, instead all I'll say is, would you like some toast?" Torien gestured at a plate piled with thickly sliced, toasted bread. "Or maybe some almond croissants? Sia's brother baked them, so you just know they'll be good."

"Anything to take my mind off tomorrow." Passea meant her words, but she knew that no one at the table had any clue what they actually implied. She pulled the plate of croissants toward herself and took two of them, along with some fried eggs and fruit from platters nearby. Next she poured herself a mug of coffee from a silver carafe, blowing on her steaming cup before she took a small sip.

"What, you're drinking it black today?" Denise asked.

Damn, she had already made a mistake. "Uh, yes. To toughen myself up before the big battle."

"Clever." Torien's partner, whose eyes had perhaps narrowed after Passea had spoken, said this. Or might she have just imagined it? She chose to ignore the tiny somersault in her stomach that this possible sight had caused.

Passea did her best to keep up with everything during the meal, learning that the younger woman who apparently had a thing for Wren was named Sia, and that the woman with Torien was called Rysha. Not that their names would matter for much longer, but knowing them would be helpful for at least the immediate future…only, she reminded herself, for the next day and a half.

Shortly after she'd eaten the last bite of egg, three tall, muscular Winged Blue who looked related to each other entered the room from the left. One was a woman, the other two men, and one of the men was far more handsome than the other. Which she decided he probably knew.

The less-handsome man sat down next to Denise, kissing her on the cheek, and she blushed a little and laughed softly. Thankfully, Passea knew Denise's happiness wouldn't last much longer. That was the only way she could hold back her rage.

"We were thinking it would be a good idea for you to go outside and train, since you've been away for a while, and we're pretty sure you didn't get any practice in while the Winged Red were holding you captive," said the female of the trio.

"Captive?" Passea said before she could stop herself. She quickly followed it with, "Yes, they didn't let me practice at all. Everything that happened there was very…disagreeable. So, of course. Take me outside, and I'll practice with my bow and arrows."

"They are already set out and waiting for you, near the targets," said the more attractive male. "Were you wanting some help? It seemed as if you already had it fairly well down, but perhaps you'd still like some pointers?"

As if she needed *pointers*. She'd been practicing with a bow and arrow since she was old enough to hold one! But she couldn't tell them that, of course. Instead, she said, "Yes, that would be very helpful." She'd had no choice but to lie about needing the help, since, unlike Wren, she didn't actually know where the practice area was located.

"Follow us, then, Wren." The female gestured toward the door they'd just entered through and started to leave, the more attractive sibling right behind her. Passea rose from the table, unable to stop herself from checking out his delightfully shapely backside. Out of the corner of her eye, she saw Sia turn to look at her, and from Sia's confused expression, she realized that Wren never would have checked out a man's ass, so Passea flashed a smile in her direction, receiving a beaming one in return. Then she followed the man out of the room, letting her eyes drift back to his behind as soon as she was out of Sia's sight.

The practice area was clearly nowhere near as impressive as the one in her own land, she noticed at first glance. And why *wasn't* it? As the leader of the Winged Blue, Torien had many resources at his disposal, so she couldn't figure out why he had such simple targets and had given Wren such a plain bow. Or at least it was plain in comparison to the one she had gifted her daughter with, when they'd first seen one another again. Memories of their reunion ran through her mind as she picked up the bow, taking an arrow from the male Winged Blue.

The tall female turned to her brother. "So, will I be tutoring her, or will you, Faest?"

"I suppose she might need to see what not to do, Speyd, so maybe you should start." The male triplet named Faest smirked in Speyd's direction, who in turn flipped him off.

Speyd stood at her right, and once the bow was strung and the arrow nocked, Speyd carefully eyed the adjustment of each part of Passea's body. Not that it was necessary, because once she was finished, she nodded, saying, "You know, Wren, your form is much better than before. I doubt you can outdo your aim from last time, though, but why not go ahead and try?"

"Sure thing, *Boss*." Almost before she was done speaking, she fired off two arrows in quick succession, and each found the exact same mark on the middle target, the second splitting the first cleanly down its center.

"Need anything else to let you know I'm good enough by now?"

A slight frown from Speyd showed her that she'd forgotten her role as Wren once more. She quickly changed her sneer to a smile and said, "I mean, since you two were such great teachers and everything, for which I thank you both."

"Y-yeah," stuttered Faest. "I think we're good, actually, Wren. Just like your aim."

Good? More like one-hundred-percent perfect. And probably much better than you two could ever do. But instead of speaking those hurtful words aloud, she told them, "I'm going up to my room, then, unless there's anything else?"

"Nope, Wren. We'll just see you later," Speyd said. "Have a nice rest or whatever you end up doing. You've earned it."

I certainly have, Passea thought to herself. She followed that thought with one wishing the two of them a nice final day of peace... and freedom. But she didn't mean it.

She couldn't find much to do up in her daughter's bedroom, although she recognized a few books on the shelf that she'd read and enjoyed when she'd last been in the land of the Winged Blue, all those years ago. Despite their being penned by authors who lived in this land, of course. She picked up the one about the delightfully deadly dragon that had killed so many fictional enemies of hers, and, sitting on the room's surprisingly comfortable couch (well, the Winged Blue had to get *some* things right), she began to read.

Hours must have passed, because the sun was much lower in the sky by the time she finally looked up from the book for the first time. She would have read a bit longer, but a knock on her door and Sia's tentative-sounding "Wren?" reminded her that she'd agreed to join that annoying young Winged for lunch.

"Coming," she called out, placing the book by Wren's bed. She would have much preferred to stay there and read some more, even if she was getting to the part in the book where, she recalled, a Winged Blue talked the dragon into stopping its slaughter of her people. If only the author had written a more pleasing ending. But it was intended for readers who didn't share her beliefs, or her knowledge. The book's unsatisfactory ending made it almost acceptable that she'd be abandoning her reading for a meal with the girl who stood on the other side of Wren's bedroom door.

Sia looked rather happy to see her, or at least to see whom she looked like at that moment, which confirmed she'd been right, that Sia definitely had an attachment to Passea's daughter. "What's for lunch?" she asked the girl as they began walking down the stairs.

"Only the best cheese-and-beef pie you're ever going to eat. My brother stayed up late making it for us, as a favor to me. He owed me one, or at least that's what he said, even if his reason for the owed favor was that I'd introduced him to the woman who's now his wife."

"Oh?" Passea answered. She was careful to keep the boredom from being around Sia out of her voice.

"Not that it has anything to do with today!" Sia told Passea, her words rather rushed. Man, she had it *bad* for Wren. Maybe she could have some fun with this annoying girl, just to pass the time during this certain-to-be-dull meal.

❖

The music playing throughout their lunch was saccharine and grossly romantic, but the pie turned out to be delicious. Passea wound up asking for seconds before she could stop herself. She'd done her best to subtly poke and prod at Sia's affection for Wren, to poke little holes in her confidence, and to prod at the weak areas of Sia's self-esteem. By the end of the meal, the girl looked far less happy than when she'd first seen Wren that morning. She still managed to work up the nerve to ask Wren to dance when an especially corny song began to play.

"I really enjoyed it when we danced last time," she said to her guest, her voice sounding hesitant as she spoke.

"I'm afraid I didn't," Passea told her. Sia's slight smile collapsed, which was a good start. "And I obviously have more important things to think about than dancing, in case you forgot."

"Of…of course, Wren. I'm sorry, I didn't think that…"

"Yes, you didn't. That's because the entire fate of your world isn't resting on *your* shoulders, is it?"

"Yes, no, of course," Sia repeated, sounding slightly shell-shocked.

Good, she'd accomplished exactly what she'd wanted with this dumb, love-struck girl. Now she could return to her room, the only place here where she wouldn't be joined or surrounded by insipid, foolish Winged Blue. "I think I'm going to leave now," she told the girl, and she was smiling proudly by the time she had reached the front door.

Because in the house behind her, she heard sounds that might have been Sia beginning to cry.

CHAPTER THIRTY-SEVEN

Things hadn't gotten any better during the hours Wren had spent trapped in her cell. And due to the lack of a window anywhere nearby, she didn't know whether it was day or night when a small rustling sound came from the darkest corner of her cell.

"I have a knife!" she shouted in its direction.

"Yes, you do," came the voice of an elderly woman. "Your brain."

"My…my *what* is a knife?" Before Wren could try to make sense of those confusing words, a puppy-sized, silver-blue raven emerged from the corner. Its glimmering feathers lit up the cell far better than the small, flickering candle outside the bars had ever managed to in the hours Wren had spent confined in the dark cell.

"Hello, Wren. Wrenny. Double-you. And you are a double you, aren't you? So powerful, so shiny, so rich and abundant with strength and sparklies." The raven squinted its eyes and ruffled its wing feathers. "Oh, my, you must forgive me. My head is so tight from being stuffed away for all these years that everything is mushed together. There was…there was…yes, I'm pretty sure I was supposed to tell someone something…"

"Tell someone? Could it be me?" Wren was a little annoyed that her hopes had soared upon first seeing this raven appear. After just their very short conversation, Wren had come to believe that the raven probably had every single screw loose she possibly could.

"Yes. Yes! It was you. That is…is…it is that you will get out of the bars—not the kind you drink in, mind you—and you will fly, and the red smoke will wispy-twisty around you, and you will get home." She cackled gleefully at the end of that statement, and Wren almost joined her, because that last part had actually made sense.

Home. That was where Wren had longed to be the whole time she'd been down in this gloomy, nasty-smelling cell. She wanted to see her father again, and Denise, and Sia, and the triplets, and—

"How's it going, prisoner?" came the jubilant voice of someone who wasn't even close to belonging on that list. The owner of the voice walked around the corner beyond Wren's cell door, carrying a large, glowing wooden torch and a red tray with large chips of its paint missing on the parts of it Wren could see. And upon seeing what sat on top the poorly treated tray, Wren was a little happier to see Ember once again: two slices of bread sat next to a small bowl of what looked to be water. And Wren was starving.

"It's safe to dine, Wrenny," she heard the raven say softly, which made Wren turn in her direction. But all Wren saw where the raven had just been standing was the last of her feathers, fading into thin air.

She decided to trust the raven's words; Wren was so hungry by now she almost didn't care if the food was poisoned. At least that way she wouldn't die on an empty stomach. When Ember shoved the tray through a slot at the bottom of the door, the water sloshed onto the bread and soaked it. She fell to her knees and began to devour the meager meal.

"Looks like you were more than a little hungry, Wren. I was almost worried you wouldn't eat, as I want you to be completely lucid when you see me kill my first Winged Blue. I was thinking of starting with your father, but I've decided that instead of him, I'll start with the girl who taught you how to fly. Sia. That was her name, wasn't it?"

Wren almost choked on her final bite of food. She didn't want to show Ember how helpless her words had made her feel, but it was too late: a feral, proud look flashed across Ember's face, and she leered down at Wren, her face lit up with delight. "It seems I struck a nerve, now, doesn't it, *Wren*? That's good. It's what I was aiming for. I want you to know, while you're trapped down here, about all the fun you're missing out on in your homeland. I want you to watch as Winged Blue fall from the sky, crash to the earth. I want you to watch as I kill every last person who matters to you. Even your mom, who did a delightfully good job deceiving you, something I'd be proud of if I hadn't been so aware of her weakness when it came to you. She wasn't up for ruling alongside Myuss and me, though, so she's on the list of the doomed. Just like you!" Ember's malicious grin spread even farther as she continued to speak. "Oh! I almost forgot to tell you: that mom of yours is disguised as you right now, and she's living in your bedroom in your pop's home. She's probably helping all the people there remember how little you actually matter to them."

Wren couldn't let Ember see exactly how intensely her verbal attacks hurt, and she realized then, as she rose, then squared her shoulders, that she *did* matter to all the people back in the land where she'd been born. She mattered immensely, and nothing this stupid, evil woman could say would convince her otherwise. "Whatever you say, Ember," Wren told her, and she found herself smiling for the first time since she'd landed in this cell.

Ember looked startled at Wren's sudden show of strength, but she quickly wiped any sign of surprise from her face, replacing it with a slightly less-happy smirk. "Well, Wren, you sleep tight, because you have only about twenty-four hours before your pathetic world is torn completely apart. Nighty-night!"

Ember had the nerve to blow Wren a kiss as she straightened up and turned to walk away. Wren found her stomach was trying to tie itself in a knot, and not just because that blown kiss had reminded her of all the times she'd kissed this heartless woman. She made a wish just as Ember and her torch rounded the corner and disappeared: that she had been able to see through Ember's perfect mask of kindness right away and recognized her for who she really was.

But it was too late now, and although her magical power might have been neat, it didn't include the much more appealing ability to make her wishes come true. It only allowed her to change into someone else, and Wren realized then that she didn't want to be anyone else. Not anymore. Being Wren, being herself, it was just fine, for the first time in all the years since her dad had disappeared.

Maybe it had been less than ideal, her blind trust of the Winged Red upon meeting Myuss and Ember and her mother. But as Ember had said, even her mom Passea loved her, in her less-than-perfect way. So at least Wren wouldn't leave this world feeling unloved. By others, or by herself. This realization was almost comforting enough for her to fully relax for the first time in hours, if not days, even in this miserable place.

She lay down on the dank-smelling, lumpy mattress in the cell's darkest corner. Just before she drifted off into some much-needed sleep, she heard her Winged cellmate speak again. "Yes, Wrenny-Wren, you will sleep well. And then, tomorrow, you'll be free! And all will be wet and watery and well."

Despite the fact that she didn't really believe any of that batty Winged's words, the seed of hope that her self-trust had planted had begun to grow. Even if now, fast asleep in her cell, Wren could just barely sense it taking root.

Chapter Thirty-eight

The night of the battle had arrived. Wren didn't know how she knew, but she could somehow feel it in her cell, feel the fact that day had ended and that there wasn't much time left before the Winged Red struck. All she could do while she was separated from the Winged Blue was hope that her father and all the rest of his people were as thoroughly prepared as they could be, because she couldn't do anything to help from here, despite what the prophecy had said.

"I guess prophecies aren't written in stone." She sighed.

"Nope, they're written in books, silly," said her feathered fellow prisoner, these words followed by an unbalanced-sounding chortle. "And everything will be fine! You will feather again, fly again, love again, *everything* again!"

"Sure, birdie, sure I will." Wren didn't bother attempting to hide her skepticism, because she was doubtful the rather off-kilter bird would even notice.

"It's 'Bez,' not 'birdie,' missy! And you'll get my help, soon enough, I promisepromise*promise!*"

In a completely different location in the Winged's realm, Torien was pacing the floor in his library. The triplets stood in a line beyond the couch that sat between him and them, all three looking like they secretly hoped he would knock off his damned pacing. None of them would have admitted to either themselves or the people in the room why, exactly, they were so desperate for him to stop. Perhaps it was of much less importance to Quiq, because at least three-quarters of his attention was clearly taken up with trying to soothe Denise's frayed nerves.

"I chose quite a time to quit drinking!" she joked, and all the triplets laughed, although Quiq laughed the softest, as he was busy sweeping her up into a hug.

Rysha stood to the right of the two other triplets, her arms crossed but her eyes full of love as she looked at him. He made eye contact with her, and finally, he slowed his pacing, stopping right in front of the chair where Wren sat.

She had been acting strangely, but he was sure she must be nervous, too. After all, they still hadn't deciphered the rest of the prophecy so it would require an enormous amount of effort *and* belief on all their parts in order to manage to defeat the Winged Red. Wren looked tense for the first time since she'd come down to breakfast the morning before. Torien knelt in front of her, taking her hands in his, an action that surprisingly made Wren flinch away from him.

Or maybe it wasn't all that surprising, Torien thought. "I guess you're a little worried, Wrenny, huh?"

"Yeah, I sure am!" There was something else behind her words, something no one in the room could quite make sense of, yet they all noticed it, even Speyd and Faest, who shared a quick, questioning look.

"You have the power within you to succeed, Wrenny. Otherwise whoever—or whatever—created the prophecy wouldn't have chosen you for the most important role in this battle. I know you may not believe that, but you already have within you all you need to help us to triumph. We all believe in you, you know." He smiled at her as kindly as he knew how, which wasn't hard considering how much love he felt for her at that moment.

"I…I…thanks, Torien. I'm glad you think so." Her words seemed to betray what she actually believed, Torien saw, her voice showing that she likely didn't have any trust in her ability to succeed, to overcome the threat of the Winged Red. But she had to be successful, Torien knew, because despite how heavily the Winged Blue had prepared for this crucial fight, he still didn't know if they were truly a match for what might be coming.

Torien had missed Rysha over these past few days, especially the reassurances that he knew she would have given often and freely. Since she was much better at training with weaponry, and the Winged Blue needed all the training they could get, she had been kept occupied with all the necessary aspects of preparing for the battle. He just had to hope that the Winged Red weren't more skilled than his people. He'd even armed Denise, giving her a short sword along with some weaponized potions Zyr had whipped up especially for her. Quiq had insisted upon keeping watch outside Denise's room. Torien had been surprised at how close those two had come to be, but it brought him great joy, all the same. She deserved to be happy.

Torien realized he'd been silent for too long, so he rose from his knees and stood, turning to look at each of the dear people who stood in front of him:

The three triplets, braver than almost anyone he'd ever met.

Denise, whose inner strength had allowed her to recover from the unconscionably hard life he'd abandoned her to.

Rysha, whose love had helped him stay strong himself, even while she wasn't by his side to remind him of her love. Love like theirs didn't weaken, even when the greatest of responsibilities kept them apart.

And then there was Wren. Even if she hadn't seemed like herself for the last couple of days, he didn't care for her any less. Instead, he cared more. No one knew what the battle would bring, and he had assumed that Wren had no idea, either. So much and so many depended on her, and yet here she was, being so very brave and looking only half as scared as he himself felt.

Now, in this moment, he felt a swelling of pride to be in such great and dear company, and his voice rang out certain and strong as he told them, "I know we will all do our best, because it's what everyone in this room, all you wonderful Winged Blue, and you, Denise, have always done. Now all we need to do is wait and try to relax."

Ember had just appeared around the corner, carrying a large, red-rimmed mirror. She looked much more excited than Wren thought she should have been, given the circumstances.

Given her violent plans.

Wren might have known she couldn't stop Ember and Myuss, but she wasn't about to cry again. Especially with Ember watching her so happily. She'd done her best, and while the pain of not being there for her family and friends and the rest of the Winged Blue was intense, she still held a small, glowing star of hope, one that told her everything might still work out.

So she chose to ignore Ember's taunts: how she'd have to watch helplessly through the mirror as her friends and family died, and that she, too, wouldn't be alive much longer. Wren's life might have been hard, impossibly hard, but it hadn't been empty of joy, and she let that knowledge warm her every inch as Ember, with one last look in Wren's direction, released her wings and stepped through the mirror's surface.

Right after Ember had exited through the mirror, Wren began to hear voices, coming from the hall beyond her cell, and soon, their owners appeared, red raven after red raven streaming into the room on open wings and all passing through the mirror as well, each of them calling out their fierce, menacing war cries. Then, what seemed like ages later, all was still once more.

"Guess it's our turn now!" Wren jumped at the sound, startled to find that she wasn't as alone as she'd thought. She turned to where the voice had come from, and there was Bez, reappearing at her feet. Wren was glad to have Bez's company again, even if that company included her apparent lightness in the sanity department. Wren knew she would have lost it too, though, if she'd been trapped down here as long as Bez likely had been.

"How'd you disappear like that? And reappear? And how long have you been down here?"

"Forever and a coupla weeks. I'm not trapped, you know, or at least not trapped now. Now, now *I* can help you, and you, *you* can let me out. Now, be a dear and stick your finger down my throat. My wingtips just can't reach far down enough."

"You want me to *what*?" Wren grimaced, but she did as she was told, because what did she have to lose, other than the contents of her stomach? She shook her head, inhaled, and held her breath. Then she bent down and stuck her finger into the raven's open beak.

Bez made a few disgusting gurgling noises, then ducked down and hopped backward, the contents of her stomach hitting the cell floor with a dull *thud*. Nothing disgusting came out, though—instead, a large, red key lay on the ground between Bez and Wren's feet.

"That…that wouldn't be the key to our cell, now, would it?"

"Only one way to find out!" Bez cackled as Wren reached down and picked up the surprisingly clean-looking key.

She went over to the door and put her fingers through the bars where a square of metal was welded to them. In that spot, after feeling around for a few tense seconds, she found what must have been the cell's keyhole, and without a moment's hesitation, she fit the key into the lock.

Perfect.

And then she was outside the cell, and she was free. She turned back to thank Bez as profusely as she possibly could, but Bez was already gone. There was nothing left to do, then, but go through the mirror.

That, and wish desperately that whatever she found on the other side wouldn't be a clear sign that she was already too late.

CHAPTER THIRTY-NINE

Is it already too late for the humans?

And the Winged Blue? Sia couldn't help but wonder this as she saw the approaching swarm of Winged Red. The upcoming battle had caused all her thoughts to follow a twisting, winding path into a dark forest within her that she didn't often visit. But if there ever was a time when those crooked trees and unpleasant wonderings were likely to beckon to her, this was it.

She knew the Blue were as prepared as they possibly could be, and Torien's pep talk hadn't exactly failed to make her ready. If she had to be honest, though, watching all those red-winged people that were quickly approaching where all her brethren hovered, watchful, waiting…if she had to be honest, she didn't know for sure that the Winged Blue would win.

Sia didn't even want bloodshed to be necessary. Couldn't they all just sit down to tea and cookies and talk it out like civilized beings? Chocolate-chip cookies, if she had a choice. An odd, surprising smile found its way onto her lips at this delicious-but-silly thought, but the red-tipped arrow that whizzed by her ear washed it away in an instant.

No, no matter how much she wanted to handle this disagreement her own way, she had to rise to the occasion. She had to fight to protect those she loved, and the humans, too. So Sia nocked an arrow against her bowstring and aimed at the throat of someone who she hoped didn't have any family waiting for them at home.

An arrow which found its mark about fifty feet away, striking through the neck of a male Winged Red who led the charge, his wings giving one last pitiful-looking flap before he plummeted to the ground.

Sia had no interest in celebrating what might be called a "victory," nor did she have time to, because the rest of the Winged Red had arrived in droves, and she knew the Blue still had a long fight ahead of them, one that they had no choice but to win.

They had to stop any Winged Red from reaching the portal. There was a cloaking spell on it, but she knew it was only a matter of time before the Winged Red found a way around it, at least if they were as powerful as Torien and Rysha had assumed. There was no reason to doubt that they would be, Sia thought as she raised her hand, using her powers to shove back a quickly approaching Winged who wielded a short sword. Then a blast of fire shot toward her feet, and she swooped away from it just in time.

Just in time to save herself, but not the Winged Blue woman whom it hit. Her screams as she burned didn't help Sia's mood any, and she knew then that she would never forget their sound as the flames bound the woman's shrieking form within their magical heat.

But then a large splash of water fell from above the woman, and Sia saw it had come from a nearby male Blue. She could also see from the tightness of his brow how much using his power was taking out of him. Too much, because by the time the flames were fully extinguished, he had nothing left to use in order to fight off the muscular Winged Red man who, his face full of ugly-looking pride, stabbed all the way through the smaller Winged's armor with his sword. Sia flinched as she saw blood spray out the startled man's back, then gasped as the Winged Red man yanked out his sword, neither the sword nor her compatriot's wings keeping him aloft any longer.

Sia decided that it couldn't possibly get any worse and that her heart could only take so much pain, but then she saw Wren's familiar face nearby. At first, seeing her friend, floating there and grinning so happily, Sia found herself almost wanting to smile back. But how could Wren look so happy in the midst of all this horror and chaos? How could she look so at peace? Before she could make any sort of sense out of Wren's apparent joy, she saw another familiar face coming straight toward her, at an uncomfortably fast-looking pace.

Ember.

If Sia had been the type to have sworn enemies, Ember would have made a good first choice, and she found that she was one Winged Red she wouldn't shed any tears for. Not one. She wouldn't allow anyone to get away with treating dear, sweet Wren the way that wicked woman had.

And if it had to come down to a fight between the two of them to settle matters, even a fight to the death, well, that would be A-OK with Sia. So she opened her mouth, screamed her fiercest war cry, and dove in Ember's direction.

CHAPTER FORTY

W ren almost lost her footing when she landed where the mirror had chosen to take her: right in the middle of Piru's living room. A shaking Piru sat on his couch, and his eyes found her instantly, first filling with dread and then understanding.

"You aren't Passea, are you? I can see someone else behind that mask you're wearing."

Her first thought was shock at the fact that she looked like her mother to him. Her second thought was to give thanks that Piru could see through her unintentional disguise. "It's me, Piru. Wren. Are you... are *you* yourself again?"

She wasn't moving any closer to Sia's grandfather until she knew she could trust him, but he looked too convincingly frightened when he answered her with a stuttery, "Y-yes. And is it ever good to be back in control of myself. My, but that was unpleasant, being trapped in the back of my head, unable to stop my body and mouth from doing things they would never normally do."

"I'm so sorry, Piru. But we haven't got much time. Do you know if I'm already too late?"

"You aren't, but...but please, don't go down there, to where they're fighting. I was never able to tell you this, but I had a vision, shortly before Ember took me over, one I was never able to tell anyone about. If you go down there—"

"I'm sorry, Piru, but I have to. I don't have a choice. After all, you can't argue with a prophecy, can you? Wish me luck!" And with those courageous words, Wren rushed toward Piru's front door, releasing her wings while she ran.

As she left, Piru called after her, but even the words he yelled weren't about to slow her down now. Not even if he had just told her that if she ventured out into the battle, she would die.

It wasn't dark yet, but nightfall was close, the moon full and the sun's last rays lighting up the sky. Wren wished it were already dark, because then, maybe, she wouldn't have been able to see the Winged that were in the air in front of her, fighting each other, wounding each other.

Killing each other.

This was nothing like watching a movie, all of it far too real. And far too painful to see. She averted her eyes from the carnage as best she could, staying below the line of rooftops as she took off and flying as fast as she was able.

The flight to her father's mansion seemed to take much longer than it ever had before; unlike other times she'd made the journey, this time the sky was filled with Winged Blue *and* Red. She had chosen to stay closer to the ground in order to avoid as much of the fighting as she could, but she still had to maneuver around two male Winged Blue's arrows and the thrust of a female Winged Blue's jagged-edged dagger.

She tried to block out the violence, the spilling of blood that was everywhere around her, but it was impossible. Still, she wouldn't let it—or her tears—slow her down, no matter how much all this pointless brutality and pain saddened her.

Once she was much closer to her father's house, she noticed two flying figures, higher than the rest of the Winged: Sia and Ember. The two were fighting, just as Ember had promised. Neither appeared to have been injured yet, but Wren was near enough to see that Sia seemed worn out; her wings appeared to take more strength to flap as each moment passed.

Wren had no other option. She had to join the fight, and she had to save Sia. It was her only choice.

She arrived at the mansion, finding the garden deserted. Wren landed near the doors that led out of the mansion to where her birthday party had occurred. Just as her feet touched the ground, a flash of blue nearby drew her eye. A beautiful Winged Blue woman had been injured somehow, her robes now stained with blood, and she tumbled through the sky. She fell close enough to Wren that she could see the woman was no longer alive when her body met the ground with a sickening *thump*.

It was too late to help her, but it wasn't too late to save Sia. Or at least to try. Finding the mansion's doors to the garden unguarded and unlocked, she went inside, rushing to the stairs and taking them two at a time. Her room was just as it had been before she'd been kidnapped, her bow lying next to its quiver on the table where she'd eaten breakfast her first day there. It seemed like much more time had passed since she'd arrived in Azyr than actually had. Far too many things had happened in that short stretch—too much pain, too much change, and too much new, unwanted knowledge.

But there would be time for all of that later, unless Piru's vision was an inevitability. Could she outrun fate, if she ran fast enough?

Back downstairs, now armed with her bow and full quiver, she headed to the front of the house this time. But just as she was about to open the front door, it swung open, and she took a few startled steps back as she watched Faest carry in her father. There was a rip in his robe near his stomach, and the blue fabric was stained dark red, the deep wound all too visible from where Wren stood.

"Dad?" Her voice shook as she spoke, and she was surprised when Faest leveled a furious glare in her direction. Then she remembered. She wasn't Wren, at least not in Faest's eyes. Or her injured father's.

But Faest's arms were full, so she took Torien's hand in hers before Faest could stop her, her fingers now covered in her father's blood.

"Is he…is he going to be okay?" she gasped out.

"Only if you get out of my way, Pass…Passe…*Wren*?" Faest's face softened, and she knew then that the strange feeling that she'd barely noticed—the one that had started the second she took her father's hand—had come with her returning to her proper form, the one she needed to transform into if the battle was going to work out in the Winged Blue's favor.

"I need you to go upstairs and get a healing potion from Denise. We left some with her, in case she got hurt. And hurry!"

Wren had started toward the stairs as soon as Faest had told her what was needed to save her father. She barely heard his last words; she was already moving as fast as her legs could carry her and was quickly up the stairs. Quiq was standing guard outside her stepmom's room.

Her "stepmom"? No, she thought with a shake of her head. Denise had been more of a mother than Passea ever had, and although she hadn't managed to get them away from her horrible stepdad, Denise was here for Wren now, and Passea wasn't.

"I need a potion from my mom," she told Quiq. "A healing potion. Torien's been badly hurt."

"He has? Here, I'll be right back. Wait right there," Quiq ordered her, in a voice that clearly announced to Wren that nothing short of complete compliance would be acceptable. Then he disappeared into her mom's room, and Wren tried to ignore the horrible thought that it was already too late.

It wasn't too late, though. After they'd rushed back downstairs, and after her father had swallowed the potion, she could see his wound begin to close, the damaged flesh weaving itself back together. "He'll be all right?" she asked Faest, and he turned to her, his face slowly showing signs that the worst of it was over.

"Yes, I think he will." Faest reached out, possibly to comfort her, but even though she wanted to, she couldn't wait for a sign that Torien was definitely going to recover. She could only barely hear Faest calling out her name as she ran, but nothing could stop her from heading straight back into the storm outside.

Not with Sia's life on the line.

She was back at the front door before she realized she'd started moving, but that was good. She didn't have any time to waste, not for her, and not for Sia. Now she would find out whether the prophecy was true. Now she would discover if she would survive the battle and if she truly was the Savior or just a girl, like she'd thought until only hours ago, a girl who wasn't capable of saving anything.

She didn't have time to wonder which was true, once she was back outside. She positioned her bow, just as she'd learned to, and her quiver's leather strap was looped safely across her chest by the time she took to the skies.

Sia and Ember were still circling and diving while they fought, but as Wren flew closer, she could now see that Sia was hurt. Her left wing seemed to have been cut, and Sia's lips were quivering just enough to let Wren know she was in pain.

Wren prepared her bow, an arrow now in place, and aimed for Ember.

Then everything changed in an instant.

Passea, her face bright with fury, was now visible in her true form, flying from Wren's direction and rushing toward Sia and Ember. It seemed that Sia had noticed the woman's approach, too, and now Sia's nocked arrow was pointing in Passea's direction instead of Ember's. She was moving so quickly that Wren was barely able to fly in front of her in time.

"Wren, no!" She heard someone cry out these words. Her beginning thoughts of relief from saving her birth mother were interrupted as a sharp pain began to bloom in the middle of her chest, and she just barely noticed the fact that Sia's arrow had found the wrong target.

Now she was plummeting toward the ground, moving faster than she'd have ever thought possible, falling much faster than she would have liked.

Suddenly, she was no longer falling, and a gentle voice, a familiar voice…Passea's voice, said, "I've got you, Wren, I've got you."

CHAPTER FORTY-ONE

Sia was in shock for only a few seconds. Then she did what she knew she had to do, aiming her bow at a distracted Ember and yanking back her bowstring. The arrow found its mark, exactly where Ember's heart lay, but Sia didn't wait to see if Ember would still be alive by the time she hit the ground.

Ember hadn't looked unhappy as Sia's arrow had struck Wren. No, she'd appeared delighted, and so Sia didn't have the slightest amount of regret at her decision to shoot Ember. Instead of taking even a brief moment to process the fact that she might have just ended Ember's life, she dove down to where Passea stood on the ground, her daughter appearing limp and lifeless in her arms.

It simply could *not* be too late for Sia to save her friend. The idea that it might possibly be was more than merely unacceptable to Sia. She wasn't able to consider that Wren's bright-as-the-sun light had been snuffed out. They'd barely begun to get to know each other, and she already felt like she'd known Wren forever—in the best way possible. It was unthinkable that Wren's time was over and that Sia had never gotten to share how she felt about her.

She touched down beside Passea and her daughter, and relief came when she noticed Wren's chest still rising and falling, the offensive arrow sticking out of her stomach and a small rivulet of blood trailing down her body. "Is she…is she okay?" Sia asked Passea, and she worried that her face betrayed her fear that Wren wasn't okay at all. She knew instantly that it was a pointless question to ask, but she didn't know what else to say.

"She is for now, but do you see how the arrow is glowing green where it is nearest to Wren's clothes?"

Now Sia looked more carefully, then hesitated briefly; she didn't really want to hear Passea's answer. "It's…poison, isn't it?"

"I'm afraid so. Oh, my poor, poor daughter. All of this was such a mistake. I just can't…" Passea choked back what must have been a sob. Her lips were trembling, and her eyes seemed about to overflow with tears any second. Then Sia spied, out of the corner of her eye, someone landing just next to them.

Piru.

He cupped his hands around his mouth and turned toward the mansion. Denise and Quiq were running toward them from Torien's home. "Do you have a healing potion?" he yelled to them.

"No, we've used them all!" Quiq yelled back.

Piru turned back toward them, his serious expression showing Sia that whatever he was about to say was of the utmost importance. "Then there's only one thing left to do. Passea, place your daughter on the ground, please. I may have a solution, but we'll have to get through to Wren if it's going to work."

Passea knelt down, gently laying her daughter on the bare earth. She smoothed Wren's hair, and then, clearly unable to hold them back any longer, she let tears begin to run down her face.

Sia held her breath as she watched Piru kneel down beside Wren. She watched intently as he placed his lips beside Wren's ear and began to whisper something to Wren that Sia was unable to hear. Whatever he was saying, Wren seemed able to hear him, Sia realized, Wren nodding slightly as he spoke.

When Piru moved away from her ear, the outline of her body began to shimmer, her features shifting into a more peaceful alignment, and then they began to fade, just as they had every time she'd shifted. Clearly this was another shift, to someone Sia had never seen before, as now an unfamiliar face had begun to appear where Wren's had been. Her hair was also growing in length, turning from dark-brown curls to a straight, shiny black mane that flowed past her chest. The wings she lay on remained the same, though, still made up of both red and blue. Then her eyes became narrower with slight folds in the far corners, and when they fluttered open, Wren's transformation seemingly complete, they were a slightly paler brown with flecks of gold and green.

"So," she suddenly asked, her new voice quiet and a bit hoarse, "will I really never look like myself, ever again?"

"I'm afraid not." Piru answered with a kind, slightly sad smile.

"But you'll be fine now, once we've removed the arrow and dressed the wound. Do you know if you can stand?"

"Yes, I think so. Sia, Piru, can you help me up?"

Sia's relief had begun to wash over her like the summer sun's warmest rays, and she allowed herself a few moments to bask in its all-encompassing calm. She had just noticed that the fighting above them had ceased, Winged Blue and Red landing one by one as she and Piru helped Wren rise from the ground. Wren's legs shook a little once she was fully standing. She took a deep breath, and then their shaking stilled.

"I think I can manage it from here, you two. And thank you, Piru," she said, turning in his direction and giving his shoulder a squeeze. "I'll never be able to thank you enough for saving my life."

Passea walked up to stand next to Wren. "Nor will I ever be able to thank you enough for saving mine, my dearest daughter. Can you ever forgive me, Wren?"

"I already had, when I decided to save you." Wren lifted her arms from Sia and Piru's shoulders and tentatively took a few slow steps forward. She turned toward Passea for a moment, then looked down at her stomach. "I guess I should wait to hug you until they've removed the arrow, huh?" These words brought a fresh flood of tears from her mother, but Sia was pretty sure these were tears of relief. After all, she'd been shedding a few of them herself.

Once the group had returned to the mansion, they placed Wren on the couch facing the one where her father rested. His eyes shut, he was snoring softly, a bandage wrapped around his stomach. Sia turned to Faest, who was standing beside him. "He'll be all right, won't he?"

"I think so. But who is this you've come in with? And why is she still able to walk, with an *arrow* sticking out of her?"

Quiq admonished him. "Faest, don't be rude. That's Wren, and she just managed to end our battle with the Winged Red."

"And saved my life," Passea added.

Upon noticing Passea, Faest reached for his dagger, but Wren raised her hand. "Don't, Faest. She's not going to do anything inappropriate, I promise."

"Yes, I wouldn't even think of it." Wren's mother looked more than a little nervous as she spoke. "We're on the same side, now."

"If you say so," Faest grumbled, but he removed his hand from the dagger and walked over to stand with the small group.

Wren lay down on the couch, then shut her eyes. "I think I'll take

a brief nap while you remove the arrow, if that's okay with everyone."
Before anyone could agree or disagree with her plan, she was asleep.
Her quieter snores were much cuter than the ones coming from Wren's
father, Sia thought as she smiled down at her sleeping friend's form.

CHAPTER FORTY-TWO

The raven was tapping its beak on the tree next to Wren's head, but strangely, it sounded more like footsteps, hurried and anxious ones at that. And yes, it *was* footsteps she was hearing, but they weren't in the forest where she stood—they were coming from farther away. The raven stopped its pecking and said, in a young woman's voice, "Oh Wren, won't you please wake up?"

"Mmm," Wren groaned, because damn, did her head ever ache. Apparently she'd been dreaming, although the raven's words might have come from someone in the room she'd just awoken in. After she opened her tired eyes, her bedroom in Torien's mansion slowly came into focus. Both of her moms were there, along with a pacing Torien, clearly on his way to making a new indentation in her bedroom's already-weathered hardwood floors. Piru, perched on the back of a sofa a few feet from her bed, was wringing his hands. And Sia was sitting beside the bed, on a stool. It was she who first noticed Wren awakening.

"Wren? Wren!" Sia encased her in a body-crushing hug, which made Wren groan again, but this time the pain was actually welcome. So was Sia's happy face when she let go of Wren. "I don't care if you'll never look like yourself again, Wren. I'm just fine with that, as long as you're okay."

"I may be okay, but does this world have some sort of magic aspirin? My head is pounding."

Piru stood and walked over to her bed. "I'll get you something immediately. Sia, your mother will have some headache potions in stock, won't she?"

"Definitely. Do I need to go get them, or...or could you do it?"

"Don't want to leave her side, do you, dear girl?" Piru looked as though he knew something Wren didn't, something about how Sia felt about her, perhaps. Did Sia care about her beyond the bounds of mere friendship? And if so, did she like Wren back as much as Wren liked her?

It seemed she might have her answer soon; after a few more incredibly tight hugs, and a large number of stated variations on how relieved everyone was, Wren's family and Piru left the room.

Now that it was only the two of them, Sia perched on the edge of the bed where Wren lay. She reached out toward Wren's forehead, and Wren held her breath for a moment. But it seemed Sia had decided against touching her, returning her hand to her knee instead of doing what she clearly wanted to do with it.

"It's okay," Wren said. "You can touch me. You can touch me anywhere you like." *Shit.* Apparently, almost dying had made her a fair amount more ballsy than she had been before her near-death experience. And was Sia even attracted to her new form?

Sia began to play with the sheets next to Wren's body, working the hem of the fabric back and forth between her fingers. "I think it'll take some getting used to, seeing you like this, looking so different."

"Oh." Wren pushed herself upright and shoved her pillows up behind her back. She spent a few moments making sure they were arranged just right. Anything to distract herself from what Sia might have meant by those words. "Guess I'm stuck like this, huh?"

"That's what Piru said at first, but now he thinks there's a chance you can change back. Your mom, Passea, told him she was pretty sure that if you worked with her, and shared each other's magic, you could. I…I mean, I'm fine with how you look now, you're pretty and all, but I do miss your real face. It won't be the same doing this, doing what I've wanted to do ever since I first laid eyes on you, but I know it's you underneath, and that's all that really matters to me. If you'll let me do it, that is…" Sia's face was suddenly inches away from Wren's, her lips parted, her eyelids slightly lowered.

Wren didn't want to hesitate, didn't want to chance Sia changing her mind, so she leaned forward the small distance it took for their lips to meet.

Sia's lips were softer than Wren ever could have imagined, and she was a really good kisser, although Wren didn't exactly have much practice evaluating anyone's kissing abilities. But that didn't matter. Nothing else mattered, nothing but the softness of Sia's lips and the fact that she wanted this, wanted to be with Wren, no matter what she looked like. Any earlier in her life, Wren would have been worrying nonstop about so many things in that moment.

She would have worried about what Sia thought of her kissing.

She would have worried if Sia really liked her, the way she'd said she did, or if this was just a brief, passing thing.

She would have worried about how the heck the Winged Blue and Winged Red could possibly work out their differences.

She would have worried about what Myuss was up to right then—if she had escaped, if she was still a threat to her and the rest of the Winged Blue.

But now all she was worried about was how long she would get to do this, to kiss Sia, again and again, because she didn't want anything to interrupt it. Not even breakfast, as hungry as her suddenly growling stomach had decided she was.

"You hungry, Wren?" Sia had stopped kissing her, a lopsided grin lighting up her beautiful face. "Or are you hiding an angry wildebeest in your tummy?"

"I am hungry," Wren told her, feeling surprisingly unembarrassed by Sia's teasing remark. "But I'll only eat if you'll join me."

"Breakfast in bed for two!" Sia rang an imaginary bell, and she and Wren laughed. Then Wren grabbed her and gently tackled her to the bed, kissing her again and again and doing her best to ignore her stomach's insistent growls. Yes, Wren had officially decided that until she'd had her fill of Sia's lips, everything else could wait.

About the Author

Maggie Morton lives in Northern California with her partner and their two cats. She is the winner of an Alice B. Readers' Lavender Certificate for her first novel, the lesbian erotic romance *Dreaming of Her*. Her other novels are *Under Her Spell* and *Out of This World*.

Books Available From Bold Strokes Books

Basic Training of the Heart by Jaycie Morrison. In 1944, socialite Elizabeth Carlton joins the Women's Army Corps to escape family expectations and love's disappointments. Can Sergeant Gale Rains get her through Basic Training with their hearts intact? (978-1-62639-818-4)

Believing in Blue by Maggie Morton. Growing up gay in a small town has been hard, but it can't compare to the next challenge Wren—with her new, sky-blue wings—faces: saving two entire worlds. (978-1-62639-691-3)

Coils by Barbara Ann Wright. A modern young woman follows her aunt into the Greek Underworld and makes a pact with Medusa to win her freedom by killing a hero of legend. (978-1-62639-598-5)

Courting the Countess by Jenny Frame. When relationship-phobic Lady Henrietta Knight starts to care about housekeeper Annie Brannigan and her daughter, can she overcome her fears and promise Annie the forever that she demands? (978-1-62639-785-9)

Dapper by Jenny Frame. Amelia Honey meets the mysterious Byron De Brek and is faced with her darkest fantasies, but will her strict moral upbringing stop her from exploring what she truly wants? (978-1-62639-898-6)

Delayed Gratification: The Honeymoon by Meghan O'Brien. A dream European honeymoon turns into a winter storm nightmare involving a delayed flight, a ditched rental car, and eventually, a surprisingly happy ending. (978-1-62639-766-8)

For Money or Love by Heather Blackmore. Jessica Spaulding must choose between ignoring the truth to keep everything she has, and doing the right thing only to lose it all—including the woman she loves. (978-1-62639-756-9)

Hooked by Jaime Maddox. With the help of sexy Detective Mac Calabrese, Dr. Jessica Benson is working hard to overcome her past, but they may not be enough to stop a murderer. (978-1-62639-689-0)

Lands End by Jackie D. Public relations superstar Amy Kline is dealing with a media nightmare, and the last thing she expects is for restaurateur Lena Michaels to change everything, but she will. (978-1-62639-739-2)

Twisted Screams by Sheri Lewis Wohl. Reluctant psychic Lorna Dutton doesn't want to forgive, but if she doesn't do just that, an innocent woman will die. (978-1-62639-647-0)

A Class Act by Tammy Hayes. Buttoned-up college professor Dr. Margaret Parks doesn't know what she's getting herself into when she agrees to one date with her student Rory Morgan, who is fifteen years her junior. (978-1-62639-701-9)

Bitter Root by Laydin Michaels. Small town chef Adi Bergeron is hiding something, and Griffith McNaulty is going to find out what it is even if it gets her killed. (978-1-62639-656-2)

Capturing Forever by Erin Dutton. When family pulls Jacqueline and Casey back together, will the lessons learned in eight years apart be enough to mend the mistakes of the past? (978-1-62639-631-9)

Deception by VK Powell. DEA Agent Colby Vincent and Attorney Adena Weber are embroiled in a drug investigation involving homeless veterans and an attraction that could destroy them both. (978-1-62639-596-1)

Dyre: A Knight of Spirit and Shadows by Rachel E. Bailey. With the abduction of her queen, werewolf-bodyguard Des must follow the kidnappers' trail to Europe, where her queen—and a battle unlike any Des has ever waged—awaits her. (978-1-62639-664-7)

First Position by Melissa Brayden. Love and rivalry take center stage for Anastasia Mikhelson and Natalie Frederico in one of the most prestigious ballet companies in the nation. (978-1-62639-602-9)

Best Laid Plans by Jan Gayle. Nicky and Lauren are meant for each other, but Nicky's haunting past and Lauren's societal fears threaten to derail all possibilities of a relationship. (978-1-62639-658-6)

Exchange by CF Frizzell. When Shay Maguire rode into rural Montana, she never expected to meet the woman of her dreams—or to learn Mel Baker was held hostage by legal agreement to her right-wing father. (978-1-62639-679-1)

Just Enough Light by AJ Quinn. Will a serial killer's return to Colorado destroy Kellen Ryan and Dana Kingston's chance at love, or can the search-and-rescue team save themselves? (978-1-62639-685-2)

Rise of the Rain Queen by Fiona Zedde. Nyandoro is nobody's princess. She fights, curses, fornicates, and gets into as much trouble as her brothers. But the path to a throne is not always the one we expect. (978-1-62639-592-3)

Tales from Sea Glass Inn by Karis Walsh. Over the course of a year at Cannon Beach, tourists and locals alike find solace and passion at the Sea Glass Inn. (978-1-62639-643-2)

The Color of Love by Radclyffe. Black sheep Derian Winfield needs to convince literary agent Emily May to marry her to save the Winfield Agency and solve Emily's green card problem, but Derian didn't count on falling in love. (978-1-62639-716-3)

A Reluctant Enterprise by Gun Brooke. When two women grow up learning nothing but distrust, unworthiness, and abandonment, it's no wonder they are apprehensive and fearful when an overwhelming love just won't be denied. (978-1-62639-500-8)

Above the Law by Carsen Taite. Love is the last thing on Agent Dale Nelson's mind, but reporter Lindsey Ryan's investigation could change the way she sees everything—her career, her past, and her future. (978-1-62639-558-9)

Actual Stop by Kara A. McLeod. When Special Agent Ryan O'Connor's present collides abruptly with her past, shots are fired, and the course of her life is irrevocably altered. (978-1-62639-675-3)

Embracing the Dawn by Jeannie Levig. When ex-con Jinx Tanner and business executive E. J. Bastien awaken after a one-night stand to find their lives inextricably entangled, love has its work cut out for it. (978-1-62639-576-3)

Love's Redemption by Donna K. Ford. For ex-convict Rhea Daniels and ex-priest Morgan Scott, redemption lies in the thin line between right and wrong. (978-1-62639-673-9)

The Shewstone by Jane Fletcher. The prophetic Shewstone is in Eawynn's care, but unfortunately for her, Matt is coming to steal it. (978-1-62639-554-1)

Jane's World by Paige Braddock. Jane's PayBuddy account gets hacked and she inadvertently purchases a mail order bride from the Eastern Bloc. (978-1-62639-494-0)

A Touch of Temptation by Julie Blair. Recent law school graduate Kate Dawson's ordained path to the perfect life gets thrown off course when handsome butch top Chris Brent initiates her to sexual pleasure. (978-1-62639-488-9)

Beneath the Waves by Ali Vali. Kai Merlin and Vivien Palmer love the water and the secrets trapped in the depths, but if Kai gives in to her feelings, it might come at a cost to her entire realm. (978-1-62639-609-8)

Girls on Campus, edited by Sandy Lowe and Stacia Seaman. College: four years when rules are made to be broken. This collection is required reading for anyone looking to earn an A in sex ed. (978-1-62639-733-0)

Miss Match by Fiona Riley. Matchmaker Samantha Monteiro makes the impossible possible for everyone but herself. Is mysterious dancer Lucinda Moss her perfect match? (978-1-62639-574-9)

Paladins of the Storm Lord by Barbara Ann Wright. Lieutenant Cordelia Ross must choose between duty and honor when a man with godlike powers forces her soldiers to provoke an alien threat. (978-1-62639-604-3)

www.ingramcontent.com/pod-product-compliance
Lightning Source LLC
Chambersburg PA
CBHW022014010726
47494CB00003B/1037